A Vicarage Wedding

A Vicarage Wedding

A Holley Sisters of Thornthwaite Romance

KATE HEWITT

TULE
PUBLISHING

Chapter One

"WE NEED TO talk."

Playfully Rachel picked a bit of ribbon out of her fiancé Dan's hair before she noticed his serious expression. The laughter welling in her chest was replaced by an all too familiar tightness…one she'd been trying to ignore these last few months, and mostly had.

"Do we? About what? I hope you're not changing your mind about the morning suit." Pale grey with pink ascot tie, the morning suit was rather formal for St Stephen's but Rachel had wanted the little girl fantasy of a Disney princess wedding, with all the OTT extras it entailed. Her own dress, with its lace overlay, full skirt, and sweeping train was certainly a match for Dan's suit.

"I'm not changing my mind about that." His voice was heavy with emphasis, the implication being that he was changing his mind about something else, something big.

Rachel stilled, her gaze sweeping over her fiancé's face, noting for the first time the look of total misery swamping his hazel eyes—eyes that were usually glinting with good humour. He jammed his hands in the pockets of his trousers and hung his head. He looked *guilty*. Her stomach cramped.

"What's going on, Dan?"

"Can we go somewhere private?"

They were standing in the foyer of the vicarage—her family home since she'd been a toddler—having just finished the rehearsal in the church, with her father officiating, a tear already glinting in his eye. Everyone was heading over to The Winter Hare, Thornthwaite's one bistro, for the rehearsal dinner, but Rachel had wanted to freshen up first and Dan had followed her back to the vicarage.

"Somewhere private?" she echoed. "No one's here." The house echoed emptily around them, its familiar rooms suddenly feeling ominous...or was that just the awful look on Dan's face? Why was he looking so miserable, when they were about to get married?

"Please, Rachel."

"Fine." She took a deep breath, trying not to show her irritation as well as her fear. Surely it couldn't be as bad as all that? Dan was so reasonable, so eminently even-tempered. Surely it was nothing. Rachel pushed open the door to the vicarage's sitting room and went inside. With its wide, floor-to-ceiling bay window, high ceilings, and ornate fireplace, it looked like something out of a Jane Austen drama on the BBC, and there had certainly been enough parishioners perched on the settee over the years, cups of tea balanced on their knees as they made chitchat with the vicar. Now the room was empty and silent, having been ruthlessly cleaned both for the wedding and her parents' imminent move to China, where her father had accepted a ministry position.

Rachel turned around and faced her fiancé of nearly six months. "What is it, Dan? You aren't…you aren't getting cold feet, are you?" She tried to make it a joke and didn't quite manage it.

"*I'm* not getting cold feet." Again with the emphasis, making Rachel feel both frustrated and fearful.

"What are you trying to say?" She let out an impatient breath and stalked forward, plucking another piece of ribbon from his hair. At the rehearsal, her sisters had thrown handfuls of ribbons from her pretend bouquet all over them, everyone laughing, but it felt offensively ridiculous in this moment to talk about something serious while festooned with bits of pink satin.

"Rachel…" Dan sighed and raked a hand through his hair, his slumped shoulders seeming to bear the weight of the world, and then only just. "This isn't easy to say…"

"Obviously." She folded her arms, barely managing to keep from tapping her foot. Better to seem irritated than terrified, surely. At least it made her seem strong. "Just spit it out, Dan, please."

"The wedding's off." Rachel blinked. "What I mean is, I'm calling it off."

She blinked again, trying to absorb what he'd said. Even now, dazedly, she wondered if he was joking, but she knew from his face that he wasn't. Still it felt too impossible to accept. The wedding was *tomorrow*.

"What… Why…" She was too stunned to ask a question, or even to know what question to ask. "Why would you do this?" she finally said, framing the words with effort, each painful syllable costing her something. "*How* could you do this? Everything's planned…" The church. The reception. Their *house*, their lovely house up on the fells, with its Lakeland stone exterior and huge fireplace, the views of Derwentwater glinting in the distance, waiting for them to move in and start living their happy life together. "How could you do this?" The cry was ripped from her, the words ringing out.

"I'm sorry, Rachel." Dan looked completely wretched, but also resolute. "I wish I'd had the guts to do it earlier, and save us both a lot of pain. I kept closing my eyes to the truth because I so, so wanted this to work out. I hope you believe that."

"I don't know what I should believe. I can't even think." Her lips felt numb, everything in her buzzing. She pressed her hands to her pale cheeks, trying to formulate at least one coherent thought when her mind felt as if it were full of static. "Dan, there are fifty people waiting for us at The Winter Hare to celebrate our marriage *tomorrow*."

"I know."

"All my relatives are here…all your relatives…my dress…our honeymoon in France!" Her voice rose on a peal

4

of despair as the realisations kept piling on top of one another, crowding each other out. All of it…everything…over. "We're meant to be flying to Nice tomorrow night."

"I *know*, Rachel."

Even in the midst of her shock she caught a flicker of something almost like annoyance or even hurt in his eyes and she stilled, dropping her hands from her face. "Doesn't any of that matter to you?"

"Of course it does, but not, I think, as much as it matters to you."

He spoke quietly, but she still heard the faint, repressive note of judgement. "What is that supposed to mean?"

"Well, let's see." Dan blew out a breath and folded his arms. "What have you been upset about since I told you I wanted to call off our wedding?" He started ticking off his fingers. "The reception, our relatives, your dress, the honeymoon." He spoke flatly, and Rachel recoiled.

"Am I not supposed to care about those things—"

"What you haven't been upset about," Dan continued in that same flat voice, "is the fact that we won't be marrying each other, after all. We won't be spending our lives together."

Rachel looked away, blinking rapidly. "Of course I'm upset about that. How could I not be—"

"Are you?" Dan cut across her quietly, those two lethal words like the snick of a blade. Rachel stared at him for a long moment, and then looked away. She didn't reply.

In truth, she didn't know what to say. What was Dan implying? That she didn't care about him? *He* was the one doing the jilting. She felt the need to rewind, to start the conversation over. "All right, let's go back to the beginning," she managed after a moment. "Why are you calling off the wedding, Dan? Is it because you...you don't love me?" She hated having to ask the question, but what else could it be?

"No," Dan answered, and now he sounded sad. "It's because *you* don't love *me*."

Rachel blinked, jerking back as if he'd struck her. His words seemed to reverberate in the silence of the room.

"You don't deny it," he remarked after a moment when Rachel hadn't said anything.

"I don't know what to say." Her mind felt like the tyres of a car, spinning in mud, getting no traction. "You call off our wedding because of what you *think* I feel?"

"Do you love me, Rachel?"

Her mouth opened and closed soundlessly several times. She felt like a fish. "Of course I love you—"

"I don't believe you."

"Well, what can I do about that?" Rachel exploded. Anger felt so much better than the other emotions skirting around the edges of her dazed brain, her numb heart. Fear. Hurt. Sorrow. *Relief.* The last one, that tiny, treacherous flicker, she pushed away instantly. Of course she didn't actually feel relieved. It was just that she was too shocked to know what to feel, and everything was coming at her so fast.

"Tell the truth," Dan urged. "Not just to me, but to yourself. Do you love me? Do you love me in that heart-stopping, spine-tingling way, where the thought of me makes you breathless with anticipation?"

"Oh come on." She tried to scoff. "You're talking like a teenager."

"Considering we're not even newlyweds yet, I don't think we need to settle for acting and feeling like an old married couple before we've even begun."

"According to you, we'll never be newlyweds!"

"I think it will be better for us both in the long run if that's the case." Dan spoke steadily but Rachel heard a break in his voice, like a hairline crack just starting to fracture.

"Dan…"

"You see, the trouble is," Dan continued, and the break was more audible now, the words themselves jagged, "that I love you. Very much. I love you with that spine-tingling, heart-stopping excitement, and nothing would make me happier than saying my vows tomorrow and making you my bride."

Rachel gaped for a few seconds before managing a word. "Then…"

"But I've been closing my eyes to how you're feeling—and more importantly, how you're *not* feeling—for too long already," Dan continued. "And I can't put us both through that misery, Rachel, not on the off-chance that you might come to love me in time. If you can't love me now, when we're supposed to be in that blissed-out honeymoon stage of a relationship, when *can* you love me? When will you?" He shook his head, both miserable and resolute. "I'm sorry. I'm sorry for waiting so long, and making it so awkward. I'm happy to take all the blame, tell everyone it was my fault—"

"That you changed your mind?" Rachel cut across him, her voice full of hurt. "And make me a laughing stock?"

"Is that what you're worried about?"

She didn't miss the slight curl to his lip. "It's not my primary concern, but it *matters*. Why are you making out everything I say and do to be selfish and shallow, Dan? Is it so wrong to care about my dress or my family or what people think?"

"It's not wrong—"

"What, then?"

"I just wished you cared more about me."

"You're making it rather difficult right now," she snapped, wanting to hurt him, and sadly succeeding in her aim. She whirled away, towards the window, the sheep pasture in front of the vicarage glinting gold in the evening sunlight. It was summer in Cumbria and the sun wouldn't set until nearly eleven o'clock at night. A night that now felt endless and unbearable.

"Everyone's waiting for us," she said dully, when the silence had stretched on for several painful minutes. "They'll be wondering where we are."

"Then let them wonder."

She let out a heavy sigh, a sound of hopeless despair. "Is there anything more to say? You seem so certain."

"I am, but…" Dan hesitated, and Rachel turned around. "But what?"

"Do you still want to marry me, Rachel?" He looked at her beseechingly. "I don't think I can feel lower than I already do, but…if you still wanted to marry me, if you really felt, deep in your bones, in your heart, that we could make each other happy, that you could love me in time…"

"Then you'd go through with it after all?" Rachel finished disbelievingly. "Are you really saying that now, Dan?"

"Do you not want me to?"

"I don't know what I want." She shook her head, despairing. It was impossible to go back to what they'd once been just a few moments ago. "I don't want to marry you whilst feeling as if I'm holding a gun to your head."

"You wouldn't be, Rach."

The nickname caught her on the raw. How could she be *Rach* in a moment like this? "I feel like everything is ruined," she said, her voice quavering. "We can never go back now." Why did he have to say anything? "What do you want from me, Dan? What would convince you that I love you enough?"

Dan sighed heavily. "Perhaps I shouldn't have put it the way I did."

You're bloody well right there. Rachel bit her lip to keep from saying something she knew she'd regret.

"It's just…" He sighed again, this time the sound heavy with sadness and regret, a burden he'd held for a long time and was now finally putting down. "Can you honestly say you love me, Rachel? Me, and not just the *idea* of me?"

She only just kept from rolling her eyes. "What is that even supposed to mean?"

"I mean…if there was no house in the fells, no Aga, no Land Rover…"

"Honestly, you're making me sound so materialistic!" She flushed, both ashamed and angry that he apparently thought so little of her. "It was never about those things."

"All right, forget the materialism then. If there was no cosy home, no Golden Retriever puppy, no house full of kids in the offing…"

A lump formed in her throat. They were meant to pick up their puppy from a kennel near Carlisle in less than a month. As for the kids…they'd always agreed that they wanted lots, and were planning to start trying soon after the wedding, since she was already past thirty. Why was he taunting her with their shared dreams now, as if she'd been somehow wrong to have them, to want them?

"I still don't know what you're trying to say."

Dan blew out a breath. "I'm saying if it was just me, take or leave all the rest, would you still want to marry me, just me?" He gazed at her steadily, waiting for her answer. Her verdict. "Tell me the truth, Rachel. Am I enough?"

Rachel stared at him wretchedly. How on earth was she supposed to answer that? And then with a thud of realisation, she understood that the answer should have been easy—and it wasn't.

She loved Dan. Of course she did. She'd known him since she was a kid, and their friendship had blossomed into romance nine months ago, when they'd reconnected at a party for one of the teachers at the primary school where she taught. They'd both been past thirty, living in Thornthwaite, looking to settle down. It had seemed simple, obvious, and she'd been so excited about planning their life together. And yet…

And yet.

"I think your silence is answer enough," Dan said quietly. "See, it really is better this way."

"It isn't," Rachel protested. "I do love you, Dan." But she heard how half-hearted she sounded, and she hated herself for it. She'd loved him enough, she knew that much. She never would have even thought about breaking it off the way he was doing. She loved him enough to be happy, and she thought Dan would have been, as well. All right maybe it hadn't been in that spine-tingling way he seemed to crave, unbeknownst to her, but so what? Who needed all that loopy, hormonal stuff? What they had was better. Stronger. More solid.

Except of course it wasn't.

How could this be happening? Her mind still resisted the

truth, insisting on the impossibility of it. Half an hour ago they'd both been stood at the front of the church while her father had cracked jokes and she'd clutched a bouquet of ribbons and everyone looked on, smiling. She'd been so happy. She'd been sure of it.

And yet.

"What should we tell everyone?" Dan asked. Somehow they'd already moved on to the damage-control stage, mopping up the mess of their wouldn't-be marriage. Rachel shook her head.

"I have no idea." Not, she hoped, that Dan had realised she didn't love him. How would everyone react to that? They'd think she was heartless, and maybe she was, because she couldn't feel anything right now.

She crossed to the settee and sank down on it, her mind both numb and whirling. She felt strangely distant from herself, as if she were watching this melodramatic scene unfold from the outside. *I wonder,* she thought, *what's going to happen next? What is that poor woman going to do?*

"I'll take care of it, if you like," Dan said. "Since I'm the one...well." He sighed. "Just let's agree on what we're going to say. That it's a mutual decision, or...?"

"A mutual decision, I suppose," Rachel said after a moment, her voice flat. Anything else seemed too awful to contemplate, to announce, and yet... She could not envision walking across to The Winter Hare and telling everyone the wedding was off. She simply couldn't.

"All right, then."

"But what about everything else?" She let her head fall into her hands, too overcome and exhausted to think through the endless repercussions. What about their honeymoon? Their *house*?

"We can tackle those later. The important thing now is letting everyone know and cancelling the imminent wedding stuff."

The wedding stuff. Rachel thought of her beautiful dress hanging upstairs, swathed in plastic. The trays of canapés in the fridge, the bottles of champagne on ice, for the after-party back at the vicarage. The hotel in Keswick ready to be bedecked with flowers for the reception, her sisters' bridesmaid dresses, her father's toast… None of it was needed anymore. None of it was going to happen.

"Dan, are you really sure about this?" She lifted her head to stare at him blearily; it felt like more than she could manage to so much as rise from this settee, never mind face fifty guests. Everything felt insurmountable, impossible.

"Aren't you?"

She stared at him, unsure how to answer. She didn't feel sure of anything. And yet even now, in the midst of her shock and despair, she couldn't deny that treacherous little flicker of relief she'd felt when Dan had first told her he was calling it off. It hadn't lasted more than a moment, a second, and yet…

It had been there. As much as she wanted to deny it, she

couldn't.

But was an elusive flicker of feeling a real reason to derail her entire life?

"I don't know anything," she told Dan. "I don't know anything at all. I'm completely blindsided by this."

"I'll handle it all. You don't even have to come over to the restaurant if you don't want to."

She didn't, she definitely didn't, and yet that felt like a cop-out.

"Rachel…" Dan hesitated by the door. "I'm sorry. Really, I am. More than I could ever say. I know this is the last way we'd want things to end…"

She nodded dumbly, because she didn't know what else to do. Maybe later she'd find it in herself to be angry, to feel wronged. Right now she just felt overwhelmed.

"I'll go tell everyone." He hesitated, and Rachel wondered what she should do. Say. This was the moment—the final moment. If Dan walked over there, went to The Winter Hare and told all her waiting family and friends the wedding was off…well, then there was really no going back, was there?

Except Rachel knew, with a leaden certainty, that they'd already reached the point of no return. Maybe it had happened when those first words had come out of Dan's mouth. *The wedding is off.*

Now she said nothing and after another endless moment Dan walked out of the room.

Chapter Two

"RACHEL, LET ME in."

Rachel wrapped the pillow around her head and scrunched her eyes shut, but her sister Esther was determined, as ever. She rapped sharply on the door for about the tenth time. "Let me in. You can't stay in there forever."

No, but she could try. She'd like to, that was for certain. Even with her eyes closed and the pillow over her head, Rachel could feel the bright summer sunlight streaming through the windows of her childhood bedroom.

After Dan had left last night, she'd walked upstairs, peeled off her dress, crawled into bed, and closed her eyes. Eventually, thankfully, she'd fallen asleep. Through the numbing fog of restless sleep she'd heard the others come in, and then a little while later a quiet tap on her door that had been easy to ignore.

Esther's determined knocking now was not.

"I'm not going to give up," her older sister informed her. "I'll just stay here knocking until you have to come out for food and water, or at least the loo."

Rachel thought she could manage all right without the first two, but the third was becoming a pressing issue. And she couldn't ignore her sister or the rest of her family forever, much as she longed to. Reality was going to intrude sooner or later, and it would need to be dealt with.

"Fine," she called, her voice croaky. She threw the pillow and covers off and staggered out of bed, the bright sunlight an assault to both her senses and sensibilities. With Cumbrian weather so woefully uncertain, the clear blue skies promised a perfect day for a wedding. Too bad there wasn't going to be one.

Rachel unlocked the door and flung it open before crawling back into bed and drawing the duvet over her head. She couldn't ignore her family forever, but she'd do her best.

"Ah, Rach." Esther's voice, so strident seconds before, was now full of sorrow, and that was far worse. A lump formed instantly in Rachel's throat and she scrunched her eyes against the threat of tears. If she started crying now, she'd never stop. She hadn't cried last night, and she wasn't going to cry now. She wasn't ready for that emotional bloodletting.

She felt the mattress dip as Esther sat on the edge of the bed and put one hand on Rachel's duvet-covered shoulder. "I'd ask how you're coping, but I think the answer's obvious," she said in her dry way, and against all odds, Rachel let out a hiccup of laughter. It was all just so endlessly awful.

Every time she got her mind around part of it, something

else leapt out of her. She'd woken up this morning thinking of the flowers—white roses and pink tulips for her bridal bouquet, and posies of miniature pink roses for the bridesmaids. Plus, all the flowers in the church that the older ladies of the flower guild had selflessly arranged yesterday afternoon. They'd looked gorgeous, festooned with white silk ribbons and trailing ivy at the end of each pew. All wasted. All pointless.

"What did Dan say, anyway? Last night?" Rachel asked, her voice muffled from beneath the duvet. Despite her desire to remain in hiding for the rest of her life, curiosity was starting to win out—and she knew Esther, of all people, would give her the unvarnished truth.

"He didn't say much, really. Just that you'd both come to the decision to call the wedding off. Which didn't surprise me all that much, to be honest."

Rachel yanked the duvet off her head. "It didn't? Because it surprised *me*."

Esther cocked her head, her eyes gleaming with understanding. "Ah, so it was Dan who called it off, then?"

Rachel groaned. She'd walked right into that one. "Yes, I suppose he started the conversation," she admitted after a moment. "But we did both…agree, I suppose. It's not as if I want to marry a man who doesn't want to marry me." She couldn't keep the bitterness from spiking her words, filling her heart. Why had Dan had to go and wreck everything?

Rachel squinted at her sister, her earlier words thudding

through her. "What do you mean, you weren't surprised?"

"Something was wrong between you, Rachel. I saw it all along. I asked you about it back in Manchester, when you were looking for your wedding dress—"

Rachel winced at the memory. She'd insisted nothing was wrong then, and she'd believed it. She'd been *happy*. All right, yes, she'd been a little tense, because getting married was a big step. But she'd still wanted to go through with it.

"You looked as if you were heading to the gallows," Esther continued bluntly. "Not like a woman about to marry the love of her life."

Rachel slid back beneath the covers, grateful for the cocoon of her duvet. She wasn't ready to hear her sister's particular brand of bluntness just now. She wasn't ready to dissect her relationship to Dan, and figure out why it had ended the way it had, or what it might have been lacking. There was far too much else to deal with, in any case.

"Don't, Esther, okay? I'm not ready to have this kind of conversation."

"Okay." For once Esther relented. The last few months, and her own separation and reunion with her husband Will, had softened her, at least a little. "I won't say anything more just now."

"How…how is everyone else taking it? Mum and Dad?"

"They're worried about you, first and foremost—"

"But all the guests? And the reception…?" Which was at a hotel in nearby Keswick. Rachel shuddered to think of all the wasted expense. It would run well into the thousands. Why on earth had Dan pulled a stunt like this? If he'd been having doubts, he should have said so, a long time ago. And if he'd thought she'd been having doubts, well, he should have said that too. He should have had it out with her when there still had been time to—what?

Misery swamped her, dousing that brief flicker of self-righteous anger she'd been longing to nurture. *Still time to call it off?*

"We can deal with all that, Rachel."

"It's such a waste."

"Yes, but marrying the wrong person would have been a bigger waste."

"You think that's what I was doing?" She flung a hand out from under the duvet. "Never mind. Like I said, I don't want to have that conversation just now. Just tell me the basics. The logistics. What's happening? How are we meant to tell everyone the whole thing is off?" She snuck a glance at the clock and saw it was already half past nine. She was supposed to be getting married in less than two hours. The photographer was meant to have been here half an hour ago, but as far as she could tell she hadn't arrived.

"We've told everyone already," Esther answered. "We had to, considering."

"Right." Rachel closed her eyes, the longing to blot out the entire world, her present reality, overwhelming. "So…"

"It was relatively easy, actually. Dad sent out a mass

email, and we put a message on the wedding website. Mum made a bunch of calls, and there is a notice on the church door." Esther rose from the bed to look out the window. "No one's out there now. I think everyone knows."

It was too horrible to contemplate. All her friends from school, where she taught Year Three, and everyone she'd known since the year dot in the village…her uni friends, who had travelled all the way from Manchester and London, and were staying in a local B&B…not to mention her family, all her relatives, even her Great-Aunt Edith who was incredibly ornery and would probably say something like 'you couldn't keep him, could you?' as soon as she saw her.

Rachel let out a groan. "I really think I'd like to just live in this bed forever."

"I understand, but that's not really possible, is it?" Esther answered, ever practical. Rachel groaned again.

"I know it's not, Esther, *obviously*. But give me more than a single morning to get over the worst thing that's ever happened to me, okay?"

"Is this the worst thing?" Esther asked quietly, and with a shaft of pain Rachel realised her sister was talking about the death of their brother Jamie, when she'd been just eleven and a half years old.

"Of course I don't mean *that*," she answered in little more than a whisper, tears stinging her eyes. "For heaven's sake, Esther. Can't you give me a break for just one day?"

"Sorry." Esther sounded genuinely contrite. "I didn't actually mean Jamie. I was just thinking that all in all, I think this is a blessing—"

"A *blessing*—"

"In a very big disguise, but yes."

Rachel shook her head. She was not ready to think that way, not remotely. Reluctantly she pushed off the duvet. She didn't want to get out of bed but she did need to escape her sister. "I'm going to take a shower and then have a lot of strong coffee. Maybe then I'll feel more like facing things."

Thankfully Esther took the hint and left the room, giving her one last bracing smile. Rachel reached for her dressing gown.

Twenty minutes later, having let the hot water stream— or rather, trickle—over her in the vicarage's ancient shower, and dressed in a pair of jeans and a summery blouse, with a little bit of make-up to give her some much-needed armour, Rachel headed downstairs to face the first hurdle: her loving family.

The hushed atmosphere of the kitchen, everyone sitting around the familiar oak table, cradling coffee cups, reminded Rachel of the hospital room of a terminal patient, or even a wake. Not good, at any rate.

Her mother Ruth looked up first, her face creasing in a relieved smile before drooping back into deep concern. "Rachel. Let me get you a cup of tea, something to eat—"

Rachel's stomach felt both hollow and queasy. She didn't think she could manage a mouthful, but she knew her mother well enough to know she needed to do something for her. Food was her mother's love language.

"Thanks, Mum." Rachel eased into the remaining chair around the table. Although her parents had had a big empty-out over the last few months in preparation for their move to China, the kitchen, with its rumbling Aga and weathered table, was still wonderfully familiar. Charlie, their elderly black Lab, was stretched out in front of the Aga although he lumbered over to her and nudged her knee as she sat down. Charlie always knew when you needed a little canine TLC.

"How are you, darling?" her father Roger asked. He gave her a smile of understanding and compassion while managing to seem as if he didn't pity her. Rachel smiled back gratefully, or at least she tried to.

"I'm all right," she said, although she wasn't. "At least, I will be." She hoped.

Her sister Anna and Anna's boyfriend Simon were both looking at her sympathetically, and Will, Esther's husband, gave her a quick, commiserating grimace. Rachel's heart lifted improbably, infinitesimally. At least no one was looking at her like they felt horribly sorry for her, even if they probably did. Unless they blamed her? Rachel's stomach went icy at the thought. The truth was, she had no idea how anyone felt, including herself.

"Here you are," Ruth said, sliding a plate of scrambled eggs and toast in front of Rachel. She must have had it ready and waiting. "And here, as well." The cup of tea came next, milky and sweet, just as she liked it.

"Thanks, Mum."

"Of course, darling." Ruth sat back in her seat. Everyone remained silent, watching her. Waiting for her cue, but Rachel had no idea how to handle this moment.

"Where's Miriam?" she asked finally.

"She's sleeping," Ruth answered. "She's so tired, poor love. Must be the jet lag." Her younger sister had arrived back from Australia a few days ago, surprising everyone by saying she might be staying for good. Miriam had followed her wanderlust for the last four years, since leaving secondary school. Perhaps her itchy feet had finally been well and truly scratched.

"Okay." Rachel took a sip of tea, savouring the warmth. "What about everyone else?"

"Who else, darling?" Ruth asked.

"Aunt Edith…my uni friends…everyone who came in from out of town." And Dan. Where was Dan? Did she want to know? Did she care? Yes, of course she did. Yesterday she had been planning to marry him. Those feelings didn't vanish overnight. Perhaps they never vanished at all.

"Everyone's fine," Roger said. "Having a nice leisurely brunch, most likely. Everyone knows, if you're concerned about that."

In a village the size of Thornthwaite, where Rachel was well known for being the vicar's daughter, the news had undoubtedly travelled with the speed of light. "That's good,"

Rachel said. "I guess."

Her head ached with all the details she couldn't bear to think about. "What about the hotel in Keswick…?"

"We rang and told them," Roger stated calmly. "As well as the caterers, and the band, and the florist." He smiled. "It's all sorted, love."

Rachel couldn't keep from dropping her head into her hands at the thought, overwhelmed by everything that had been lost and wasted, including her own dreams. "All that money…" she whispered.

"Don't worry about the money, Rachel," Ruth said firmly. "That's not important now."

"But it is." She couldn't keep from saying it. She and Dan had paid for most of the wedding costs, but her parents had shouldered what they could, and it ran into the thousands. All wasted. All because she'd wanted such a bloody big wedding. Rachel winced, her face still hidden by her hands, the realisation thudding through her. She'd wanted the fairy tale, and look how it had turned out.

"Rachel, please don't worry about the money," Roger said in that same unruffled voice. It didn't surprise her; her father had never been much concerned with money, and had happily foregone holidays and extravagant presents for a life of simple pleasures—family around the table, fell walks with their dog, laughter and sharing and joy. And she felt the same—of course she did, but *still*.

"How can I not worry about the money, Dad?" Rachel

looked up, blinking the world and all the worried faces back into focus. "It was a lot. Most of your savings, probably…"

"I don't think you know the first thing about my savings," Roger returned mildly, "and in any case, we've been able to get some things refunded."

"You have?" Curious now, Rachel asked, "Who gave a refund? I mean, so late…?"

"The hotel gave back our deposit, and the band did as well. People want to help, Rachel."

She stared at him for a moment, realisation dawning slowly, like a clearing mist. "You mean they feel sorry for me."

"Is that so wrong?" Ruth interjected quietly. "Compassion is no bad thing, darling."

"Pity is," Rachel returned, grimacing. She hated feeling like she was a cross between a sob story and a joke. "But I am glad about the money." Her grimace deepened as she thought about the flight from Manchester she was meant to be on tonight, and the honeymoon suite in a luxury hotel in Provence that she and Dan were meant to be enjoying, with all the treats and tours she'd happily booked, picturing them strolling hand in hand down narrow, cobblestone streets, walking into their future. "That's not going to be the case with the honeymoon, though, is it?"

"Well, actually, I have an idea about that," Esther said as she came into the kitchen, looking as brisk and no-nonsense as ever.

"You do?" Rachel regarded her sister warily, having no idea what she had planned.

"Yes, I do. Obviously, you should still go. Your name is on the ticket and the whole thing will go to waste otherwise."

"Go on my honeymoon alone?" Rachel couldn't think of anything worse. Well, she could, but it had already happened.

"No, not alone, that would be beyond sad. No, I think you should go with someone."

"Who…?"

Esther smiled. "Me."

The silence fell like a thunderclap while everyone stared at Esther in surprise.

"I fancy a holiday," she continued breezily, "and since I don't have a job at the moment, I can take the time off. Plus, I think we could use some sisterly bonding time. Will can manage the farm on his own, can't you?"

Will's smile was slow and easy. "Just about."

Esther turned to Rachel, eyebrows raised. "What do you say?"

What could she say? "But Dan's name is on the plane ticket…"

"He'll have to forfeit his ticket, which he's perfectly happy to do. And I can book my own. It's not that expensive, about a hundred quid."

Rachel didn't want to think about Dan being perfectly happy *not* to go on their honeymoon. "What if someone else wants to go? Anna or Miriam?"

Anna shook her head decisively. "I can't take time off work, and I want to spend what holiday time I do have with Simon." She gave her boyfriend, the former curate who had now taken over both vicar's role and vicarage, a loving smile.

"Miriam's travelled loads," Esther scoffed. "And she's still recovering from jet lag."

Everyone turned to look at Rachel expectantly.

"It does seem like it could be a good idea, love," Ruth said hesitantly. "A chance to get away, have a rest…"

What could she say but yes? And it wasn't as if she didn't want to go on her honeymoon with her older sister…well, it sort of was, but *still*. She loved Esther, even if she didn't always appreciate her brand of bossiness. And getting away from Thornthwaite, as her mother had suggested, and all the prying, pitying eyes for a week while the wreck of her would-be wedding was swept away…that was seriously tempting.

"All right then," Rachel said. "Sounds good."

Chapter Three

"WOW, THIS PLACE is seriously deluxe."

Rachel stood in the doorway of the honeymoon suite, wilting with exhaustion, while Esther strolled around the huge room and then plucked a strawberry from the fruit bowl taking pride of place on a coffee table in front of a huge, squashy sofa.

"I think it's bigger than our downstairs. Our entire house, maybe."

"Yes, well it was meant to be our honeymoon."

"Don't be grumpy," Esther chided. "Let's enjoy this."

"I think I'm allowed to be a little grumpy," Rachel returned. "Considering."

"You were grumpy all the way over on the plane."

"I was *asleep*," Rachel shot back. "And who are you to talk, Esther? You were grumpy for about three months after you left Will." Her sister had been reconciled to her husband of eight years for four months, and now they seemed stronger than ever, but Rachel wasn't the only who had let herself derail after a major bump on the road. And she wasn't even derailing the way Esther had—leaving her husband, quitting her job, moving back home. All Rachel was doing was indulging in a bit of a bad mood. Was that a crime?

Fortunately, Esther had the grace to look a little abashed. "Sorry, you're right. I'm rubbish at cheering people up, that's all."

"Maybe I'm not ready to be cheered up. You did watch *Inside Out*, didn't you? Remember it's okay to be sad?"

"Ye-es…" Her sister did not sound convinced.

"Well, I'm sad. Let it lie, at least for a few days. Okay?"

"Okay." Esther nodded solemnly. "I will. But can we have these his and hers massages that were booked for tomorrow morning?" She waved a notice that had been left on the coffee table, next to the fruit bowl. "There's nothing creepy about his and hers massages, is there?"

Rachel rolled her eyes. "No, it's not the massage version of the *Kama Sutra* or something. It just means having them at the same time."

"Phew. I was a little worried there. I'm already a bit concerned about the double bed, king-sized as it is." She nodded towards the huge bed on its own dais. "You kick in your sleep."

Rachel let out a little hiccup of laughter. Surprisingly, her sister was cheering her up…whether she meant to or not.

They hadn't talked much on the train to Manchester, or the flight to Nice; Rachel had been too exhausted, and Esther had seemed happy enough to read her book. It had been an unutterable relief to leave Thornthwaite and all the sympathetic smiles. Ruth had hugged her tightly before she'd left.

"I'm glad you're getting away," she'd whispered fiercely, "but you know I can stay on, Rachel, if you'd like me to. If you need me…"

"It's okay, Mum." Ruth and Roger were due to leave for China a week after Rachel got back from her would-have-been honeymoon. "You need to be with Dad."

"Still…we'll talk about it when you get back." Her poor mother looked so anxious, and Rachel couldn't keep from feeling another spurt of resentment at her former fiancé for putting so many people in such an untenable position. She'd have liked to get a proper head of steam on her anger towards Dan, because that felt so much simpler and easier, but whenever she tried, she remembered that little flicker of relief she'd felt when he'd told her the wedding was off, and she knew she couldn't.

It had only lasted a second, and she'd barely recognised it for what it was; yet still it remained, a most inconvenient truth, and one she was not yet ready to examine too closely.

She'd been fully prepared to marry Dan. She'd been planning on it. She'd bet her whole life on it, and yet…

And yet. When Rachel let herself think about it, she couldn't suppress a cold, creeping suspicion that while Dan had been the instigator of the decimation of all her hopes, she had been the architect. And that was a fear that was not only inconvenient, but also deeply uncomfortable. Downright terrifying, in fact, and so she didn't let herself think about it. The point was, she'd loved him, and he'd loved her, and they'd been planning on building their life together.

Soon after they arrived at the hotel, she and Esther both fell into bed; it had been an endless, emotional day and they needed their sleep. Rachel woke in the morning to bright summer sunlight streaming through the French windows; the air was drowsy and warm and she lay in bed, stretching indulgently, before reality crashed in and she tensed all over.

She wasn't married. She wasn't getting married. Everything she'd thought was going to happen, all that her life was going to look like, wasn't.

She closed her eyes, breathing in the sweet smell of lavender and honeysuckle, before throwing off the silky duvet and rising from bed. Esther was already awake, showered and dressed, by the looks of the open suitcase and the towel hanging on the bathroom door's rail.

Rachel reached for one of the hotel's complimentary dressing gowns, made of a thick white terrycloth as soft as velvet. She found Esther sitting outside on the private terrace, spreading jam on a croissant.

"This place is amazing. They just delivered breakfast at ten, without me even asking."

"It's past ten?" Rachel squinted in the bright, Technicolor sunshine; from their terrace, she could just glimpse the hotel's pool, the placid aquamarine water shimmering with sunlight.

"Yes, I didn't want to wake you, because you seemed absolutely knackered."

"Did you sleep all right?" Rachel asked as she sat opposite Esther on a delicate wrought-iron chair.

Esther poured her some hot, fragrant coffee and pushed a little pitcher of foamed milk across the table. "As well as can be expected, considering how much you kick. Dan had a lucky escape." She grimaced quickly. "Sorry. Too soon for jokes?"

"Definitely." Rachel busied herself making her coffee milky and sweet, her hair thankfully falling forward to hide her expression, which she couldn't quite trust or judge.

"I won't mention him again, promise. So, we've got the massages booked in an hour, and according to the itinerary left in the room, there's a walking tour of the old town of Aix booked for this afternoon—apparently we don't want to miss Les Cours Mirabeau, or the birthplace of Cézanne."

"Right."

"And then tonight we have a reservation for the tasting menu at a Michelin-starred restaurant." Esther raised her eyebrows. "Did you plan all this or did the hotel?"

"I did." Rachel took a sip of coffee, avoiding her sister's gaze. "It was meant to be my honeymoon, you know."

"I know. I'm impressed. Will and I never had a honeymoon, so I'm glad to finally get one in, even if he's not here. Rather appropriate, considering—sorry." She shook her head. "I really must stop that."

"Yes," Rachel agreed. "You really must."

Yet as low as she felt, it was hard to stay down in the dumps when she was sitting on a lovely little terrace, sipping delicious coffee, in the south of France. Everything was perfect—from the rich, slightly bitter coffee, to the sweet strawberry jam on her flaky, golden croissant, to the honeysuckle-scented air and the sunlight pouring over everything like golden syrup. Despite herself, Rachel started to relax.

She continued to relax as they went for their massages at the hotel's luxury spa; it was impossible to tense up when a very competent Swedish masseuse was digging deep into her stressed and knotted muscles. Rachel came out feeling as if she'd been melted like butter.

They spent an hour lounging by the pool, and Esther ordered sandwiches from the pool bar for lunch, before they headed upstairs to change for their walking tour.

Thankfully, Esther had not felt the need to make much conversation, and Rachel was content simply to be and let herself be pampered by all the luxurious treats she'd planned several months ago, when she and Dan had decided on the south of France for their honeymoon.

It was good of him, she acknowledged in a rare moment of empathy, to have forsaken his place on this trip, although perhaps he really hadn't wanted to go. Perhaps he'd never wanted any of the things she had. She felt as if she had to question everything now, and it was an awful feeling, like dangling in mid-air, the solid ground she'd assumed had been right under her feet now miles below.

She wondered how Esther had handled the conversation with Dan about the honeymoon, and then decided not to ask. She wasn't ready for grim details yet.

The old town of Aix was lovely, with a wide, pedestrian thoroughfare lined with elegant mansions with wrought-iron railings that dripped with brightly coloured bougainvillea, interspersed with upscale boutiques and outdoor cafés where tourists and locals alike lounged, sipping their lattes and reading newspapers or simply watching the world stroll by.

By the time they got back to the hotel Rachel's feet were aching and she was tired but a little bit happy—strangely so. Everything was so beautiful, and it felt good, after weeks of frantic stress, to relax. All she had to do was not think and she could enjoy all this week had to offer. Hopefully.

But of course it couldn't last. Over dinner that night, both wearing their nicest sundresses, sipping wine, Esther started at it again.

"So why do you think Dan called it off, really?"

"Esther." Rachel put down the tasting menu of ten courses she'd been perusing. "I thought we weren't going to talk about this? Too soon, remember?"

"But don't you want to know?"

"Not really. Not yet."

"I would, if I were you."

"Well, you're not me, are you?" Rachel answered with

some asperity. "And, in any case, you stuck your head well in the sand when it was your marriage that was at risk. Didn't want to talk about it to anyone, didn't even want to think about it yourself. So please don't push me, okay?"

Esther looked abashed. "You're right, you're right. Sorry."

Rachel wondered how long it would be before her sister couldn't keep herself from asking another prying question. Five minutes? Ten?

Amazingly, Esther controlled herself the whole meal, making sure only to talk about innocuous subjects—food, wine, France. She touched briefly on family—Anna and Simon, and when they might get engaged, before discreetly skimming away from that potentially fraught subject, although Rachel didn't actually mind thinking about Anna and Simon and their undoubtedly forthcoming engagement; she wanted Anna to be happy. Someone should be, at any rate.

Tonight, however, Rachel focused on enjoying the food and drink, as well as the lovely ambiance of the restaurant, all shadowy candlelight and murmuring customers.

She kept up the mind-blanking enjoyment for the next few days, going from beauty treatment to leisure activity to decadent meal and back again, spending time in between lounging by the pool, supplied by Esther with a series of frothy blockbusters to read that did a very good job of keeping her thoughts otherwise engaged.

And while Esther was as good as her word, keeping silent about Rachel's marital woes—or lack of them, really—as the week wound to a close reality began its inevitable, relentless intrusion.

She was heading back to Thornthwaite in two days, and she had no plans whatsoever for the rest of the summer holiday. She also had no place to live…yet another aspect of this whole tragic debacle that she'd kept herself from thinking about.

Now, their departure forty-eight hours imminent, Rachel felt brave enough to tackle the subject with her sister.

"Nowhere to live?" Esther raised her eyebrows so they appeared above her sunglasses, two dark arcs. "What about that pile up on the fells?"

Rachel grimaced. Thinking about that house—her absolute dream house—hurt, a lot. "We'll have to sell it, I suppose. It was a stretch with both of us living there, but now…" She shrugged, trying to dissolve the lump that was rapidly forming in her throat. She'd been going to have her children in that house. Their BabyGros were going to hang on the Aga railing, neatly drying. Their laughter would ring through the wide corridors and up the sweeping staircase. There was a big gnarled oak tree in the back garden, perfect for climbing, and a rope swing.

Tears stung her eyes and she looked away, not wanting Esther to see how much losing that house pained her. Her sister had confronted her once before, when Rachel, in a frenzy of excitement, had shown it to her, before they'd bought it. Esther had been quietly wary, even disapproving, knowing the house was beyond their means, and sensing, even then, that Rachel cared more for the house than her husband-to-be.

She didn't, of course, but the house had been important. It had been the place where all the wonderful things she'd had planned were going to happen not just for her, but for her and Dan and their family, as well. Things she thought they'd both wanted, had both valued. Had she been wrong? Did Dan care more about temperamental, fizzy feelings than the reality of day-to-day life together? Based on his reason for calling off the wedding, it seemed so.

"Can you keep your current place?" Esther asked, bringing Rachel out of her circling thoughts. She had been living in a cosy terraced cottage a stone's throw from the vicarage for the last five years, having bought it on the cheap, because it had needed complete doing up. As DIY was not her strong suit, she'd only managed to do the absolute minimum.

Still, it had sold—to a lovely young married couple with a baby on the way. The husband was a joiner, and keen to get cracking on the renovations. They'd already moved in, since Rachel had been living at the vicarage for the last few weeks, and she'd seen most of the kitchen fittings in a skip outside. No, she definitely couldn't move back to her old place.

"It's sold," she told Esther. "You know that."

"But sometimes you can negotiate—"

"No, they're already living there." She shook her head, her throat tightening again. "It's completely impossible."

"Could you rent…?"

She wasn't sure she could afford to rent anywhere, not at least until the dream house sold. As it was, she and Dan were going to have to sit down and hammer out all the awful financial implications of their wedding-that-wasn't.

"Maybe," she said, because she didn't want Esther to know how skint she really was. Her parents had put a lot towards the wedding, but she'd wanted the best and so she'd paid for plenty out of her own pocket. She'd wanted the blasted fairy tale, and she most certainly hadn't got it. Perhaps it had been foolish to want those kinds of dreams, to live for the castles-in-the-air expectation that could—and did—so easily fall flat. But she'd thought her dreams had a solid foundation, a basis in reality. She hadn't realised how flimsy they had ended up being.

"You don't sound too enthused," Esther remarked. "You could live with us, if you wanted."

Rachel tried not to show how appalling she found that prospect. She knew her sister meant to be kind, but Esther and Will were just re-establishing their blissful married life, and Esther had mentioned, cautiously, that they were trying for a baby. Rachel would be third-wheeling in the extreme.

"I'm sure I'll find something," she murmured, although she wasn't sure at all.

Esther nodded and Rachel gazed out at the shimmering pool, wishing she could just stay in the lovely sun-soaked and surreal beauty of Aix-en-Provence. She had three more weeks of summer holiday before she had to start teaching Year Three again. Maybe she could rent a place here, hide out for another few weeks…

As tempting a prospect as that seemed, Rachel knew she couldn't afford it, and it wasn't realistic anyway. She needed to face up to her life—or what was left of it—back in Thornthwaite. And somehow, amidst all the wreckage and rubble, she needed to figure out how she was going to go forward.

"Rachel," Esther asked abruptly, startling her out of her thoughts, "do you ever think about Jamie?"

Rachel stiffened automatically. "Jamie…?" She gazed at her sister in wary surprise. "Why are you asking about him?"

"He was our brother."

"I *know* that." She couldn't keep from bristling, despite her best attempts to sound calm and reasonable. "Of course I think about him, Esther. Like you said, he was our brother."

He'd been *her* brother. She and Jamie had been only sixteen months apart, the closest of all the siblings both in age and spirit. They'd shared a room until a year before he'd died. The day he'd died… But she didn't want to think about that. She never thought about that morning, even if she often thought about him.

"Don't you think it was a big thing in our lives?" Esther

asked quietly. "His death?"

"Don't I *think*?" Rachel stared at her sister in disbelief. She knew Esther was blunt and brusque at the best of times, even callous, but this was cruel. "Of course I think it was a big thing, Esther," she said in a carefully controlled voice. "It was the biggest thing. Our brother *died*. I saw him die." But no, she didn't want to go there. "I was in counselling all through high school. Don't you remember that?"

Esther had the grace to blush. "I remember that," she said, but Rachel could tell that she hadn't, not until she'd reminded her.

"I'm sorry, this is coming out all wrong," Esther tried again. "I'm not trying to sound insensitive, even for me."

"You're doing a good imitation, then."

"It's just…when Will and I had our…issues…" Each word came with painful slowness, the verbal equivalent to mountain climbing. "I realised that a lot of my feelings…my fear and anxiety and stuff like that…they came from Jamie's death, and how I handled it. Or rather, how I didn't handle it."

Rachel stared at her sister for a long moment. She knew this was a big confession for Esther, who of all four Holley girls was the most emotionally closed off. Rachel was probably the least. She'd worked her way through Jamie's death through years of counselling—the grief, the guilt, the sorrow, the loss. She'd felt it all, over and over again, in an all too familiar cycle. And she'd finally come to a place, some time in her early twenties, where she'd felt at peace with it all, at least as much as she could.

She still missed Jamie; she still thought about him nearly every day, and she made a birthday cake on his birthday every year. She'd got to a point where she could talk about the fun times with a smile and recount funny stories about him with a laugh. Really, she'd done all she could. And if Esther thought Dan calling off her wedding had anything to do with her brother's death…

Well, she was crazy, that was all. Just plain crazy.

"Look, Esther," Rachel said after a long moment. "I appreciate your honesty. But we're different people and we have different issues to deal with. And right now, mine is facing up to the fact that my life just collapsed all around me, as well as figuring out where I am going to live, and how I'm going to face two thousand people back in Thornthwaite, all of whom know I've been jilted."

A funny look came on Esther's face, making Rachel's skin prickle. "What?" she demanded when the silence stretched on and her sister's expression didn't change.

"It's just…your issue to deal with isn't Dan leaving you? Or mending your broken heart?" There was a gleam in Esther's eye that made Rachel feel as if she'd just stepped into a neatly set trap and sprung it.

"Of course I meant that too," she snapped, but her sister didn't look convinced.

Chapter Four

A S THE TRAIN pulled into Thornthwaite's tiny station, Rachel felt a very real sense of dread swirl in her stomach. It had been easy, or at least easier, to put aside all the pressing worries and concerns when she'd been sunbathing in the south of France, with a seemingly limitless supply of escapist novels and frothy cocktails to lose herself in, but now that she was back home, surrounded by the familiar grey-green fells, the church and vicarage looming in the distance, reality was impossible to avoid.

She and Esther hadn't spoken much on the train; in fact, they hadn't spoken much since that unfortunate conversation about Jamie two days ago. Rachel felt she might have been a bit snappish, and she was sorry for it, but Esther never knew when to stop. Still, she felt a needling of uneasy guilt as she stepped off the train and onto the platform, a brisk Cumbrian wind buffeting her the instant her feet touched the pavement. They weren't in the South of France anymore; that was for certain.

It was only a five-minute walk from the train station to

the vicarage, and so they both lugged their suitcases towards their family home, where Esther had left her car and Rachel had left her life. Even in that short distance they managed to walk by half a dozen people Rachel either knew or recognised, and every one of them gave her an all too sympathetic smile, pity visible in their eyes. When was *that* going to let up?

"Hello?" Rachel called as she stepped into the cool, dim entry hall of the vicarage, with its floor of inlaid Victorian tile in a range of reds and yellows. She took a deep breath, but instead of the usual comforting scents of home baking and furniture polish, she inhaled the musty, dusty smell of emptiness, and it shocked her.

In the week she'd been gone her parents had obviously done the last of the clearing out, getting ready for Simon to move in. Although they were leaving the bigger pieces of furniture for him, there could be no doubt the house looked emptier; there were bare patches on the walls where there had once been pictures, the paint underneath several shades brighter than the rest of the wall.

"Rachel!" Her mother Ruth rounded the hall from the kitchen, her lovely, familiar face breaking into a wide smile as she came towards Rachel with her arms outstretched. "How lovely to see you, and Esther, too." She hugged them both in turn, putting her hands on their shoulders one after the other to inspect them, just as she used to when they were little, on a Sunday morning before church, to check for toast crumbs on their chins or tangles in their hair.

"You're both looking remarkably well. So tanned!"

"It was very relaxing." Rachel put her carry-on bag down with a thud. "How have things been here?"

"Oh, fine. Busy. Last-minute preparations and all that."

"You're all ready?"

"Just about," Ruth said brightly, but her smile faltered a little bit. Rachel wondered if her mother was having cold feet about their move to China, which seemed to be far more her father's dream than hers.

"Hey, guys." Miriam came down the stairs, dressed in yoga pants and a faded T-shirt, her hair in a tangle. Esther's eyebrows rose.

"Did you just get up, you lazy cow?"

Miriam yawned and stretched. "So I did."

"Tell me you're not still jet-lagged?"

"It takes a long time to get over."

"Right, I'd better get back home." Esther kissed her mother's cheek. "I'll come by tomorrow for a cuppa, okay? Got to get them in while we can."

"Yes, lovely." Ruth's lips trembled only slightly as she smiled. "Thank you, darling. Rachel? Cup of tea?"

"I could murder one," Rachel admitted, and Ruth turned to her youngest daughter.

"Miriam?"

"No, I need to have a shower." Miriam turned back upstairs and Rachel followed her mother into the kitchen, stopping short when she saw the beloved old oak table and mismatched chairs were gone, replaced by a pine table with four matched chairs, that looked as if it was straight out of an IKEA flat pack. "What happened to the table?"

"It was too big for Simon," Ruth explained. "With just him rattling around in here."

"He asked for it to be moved?" Rachel couldn't keep the indignation from her voice.

"Rachel, it's about to be his house now," Ruth said gently. "But no, he didn't ask. He's been so gracious about everything, offering to keep anything we wanted. You know he's keeping Charlie?"

"Yes, I know." Their poor old dog had known no home but this one. Even now he was stretched out in front of the Aga, snoring quietly. Rachel bent to fondle his ears and he snuffled in his sleep.

"Simon's been the soul of consideration," Ruth said as she put on the kettle. "Don't be cross with him."

"I'm not." It was just about impossible to be cross with Simon, because he was so kind and good-natured. "But where's the table?" Rachel pulled out one of the flimsy chairs and sat down on it with a little moue of distaste. Definitely not the same.

"It's in storage, in one of Will and Esther's barns. Anna was adamant that we not give it away. You're not the only one who is sentimental about these things."

"And you're not, Mum? That table must mean something to you. It has teeth marks on one end from when Miriam was teething, and a dab of green paint from Jamie's Incredible Hulk costume in Year Four." Her voice caught and after a second she continued more steadily, "You and Dad bought it in a car boot sale when you'd only just got married."

"I know." Ruth's back was to her as she got out cups so Rachel couldn't see her expression. "That table has a lot of wonderful memories. But people matter more than things, Rachel. You know that."

"Yes, of course I do, but things matter too. They hold memories. They remind us of the people we love, the life we've had." Her voice trembled with the force of her emotion. Wasn't that what all the trappings Dan seemed to think were materialistic had meant to her?

"Yes, that's true." Ruth's voice wavered and she turned to give Rachel a sad smile. "You're right, of course, but at the end of the day, they're still just things, and you can't take them with you the way you can take the memories. Now Earl Grey or English Breakfast? I know you like them both."

"English Breakfast, please," Rachel answered after a moment. She considered dropping the whole subject, but something made her ask, "Why *are* you going to China, Mum? You and Dad?"

"This again?" Ruth said, raising her eyebrows.

"I haven't talked to you about it before, not really."

"Your sisters have checked and double-checked that I'm

happy to go, and I am. Please believe me."

"Yes, all right, but *why* are you going? I mean, Dad has thirty years of experience in rural ministry in the UK, and he's always saying how China is sending missionaries to us these days. Why is he going over there?"

Ruth smiled faintly as she passed Rachel her mug. "That's a refreshing question, actually. I think all of you girls have been so gobsmacked by our move that you haven't really asked why we're doing it, or even what we'll be doing, exactly."

"Sorry," Rachel murmured, chastened. It was a big move for her parents, different and exciting, and she had a feeling that she and her sisters had been far more concerned with how it affected them than why her parents were going in the first place, which was really rather self-centred of them.

"As it happens," Ruth said as she sat opposite Rachel at the table that really felt far too small, "your father was asked to teach a course to training pastors on the challenges and opportunities of rural ministry. You might think it would look very different in China compared to here, but some things are the same."

"But I thought you were moving to the city? Jinan?" Her parents had shown her pictures of the tiny flat in an enormous high-rise where they would be living, the exact opposite of their home now.

"Yes, because the theological college is in Jinan. Although I expect we'll be travelling out to the rural areas fairly often, and perhaps we'll even move to one of the outlying villages one day."

"Wow." Rachel shook her head slowly as she considered her mother's reality; in less than a week, she'd be living in Jinan, in an area and home that was about as far from this rambling old vicarage tucked among the fells as was possible. "I'm really going to miss you."

"And I'm going to miss you all terribly. But we will be back for Christmas, you know, and after that, as well."

"Yes." Although that seemed ages away. But maybe by Christmas her life would be on a more even keel. Which brought Rachel to the questions she knew she needed to ask. "Have you seen Dan?"

"Yes, he stopped by the day after—the day after you left." The day after her wedding, as was. "To apologise. He was very contrite, very gracious."

"Did he explain…?"

"Only that you'd both agreed to call it off." Ruth frowned at her in worry. "Is there something more you want to tell me, Rachel? Because I must admit, I was terribly surprised by the whole thing."

Rachel sighed. "So was I, really."

"So it was Dan—"

"Yes, but I suppose it ended up being a mutual decision, sort of." And sort of not. She paused, debating whether to confide in her mother about what Dan said. *It's because you don't love me.* It sounded so awful, so damning, as if she was some heartless mercenary, and she *wasn't*.

She'd wanted to build a *life* with Dan, one based on shared beliefs and values and affection. And yes, she'd wanted a lovely house to raise her family, and a big wedding to celebrate the start of it, but were those things so bad? So wrong?

While Rachel knew absolutely that her mum would be sympathetic, she still didn't want to admit to what Dan had said—and she didn't want to worry her mother more than she already was. "Although it was his idea," she said finally, "in the end, I agreed." Because what had been the alternative?

"Why, though? You both seemed so happy."

"Did we? Because Esther doesn't seem to think so."

"Oh, you know Esther. Prickly as anything."

"Yes, but…" Rachel took a sip of tea, her thoughts all jumbled, and in truth she didn't know whether she wanted to sort them out. "I thought we were happy," she said. "Happy enough, anyway."

"Happy enough?"

"That sounds worse than I meant it to. I mean, no one is happy all the time, are they? All I'm trying to say is, I wanted to marry him. I was planning on spending the rest of my life with him."

"But…" Ruth looked troubled. "Did you love him, Rachel?" The question was quiet and sad, and Rachel had to look away. Her mother, in typical fashion, had got right to the heart of the matter, and with characteristic gentleness. Rachel knew she would have to tell the truth.

"Yes, I did," she said after an endless moment. Her throat felt almost too tight to get the words out. "But it seems Dan didn't think so." Hurt spiked her words. What had he *wanted* from her? "Maybe I don't know what real love is. Romantic love, anyway. Whatever I felt wasn't enough for Dan."

"You've had a few boyfriends through the years…"

"No one serious, though." She'd been happy enough to lose herself in a relationship, become over-the-top obsessed even, but it had always felt like a game, the chase rather than the catch, and each relationship had run its course after a couple of months if not weeks. When they'd ended, she'd never been more than melodramatically broken-hearted for a few days, simply because it had always felt rather luxurious to indulge in those kinds of theatrics for a little while, like something out of a rom-com—permission to have a tub of Ben and Jerry's and a whole evening of Netflix for a few weeks, at the very least, before someone else caught her eye. If she was honest, which she had to be now, her heart had never been involved. But it had been with Dan.

"But Dan was serious?" Ruth asked.

"Yes, of course he was." They'd only dated for three months before getting engaged, but Rachel had felt certain. Dan was everything she'd wanted in a husband—kind, attractive, gentle. Someone with good humour as well as faith, who wanted to have loads of children, just like she did. And she'd loved him…even if Dan hadn't thought she had.

Although Rachel was honest enough to admit now that after they'd become engaged, planning the wedding had taken up far more of her time than actually maintaining their still-new relationship, never mind deepening it. "I don't know, Mum," she said restively. "When he said he wanted to call it off, it blindsided me, but in some weird way I wasn't surprised, either. I was horrified and hurt and completely shocked, but not totally…surprised. Which doesn't make any sense, I know."

"Relationships are complicated," Ruth murmured. "And so are our emotions."

Or lack of them? Rachel propped her chin on her fist. "Complicated or not complicated enough? Dan wanted something from me that I'm not sure I even have to give." Which was a terrifying thought. What if she just didn't have it in her to love someone the way you needed to in a marriage? Or could she find someone who was happy with her happy-enough?

"Perhaps that's just a sign he wasn't the right person," Ruth said gently.

"He seemed like the right person."

"Yes, but our hearts don't believe in box-ticking. A person can have all the right traits and characteristics, but something fundamental might still be missing."

"But you and Dad always say how love can grow," Rachel returned. "Dad always says he loves you more with every year. What if Dan and I had been like that?" A lump formed in her throat at the thought. "Maybe I didn't feel what he wanted me to feel now—I can admit that. But what if I felt it later? What if what we'd had would have been enough, after all?"

Ruth regarded her sadly. "I don't think Dan came to this decision lightly, Rachel. What you say might have happened, but it also might not have. There needs to be a certain, solid foundation—"

"And I thought we had that!"

"But Dan didn't think you did. And the fact that he thought that suggests something was missing."

"So you think he was right to call it off?"

Ruth sighed. "I don't know if there is a right or wrong in this situation, darling. It simply is. Dan is a good man and you are a lovely woman, and if the two of you don't marry each other, then I pray you'll both find someone else, in time."

In time. Rachel couldn't imagine dating again, ever, even though she still longed for marriage and family, as she always had. As for Dan… "Yes," she said rather dutifully. "I'll pray for that too." She tried for a wry smile and thought she managed it. "Thanks for the tea. I'd better go unpack." And figure out where she was going to live once her parents left and Simon moved into the vicarage.

On the way to her bedroom, Rachel stopped by Miriam's, glancing at her sister, who sat on the edge of her bed, running her fingers through her damp hair, a distant look on her face.

"Everything okay, Miriam?"

"Hmm? Oh, yeah." Miriam gave her a quick smile, but it didn't quite reach her eyes. Although she'd been flat out with wedding stuff since her sister had come back from Australia two weeks ago, Rachel had still managed to notice that something was a little off with Miriam, who was usually sassy and cheerful and full of bouncy energy.

The very fact that Miriam had indicated she might be staying in Thornthwaite for good had given everyone pause, but her sister had refused to say anything more about it, and she had, more or less, been keeping to herself since her return.

Now Rachel braced her shoulder against the doorframe. "Have you decided what you're going to do, Miriam? I mean, long term? You mentioned you might stay in Thornthwaite…?"

"I don't know." Miriam shrugged. "There's not much for me back in Australia, to be honest. And I've run out of money." She gave an insouciant smile, or tried to, but it wobbled.

"Right…" Rachel frowned. "What do you mean, there's nothing for you back in Australia?"

"Minimum wage work in a bar. Hardly something to fly across the world for."

"And friends…?"

Miriam shrugged. "Backpackers who have moved on. I liked my life, but it wasn't ever going to be permanent, was it?"

"No…" Rachel's frown deepened as she realised Miriam's situation was just as precarious as her own, if not more so. "Mum and Dad are leaving in less than a week," she said, pointing out the glaringly obvious. "You can't stay here, can you?" And neither could she.

Miriam's glance slid away. "I suppose not."

"So have you thought it through? Where are you going to stay, Miriam?"

She shrugged. "I'm not sure. I could bung in with one of my old mates from school, if worse comes to worst."

"But are any of your old school friends living in their own places around here?" Miriam was only twenty-three, the surprise baby, born five years after Anna and thirteen years younger than Esther. Her friends were surely finishing uni or had moved on.

Miriam just shrugged. "Dunno."

"Seriously, Miriam—"

"Oh lay off, Rach, okay? You've got troubles enough of your own, haven't you? I'm fine." And to Rachel's surprise, her sister rose from the bed and, nudging her out with a determined foot, she closed the door firmly in her face.

Well, that wasn't like Miriam. She was the most laid-back of them all, the opposite of Esther. Maybe Rachel had been a bit naggy, but it seemed as if something was going on, yet what? Worry cramped her stomach as Rachel retreated to her own room. She wished Miriam had more of a plan…heaven knew, she needed more of a plan. Miriam was right; she had troubles enough of her own, and they weren't going to go away anytime soon.

The next day, despite her deep reluctance, Rachel did what she knew she had to do. She went to see Dan. She texted him first, preferring that to an actual phone call, and he texted back promptly inviting her to come to his house that evening. All very civilised, she acknowledged rather sourly.

And it *was* very civilised, she thought as she pulled up in front of his barn conversion on the other side of the village, the air surprisingly balmy for a Cumbrian summer, the sun still shining high above at eight o'clock at night.

Dan greeted her at the door, his dark hair rumpled, his hazel eyes glinting, and Rachel's heart didn't roll over in remembrance. It didn't even so much as twitch, and that made her feel oddly guilty. Surely she should still feel a rush of emotion, of desire? Or was she just still so hurt, so desolate, at the way things had ended, or the fact that they'd ended at all?

"Hi, Dan."

"Rachel." His gaze rested on her briefly, taking in the tan. "You had a good ho—holiday?" Had he actually been going to say *honeymoon*? Rachel stepped across the threshold, sidling past him.

"As good as can be expected, I suppose." That came out a little more bitter than she meant it to, but she *was* bitter. She was trying not to be, heaven knew, but it was there all the same, a dark little root burrowing deep into her heart. It would take a lot of strength, a lot of healing, to pluck it out.

"I'm glad. Would you like a drink? I have wine, or if you'd rather something soft…?" He knew she didn't like beer, and so he didn't offer it, something that made Rachel feel sad. No matter what Dan thought they had or hadn't felt for each other, he knew her and she knew him. They'd been going to spend their life together, and she'd been looking forward to it.

"I'll have a glass of wine if there's a bottle open, but don't go to any trouble."

"It's no trouble."

Rachel stood in the kitchen doorway while Dan opened a bottle of red. She'd been in this room many times, had eaten dinner at the table in front of the French windows; she had relaxed outside on the little terrace overlooking the fells. Dan had wanted her to move in here after the wedding; he hadn't seen the need to buy their dream house right away, but Rachel had been adamant…and now they were here, dismantling their dreams. She sighed, the sound heavy.

"So I guess we need to hammer out some details."

Dan handed her a glass of wine, his eyebrows raised. "About what?"

"Well, the house, for one. And all the wedding presents." Her mother had been old-fashioned, displaying them on the dining room table—twelve place settings of fine china, linens and crystal vases, a state-of-the-art coffeemaker and several toasters, although they'd only registered for one.

"I suppose we just send the wedding presents back?" Dan suggested uncertainly.

Box up one hundred gifts? Yet what else could they do? The gifts definitely had to go back. Rachel sank into one of the chairs at the kitchen table. "I suppose so." That would fill a lot of her summer holiday, at any rate. "I can do that."

"I'm happy to help…"

"No, they're all at the vicarage, anyway." She didn't fancy working together on that project, like some honeymoon period in reverse. "What about the house?"

Dan sighed and raked a hand through his hair. "Yeah, that one's not so straightforward."

"Except it rather is, isn't it?" Rachel's mouth twisted grimly. "We could barely afford it when we were both going to live in it. We certainly can't afford only one of us to live in it now."

"But you love that house…"

Rachel stared at him, trying to control the expression on her face. Did he think it had just been about a house for her? It had been so much more than that, a dream house for both of them, the place where they were going to build their lives.

"Do you want to live in it?" Dan asked.

"No," she said, unable to keep the horror from her voice. "Of course not." Living by herself in her family dream home would be just about the most depressing thing, ever. "Do you?"

Dan looked startled. "I haven't even sold my house yet."

"Oh, right." Unlike her, he had a place to live. His life could go on the same. "Have you taken it off the market?" she asked as she took a sip of wine.

"Well… yes." Dan shifted, looking uncomfortable. "It seemed for the best, considering…"

She nodded, trying to school her face into an understanding expression. Of course he'd taken it off the market. Why wouldn't he? She shouldn't feel resentful, she knew that, and yet…

Rachel took a deep breath and let it out slowly. There was no point being angry with Dan. He already looked miserable; she didn't need to make it worse for both of them. He'd done what he'd thought was right, even if she still felt like railing against it.

"So we need to put the house—the other house—on the market." She tried to speak practically but her voice wobbled and she felt her face start to crumple. She looked away, blinking rapidly, willing herself not to break down in front of Dan.

"Oh, Rachel." He put his wine glass on the table before coming over and wrapping his arms around her. Rachel breathed in the comforting scent of him—aftershave and animal, from his work as a vet—and then pushed him away.

"We shouldn't."

"We're still friends, aren't we? We can be friends at least, given a little time?"

"I...I don't know."

"Sometimes I think we worked better as friends than fiancés," Dan said with an attempt at a wry smile.

Rachel prickled. "What is that supposed to mean?"

"Just...sometimes you didn't seem to really like me, Rachel. That way." To her shock Dan was blushing, and she realised she was, as well.

"You mean..."

"Physically. You know, I get that attraction can grow between people when they love each other." Dan looked away, his cheeks now nearly scarlet. "But sometimes I felt as if you were just...tolerating things. When I kissed you."

Tolerating...? Rachel didn't know where to look. She'd never even considered that aspect of their relationship...which, in its own way, was rather telling, but still. It had been fine. It had all been *fine*. Hadn't it?

"What did you want from me?" she asked. "I loved you, Dan—"

"I think you loved the idea of me," Dan said quietly. "But did you love me? I'm not sure about that."

She shook her head, hurt. "Just because I wasn't crawling all over you?"

"I'm not saying that—"

"Aren't you?"

"It's just...sometimes it felt as if you were avoiding...me." He raked a hand through his hair as he shook his head. "I could tell, Rachel. That's all. Don't you know what I'm saying?"

She bit her lip as she looked away. All right, yes, *maybe*. She hadn't felt that pulse-pounding tingle he'd mentioned before, the kind she'd only read about in romance novels or seen in chick flicks, but did it really matter? Was that so important? She thought they'd had something better, something stronger.

"Yes, I know what you're saying," she said at last. "But I'm not sure how important it was. I still wanted to spend my life with you."

"But don't you think that would have changed, in time? When you realised you didn't feel that way about me?"

"We'll never know now, will we?" Rachel couldn't keep from saying bitterly. "Although you seem to have worked it all out for yourself."

"I just didn't want to take that risk."

"And I did."

"Are you sure about that?" His words were quiet, lethal. Rachel turned to look at him, her heart somersaulting in her chest.

"Pardon...?"

"When I told you the wedding was off...for a second...before the shock set in...you looked relieved, Rachel. I saw it. I felt it."

She stared at him, slack-jawed, unable to form a reply. He knew her so well, and yet sometimes it felt as if he didn't know her at all.

"Do you deny it?"

"No," she admitted painfully. "But…but…" To her shame, she found she couldn't say anything at all.

"I'm sorry, Rachel. I'm sorry it ended the way it did, as late as it did. But I still think it was the right decision, and I hope you come to realise that, as well."

Tears stung her eyes and she blinked them back. How could she be angry with Dan now? How could she be bitter? "I'm sorry too," she whispered, and she meant it with every fibre of her being.

Dan sighed heavily and nodded. "As for the house, I can call the estate agent and list it this week."

"Thank you." She released a shuddery breath. "The sooner the better, because I don't think I can afford to rent somewhere until that place is sold."

A look of concern crossed Dan's face. "Where are you going to live?"

"At the vicarage for the next week. After that, I'm not sure. Maybe in Will and Esther's spare room," she added with a wry grimace. She could share with Miriam, who was looking to be as potentially homeless as she was.

"You can always stay here, Rachel—" Dan began, and Rachel shook her head.

"No." Her response was immediate and definite. "Thank you very kindly for the offer, but no. That's not a good idea."

"No, it probably isn't." He smiled sadly. "Sorry, I guess I wasn't thinking."

"It's just…it will take a little time, Dan." She tried to smile. "To get things back to being friends. But I think we will get there one day. One day soon, even."

"Good."

They stared at each other, a little bit at a loss, sad and silent. The bitterness Rachel had been feeling was starting to wither. She'd loved this man. She couldn't start hating him just because he'd hurt her. She didn't want to, and yet she didn't know what to feel.

Finally Rachel stood up. "I should go."

"All right." Dan took a step towards her, one hand outstretched. "You're…you're okay, though, Rachel? I mean…" He shrugged helplessly. "I really am sorry."

"I know you are, and I am, too. But I am okay," she said as firmly as she could. "At least, I will be." She tried to smile. "I suppose you'll want this back?" she forced herself to ask, gesturing to the modest diamond on her ring finger. They'd picked it out together.

"No, you keep it," Dan said hurriedly.

"I don't know what the etiquette is, but I think you should have it." With effort Rachel slipped it off and handed it to Dan. "You take it, Dan. It's only right."

Reluctantly he pocketed the ring. "I never meant it to happen this way, you know. I really didn't."

"I know." And she hadn't, either. "I guess I'll see you around?" she asked instead, although belatedly she realised she'd made it sound like an invitation to get together, and she wasn't ready for that yet.

"Yes, definitely." Dan nodded quickly. "Anytime you want to talk…"

"Thanks." She wasn't ready for that either, though. With a nod of farewell Rachel headed towards the door. She knew there had to be other things they needed to talk about, but she couldn't think about them now. This had been hard enough.

Outside the sun was sinking behind the fells, casting long, cold shadows across the rolling sheep pasture. Even though it was late July, right now it felt like November, which was on par with her mood. She didn't look back at Dan's low, snug house as she pulled onto the narrow lane and headed back towards the vicarage.

Everything was quiet as she came into the house, and even quieter as she headed back to the kitchen. Anna and Simon were sitting around the table with Ruth and Roger, and they all fell ominously silent as Rachel rounded the corner. She clocked their guilty expressions with a ripple of dread.

"What is it?"

Anna glanced at Simon, and then at her parents. No one

spoke. What on earth was going on? Anna had only arrived in Thornthwaite that *afternoon*. Surely something hadn't happened already?

"Hello…?" Rachel tried to sound light and teasing. "Why are you all looking so guilty?"

"Not about *you*," Anna said quickly.

Uh-oh. "Then why have you all gone so quiet?"

"It's just…" She gave another helpless glance at Ruth and Roger, who both smiled at her encouragingly. "The truth is, Rachel…Simon and I are engaged."

Chapter Five

THE THING WAS, Rachel didn't mind. While her parents, her sister, and her sister's boyfriend—now fiancé—were all looking at her in fearful concern, as if she might break down sobbing, Rachel knew she wouldn't. She really was happy for Simon and Anna. Of course she was.

Yet somehow she couldn't convey that in her voice.

"Oh wow, congratulations!" Her voice came out high and brittle. "That's so exciting, both of you. Really." Anna and Simon both looked miserably unconvinced, and her parents were staring at her in open pity. Rachel couldn't stand it.

"Seriously," she continued, now clearly over-egging the pudding to convince them. "I'm *so* thrilled for you. When did it happen? And how? I'd love to know all the details." To prove her point, she leaned against the counter—there were no more chairs at Simon's dinky little table—and folded her arms, eyebrows raised expectantly.

"Are you sure…" Anna began, looking around everyone at the table as if for permission to go ahead. They were treating her like some terminal patient who didn't know her diagnosis.

"Tell me," she urged, her voice coming out almost aggressively despite her best attempts to monitor it. Honestly, why couldn't she act normally? She was happy for them. She knew she was. "Please, Anna. I really want to know."

"Well…Simon proposed to me on top of Scafell Pike, after we'd been hiking. He hid the ring in a Kendal Mint Cake."

It sounded rather ridiculously romantic. "Good thing you didn't swallow it by accident."

"I know!" Anna giggled. "I wondered why Simon was looking so nervous as I unwrapped it!"

"I really didn't want you to swallow it, because we'd have a rough time getting it back," Simon joked. They shared a loved-up look, their hands sliding along the table and finding each other, fingers twining. Rachel kept smiling, determined not to look away. Not to seem as if she minded, because of course she didn't. She'd have to be a complete shrew to begrudge her sister her happiness.

Her smile had started to turn into a rictus before Simon spoke again. "Fortunately she didn't swallow the ring and she said yes. Wins all around."

"Absolutely." Rachel nodded, and then couldn't seem to stop. "So have you set a date?"

Another one of those shared, silently meaningful looks. "Yes, Christmas. December twenty-second, actually, which is the day we met last year."

"Oh, how perfect!" Rachel's over-loud voice echoed through the kitchen. Everyone stared at her. She was acting as if she wasn't handling this well, and really, she *was*. She was happy for Anna and Simon, and their marital bliss had no impact or effect on her own. She knew that. She felt it. And yet somehow she couldn't seem to stop acting as if she were dying on the inside.

"Well, it's getting late. I'd better go to bed." She didn't miss the look of relief on Anna's face as she straightened. "But really, congratulations. I'm so happy for you both." For good measure, she kissed Anna and Simon's cheeks, and then Ruth and Roger's as well, even though she didn't usually do that sort of thing. Ruth pressed her hand, giving her a look of such sympathy that Rachel wanted to cringe—or scream. When was she going to stop being Thornthwaite's pity case? Since it had only been a week since she'd been jilted, she had a feeling it would be a while.

The next morning she came downstairs to hear her parents' hushed voices in the kitchen; it sounded as if they were arguing, which they never did.

Rachel hovered by the turn in the corridor, guiltily eavesdropping.

"Of course I understand your concerns, Ruth, and you must follow your own conscience in this—"

"Oh, Roger, don't talk to me as if I'm one of your parishioners," Ruth snapped. "I'm your wife, and these are your daughters, who are each, in their own way, going through a very challenging time—"

"I accept all that, of course. But they are also all adults, and I don't think it would help any of them if we were to—"

"Not *we*."

A heavy silence fell on the room, so oppressive that even Rachel could feel it, out in the hallway, smothering her.

"Oh," Roger said after a moment, his voice quiet and sad. "I see."

"Do you?" Ruth asked despairingly. "Because sometimes I think you don't."

"Perhaps you should enlighten me, then."

"It just feels…hard," Ruth explained haltingly, "to leave when everyone is in such an uncertain place."

"Is everyone *in* an uncertain place? Anna is happily looking forward to her wedding, and Miriam is home now—"

"Something is going on with Miriam, surely you can see that? She's been so silent, so closed-off—"

"Perhaps," Roger allowed, "but if she doesn't want to tell us—"

"She can't tell us if we're not here."

A ripple of shock went through Rachel as she realised what her mother was implying. They were due to leave for Jinan in four days but Ruth sounded as if she now wanted to stay in Thornthwaite…without Roger.

"I don't know if that's true," Roger said quietly. "But if you feel you need to be here…"

"Oh, Roger, I don't know what I want." Her mother sounded near tears. "Perhaps just for you to understand how difficult this is for me sometimes."

"I do understand that," Roger said, and Rachel heard him move across the kitchen as her mother gave a loud sniff. Feeling as if she were really intruding now, Rachel tiptoed away, her heart thudding.

Of course, she'd known her mother had some worries about moving to China after thirty years in a comfortable vicarage in the Lake District. Her four daughters certainly had had concerns—her mother *fit* here, bustling about, baking, making tea, always listening and offering advice. All skills that could translate, in one way or another, to her new life in China, but still. Rachel hadn't been able to shake the feeling that her mother *belonged* here, and she knew her sisters felt the same way.

Yet it still jolted her with both fear and shock to think her mum might *not* actually go to China. Where would Ruth live? What would she *do*, without her vicar's wife role that she wore like a second skin, or even a first one? And how would her father cope on his own? He was a wonderfully capable man, but he depended absolutely on his wife. They were a team, rock solid and inseparable. It was the only way Rachel could imagine them being. She didn't like thinking of them being apart, even temporarily. It felt inherently, innately wrong, like something split or missing.

She went back upstairs, only to run into Miriam standing at the top, swathed in a dressing gown and looked bleary-eyed and tangle-haired.

"Are you *still* jet-lagged?" Rachel asked in surprise. Her sister had been home for more than two weeks, yet she'd barely been out of bed at lunchtime most days.

Miriam shrugged. "Something like that."

"Are you okay?" Rachel asked in concern. She didn't feel like getting her head bitten off again, but something was so obviously up with her little sister that she couldn't not ask. To her surprise, Miriam's eyes filled with tears and she shook her head.

"No, not really."

"Oh, Miri." The childhood nickname slipped out naturally and Rachel pulled her sister into a quick hug. "What's happened?"

"You don't want to know."

"But you can still tell me. Look at my life," Rachel only half-joked. "It's all gone to pieces. Whatever is going on with you, Miriam, I'm sure I can take it. And you look as if you need to tell someone. A trouble shared is a trouble halved, isn't that always what Mum says?"

But her sister just shook her head and stepped back, sniffing. "I'll be okay."

"You need to find a place to live, though, and so do I." Rachel eyed her with growing worry; her sister really did look rough. What was she not saying? "We could let a place together, you know."

"In Thornthwaite?" Miriam looked sceptical. "Is there anything?"

"There might be. Or we could be really daring, and live in the big city. Keswick." That brought a smile to her sister's face, but then she shook her head again.

"You'd have to commute to work every day."

"I can manage—"

"I'll be fine." Miriam was clearly shutting the conversation down, and so Rachel could do nothing but gaze at her helplessly, wishing she could say or do something that would breach her sister's brittle armour.

"What's going on?" Anna came out of her bedroom, towel-drying her damp hair. For the first time Rachel noticed the small diamond glinting on her ring finger. She should have asked to see the ring last night, but she'd been so intent on acting as if she were fine, which she *had* been.

"I came upstairs because Mum and Dad are having a bit of a pagger downstairs," Rachel whispered.

Miriam wrinkled her nose. "A what?"

"It's Cumbrian," Anna explained with a little laugh. "Have you been away that long? It means a fight." She frowned as she glanced at Rachel. "Not seriously, though? Mum and Dad?"

Rachel shrugged. "They're arguing. Mum wants to stay here."

"What?" Anna looked shocked. "She's been absolutely determined to go—"

"Well, I think she's having a wobbly now, because of you getting engaged and me not getting married." Rachel tried to smile. "She wants to be here for us."

"I knew we should have waited." Anna looked distraught. "I told Simon we should have waited to announce our news until Mum and Dad were in China and—" She stopped abruptly, biting her lip.

"And I was a little less wounded?" Rachel filled in. "It's okay, Anna. I understand. And I don't think you should have waited, in any case. Mum and Dad would want to be here for your engagement, and I'm fine with it, honestly. I know I sounded a bit strange last night but it was just because everyone is always so worried about me and how I'm going to react. I'm absolutely a hundred per cent thrilled for you."

"Thanks, Rachel. I know you are."

"Good."

"So Mum might just stay in Thornthwaite?" Miriam said. "And Dad will go to China alone?" She sounded shocked and not all that thrilled by this news.

"I don't think she will, really," Rachel answered slowly. "I think it's just a knee-jerk reaction—and maybe a bit of cold feet."

"Still." Anna shook her head. "Mum and Dad *never* argue."

"I know. That's why I came upstairs. I don't want to go down and walk in on them."

"Well, I'm going to take a shower." Miriam yawned and strolled off towards the bathroom; a few seconds later the vicarage's ancient pipes began to creak and clank as the water started to heat up.

"Do you think she's okay?" Rachel asked in a whisper. "Miriam? She seems a bit…"

"Yes, she does, doesn't she? I don't know." Anna chewed her lip. "Maybe something happened out in Australia?"

"I asked her if she wanted to find a place to let together. As of next week, we're both officially homeless."

"Oh, Rachel. You don't have to leave the vicarage—"

"We kind of do," Rachel said as gently as she could. "I mean, it wouldn't quite be fair to Simon, would it? To have a couple of squatters when he moved in?"

"He wouldn't see it like that."

"Still. New start and all that." Rachel tried to sound chirpy about the prospect, and thought she probably failed. "What are you and Simon up to today?"

"We're going to Keswick to look at some reception venues," Anna said with a little, apologetic smile. "And register for gifts."

"Get right on top of those things," Rachel returned with a little nod of approval. "That's the way to do it. Which reminds me, I need to box up about a hundred wedding gifts and send them back."

"Rachel, I'm so sorry…"

"Please, Anna. Don't be. And don't let what happened to

me spoil your plans. This is your moment. Enjoy it, for all it's worth." Rachel widened her smile. "Seriously. I'm okay."

"We were thinking about going out for drinks tonight, to celebrate," Anna said cautiously. "Nothing big…"

"That sounds great. Count me in."

"Okay. As long as you're sure…"

"Wouldn't miss it for the world." Rachel made herself sound as cheerful as possible, but as soon as she could she escaped to her room, closing the door behind her with a grateful click as she let out a heavy sigh. When would this get easier—for her family as well as for her?

She spent the rest of the day boxing up her wedding presents, which wasn't as hard as she'd expected. In the end, they were only things, just as her mother had said, and Rachel knew she didn't actually care that much about *stuff*. It had been about what it had represented—the waffle maker for lazy Saturday mornings making a big cooked breakfast for her children; the croquet set they'd all play with outside.

She didn't need any of it anymore, and therefore she didn't want it. As long as she kept herself from envisioning those wished-for scenarios, she was fine. Mostly.

Having boxed everything back up in its original packaging, which they'd thankfully kept, Rachel didn't feel brave enough to lug all the boxes to Thornthwaite's tiny post office, which was a hub of gossipy news for the village, and so she loaded up the car and drove to Keswick instead, returning everything by post even as she acknowledged how much easier it would have been if she and Dan had registered somewhere local, instead of the upscale online service she'd wanted. Hindsight was twenty-twenty, she reminded herself with a sigh.

Her spirits lifted a little as she drove back to Thornthwaite, the sky a hazy blue, the sun gilding the fells in gold, sheep contentedly munching grass on the steep slopes criss-crossed with drystone walls. She was glad she'd finished with that particular job; she'd been dreading it. It felt like one more important step towards a future she couldn't quite envision, but it was slowly amassing an amorphous, uncertain shape.

Back at the vicarage the house was quiet; Anna had gone out with Simon, and Miriam was in the garden, lounging in the sunshine, a magazine over her face. Rachel peeked into the kitchen and saw her mother at the little table, a cup of tea forgotten by her elbow as she stared into space.

"Mum?"

Ruth started and then smiled. "Hello, darling. You managed with the gifts?" She'd offered to help but Rachel had kindly refused, feeling she needed to do it herself.

"Yes, thankfully. Everything's been returned, down to the last toaster. Two of them, as it happened."

"Your father and I received two blenders," Ruth recalled with a smile. "And we argued about which one to keep. Isn't that silly?"

It seemed like the perfect opening. "Is everything okay

with you and Dad, Mum?"

Ruth looked surprised. "Why would you ask such a thing?"

"I overheard you this morning." Rachel hunched her shoulders guiltily. "Sorry for eavesdropping."

"Heard us…" Ruth sighed. "Oh, yes. That was only a moment, Rachel. Your father and I are fine. Please don't worry about us."

"So you're both going to Jinan…?"

"Yes, I think that's probably best." Ruth smiled tiredly. "I admit, I feel torn at the moment, because you're all here and you're all going through such different things. I want to be here to support you, to help—"

"That's understandable, but there would always be something to stay back for, wouldn't there, Mum? And you will be back at Christmas."

"Yes…"

"Of course we'll all miss you. Terribly. You know that, don't you?"

"Yes." Ruth smiled, the curve of her lips just a little wobbly. "Yes, I know that."

Rachel smiled back, and hers was just as wobbly. Ruth sniffed and then reached over and squeezed her hand.

"It will get better," she said quietly, and Rachel had to work hard not to let the tears fall.

"I know."

A few hours later everyone was heading out for celebratory drinks at Thornthwaite's 'rougher' pub, The Bell.

"Why not The Queen's Sorrow?" Miriam asked. She looked marginally better than she had that morning, her dark, wavy hair caught up in a messy bun, her lanky form encased in skinny jeans and a loose jumper, but there still seemed something pale and haunted about her, and Rachel's attempt to ask her sister what was going on had been rebuffed again.

"Simon and I met at The Bell," Anna explained. "Didn't I tell you that story?"

"No, I don't think you did."

Rachel, having heard it all before, walked slightly behind Anna, Simon, and Miriam as they headed over to The Bell, across the little stone bridge that spanned St John's Beck, and then up the street to the weathered Victorian building on the corner of Finkle Street that housed Thornthwaite's other pub.

The sun was just starting to sink towards the jagged edge of the fells on the horizon, and the evening was still warm, the buildings and houses of Thornthwaite bathed in golden, syrupy light.

It was a beautiful scene, and yet it gave Rachel a little pang of melancholy. In her alternative reality, the one that was supposed to happen, she and Dan would be walking together, hand in hand, happy and secure in their newlywed status. Perhaps they would have been teasing Simon and Anna, giving them well-meaning and jokey pointers.

As it was she stayed silent, only half-listening to Anna regale Miriam with how she'd met Simon at The Bell, but hadn't realised who he was, and trying to stave off that pang of melancholy that threatened to swamp her completely. Behind her Will and Esther were chatting quietly, and her parents were holding hands. Everyone seemed happy except for her.

Rachel didn't want to bring the evening down, but as she stepped into the crowded warmth of The Bell, she decided she could definitely use a drink…or three.

Chapter Six

ROGER SHOULDERED HIS way to the bar as they all sat around a few tables squeezed together in the back. Rachel had only been in The Bell a couple of times, for a friend's hen do and another teacher's birthday drink.

It was known as the village's rougher pub, but it wasn't *that* rough—not really. Admittedly a bunch of rowdy lads were standing in the front, slopping their pints all over the floor, but everyone else seemed quiet and friendly enough, and the pub had an old-fashioned feel to it, with plaster walls and a bar of old, scarred wood, a well-used dartboard on one wall and, refreshingly, no loud music, just the normal chatter and laughter that accompanied an evening in a pub.

The Bell did lack the gastro-pub décor of The Queen's Sorrow, and the only food on offer was packets of crisps or pork scratchings. There were no micro-brewed ales or tapas plates, but that was fine by Rachel—and better yet, there was no one she knew here, besides her family. No sympathetic-looking teachers, parishioners, or friends, which was a huge relief.

"Here we are." Roger came towards the table brandishing a bottle of the pub's best champagne, which was more of the supermarket variety, but who cared? He uncorked it with a satisfyingly loud pop and then set to pouring glasses.

"To Simon and Anna!"

"To Simon and Anna," everyone returned, and Rachel glugged half her glass in one go.

"Easy there," Esther murmured, and Rachel smiled and ignored her.

The conversation wafted over and around her while Rachel tried discreetly to pour herself a second and then a third glass of champagne, hoping no one noticed how fast she was downing them. She deserved a little Dutch courage, surely, after everything she'd been through? Especially when everyone else was so happy?

She wasn't a big drinker normally; a glass of wine on the weekend, maybe, or a cocktail out with friends was all she was usually up for, and it didn't take long for her to realise that three glasses of champagne was at least one and possibly two too many.

Her head was spinning and so was the room, and everyone's voices started to sound very loud.

"You all right, darling?" Ruth asking, touching her shoulder, and Rachel had to blink her mother into focus.

"Yesh." She tried again. "Yes, I'm fine."

Ruth frowned, and from the corner of her eye Rachel saw Esther smirk. Suddenly she felt near tears. How stupid was she being, getting tipsy with her *family*? It just made her feel even more pathetic.

"I just need the loo," she murmured, and walked as steadily as she could from the table towards the bathrooms in the back. Someone was having a crisis in the ladies'—Rachel heard raised voices and then sobbing and so she decided to give the loos a miss. Despite the three glasses of champagne she didn't need to go, anyway; she'd just wanted to escape her family's pitying, eagle eyes.

She didn't want to go back to the table yet, though. The thought of being around all that blatant happiness made her feel even more miserable—and the fact that it made her miserable, even worse. What sort of cow was she, that she couldn't put her own problems aside to celebrate her sister's engagement? A miserable cow, apparently.

She walked past the loos to the door at the end of the hallway that led to a little enclosed courtyard behind the pub, where the bins were kept.

Rachel stepped outside and breathed in deeply the smell of rubbish and coal smoke with just a whiff of fresh summer air. She leaned against the brick wall and closed her eyes, willing the world, if it couldn't change, then at least to stop spinning.

"Are you areet?"

Her eyes flew open as she took in the shadowy, hulking figure that took up the entire doorway. "Sorry...?"

"Are you areet?" The voice was low, the accent decidedly

Cumbrian, although Rachel recognised what he was asking. Was she all right? She scuttled out of the way as the man came into the courtyard and heaved a black bag full of rubbish into the bin, his impressive biceps bulging.

"Yes, I'm fine." She tried to smile. "Just getting some fresh air. Sorry, am I not supposed to be out of here?"

"I don't mind." The man shrugged, his gaze assessing her, probably trying to figure out how drunk she was. Rachel recognised him now—he was the man who had been behind the bar, pulling pints.

He had very closely cut dark blond hair, piercing blue eyes, and a muscular figure that undoubtedly helped in his line of work: bartender cum bouncer. He folded his arms, an intricate tribal tattoo swirling across one bicep, and gave her a level look.

"How much have you had to drink?"

"Three glasses of champagne, but I'm a lightweight." She tried to sound airily insouciant. "Don't worry, though. I'm not going to embarrass myself."

"I'm not worried, but you look as if you could bowk all over my shoes."

"Bowk…?"

"Vomit."

"Oh. Right." Her stomach was feeling a bit queasy, now that she thought of it, but Rachel didn't think she was going to be sick. She was known in her family for having a stomach of steel. "I think I'm okay," she said, but the bartender didn't look convinced.

"How about a glass of water?"

"Seriously, I'm fine." Rachel straightened, keeping her chin tilted at a slightly haughty angle as she sought to move past him and back into the pub. Unfortunately, with her first step, the world spun a little more and despite what she'd just assured him, her stomach heaved in protest.

The man grabbed her elbow to steady her. "Careful," he murmured and Rachel closed her eyes, willing the ground to stop moving underneath her feet. She'd only had three glasses of champagne, after all. Three *small* glasses. Her stomach heaved again, her insides twisting viciously, and she tried to take another step, back to the safety of the pub.

"I'm fi—" But she wasn't. Rachel clapped a hand over her mouth but it was too late. Unable to stop herself, she *bowked* all over the bartender's work boots, just as he'd been afraid of.

Tears sprang to her eyes as she retched helplessly, horrified and humiliated, while he watched. Finally, the unbearable episode came to an end.

"I'm so sorry," she gasped, doubled over, her hands on her knees, her stomach feeling as if it had been wrung inside out. "I really didn't think that was going to happen."

"I did," the man returned dryly. "Stay right there." He left for only a few seconds, returning with a glass of water and a roll of paper towel. "Here," he said, passing her over a sheet. "Wipe yourself off and then have a drink."

Rachel tidied herself up while the man rinsed his boots under the outdoor tap in the courtyard. She felt utterly wretched.

When he'd finished, he silently handed her the glass of water. "Drink."

"Thank you," she murmured, and took a a few sips of water. Her stomach, thankfully, had settled right down and the world no longer spun. She felt astonishingly sober all of a sudden, which was both a good and bad thing in that moment. She wouldn't have minded a little blurring at the edges of everything right about now.

"Does this happen to you fairly often?" she asked with an attempt at a smile. "In your line of work?"

"No." The man regarded her stonily. "I toss anyone out who has had one too many. I don't run a pub for drunks."

"Ah." She felt suitably chastened. "I really didn't have that much to drink—"

"Obviously, you'd had enough."

Unable to disagree, she nodded. "Yes, I suppose that is true." She took another sip of water, trying not to cringe under the man's unsmiling scrutiny. She felt even smaller and more miserable than when she'd been sitting with her family, swilling champagne.

"Whatever it is," he said abruptly, "it's not as bad as all that."

Rachel looked up from her glass of water, shocked. The man still wasn't smiling; he stood with his arms folded, biceps rippling, a resolute look on his face. "I'm sorry...?"

"Most people get kaleyed because something's gone wrong in their lives and they don't want to face it. All I'm saying is, it's not that bad."

It took Rachel a second to recognise the Cumbrian word for drunk. "How would you know?" she retorted, both stung and touched.

He shrugged one powerful shoulder. "Because nothing is."

Okay, now she was just stung. "Speak for yourself, then."

"Because," he continued implacably, "when the buzz wears off and the puke is cleaned up? The problem is still there. You haven't done it or yourself any good."

"Wise words from a bartender," she managed. "Clearly you're in the wrong profession."

"Maybe so," he agreed, unruffled. Rachel felt petty and childish for snapping at him, especially considering what she'd just done to his boots.

"I'm sorry," she said after a moment. "You're right, of course. Getting drunk doesn't help at all. And it was dreadful of me to be sick all over your boots. Thank you for—for everything." The man inclined his head, as unsmiling as ever. Rachel felt even more cowed. "I suppose I should be getting back."

"I suppose you should."

She bit her lip, discomfited by this man's quiet stillness. Who was he, anyway? He looked vaguely familiar, but she'd never been in The Bell before and she didn't think she'd seen him around the village.

"Thanks," she said again, and then she slipped past him back into the pub.

She made her way back into the table, everyone exclaiming as she sat down.

"Rachel, where were you?"

"Are you all right, darling? You look a little peaky."

Esther simply gave her one of her narrowed, knowing looks, as if she'd witnessed the whole uncomfortable scene out in the courtyard—a prospect that nearly made Rachel shudder.

"I'm fine," she said wearily. "Just needed some air." She felt flat suddenly, and so very tired. All she wanted to do now was go home and sleep.

Miriam gave her a beaming smile. "More champagne?" she asked, and suppressing a shudder, Rachel shook her head.

The next morning, she felt rather ridiculously hungover, and after making herself a strong, sweet cup of tea, she sat at the dining room table with a pad of paper and a pen, determined to make a list of everything she needed to do to end the wedding period of her life. Once she'd done that, maybe she'd be able to move on. See the bright side of life. Make lemonade with the lemons she'd been given, and all that banal nonsense. She sighed and pulled the pad of paper towards her.

Put house on market, she wrote first, the words still giving her a pang of sorrow. Letting go of that house and all it had represented would always be a wrench. *Store dress. Write to family and friends.* She chewed the end of her pen, wondering what else she needed to do. Hold head up high? Soldier on?

With a dispirited sigh Rachel pushed the pad of paper away from her and took another sip of tea. She wanted to jump to the next, happier stage of her life but she knew she couldn't. She just had to slog through the muck and mire of this one, and some day, she'd hope and pray that it would come to an end. She'd look up and the sky would be brighter, the sun would be shining. Philosophically speaking, of course. This was Cumbria, after all.

"Feeling better this morning?" Anna asked as she came into the dining room cradling her own cuppa.

"Yes, a bit. Sorry, I hope I didn't bring your evening down." Rachel grimaced. "I had a bit too much to drink. Stupid of me, I know. I'm such a lightweight."

"Don't worry, you didn't," Anna answered. "And I understand why you might have—"

"Don't, please." Rachel held up her hand. "I know you mean it well, everyone does, but I'm getting tired of everyone treating me as if I'm a terminal cancer patient who isn't accepting her diagnosis. What happened was hard and horrible and it will take me a while to get over it, but I just want to move on and be seen as normal again."

Anna ducked her head. "Sorry…"

"And I'm sorry for snapping," Rachel said on a sigh. "I seem to be doing a lot of that lately." She let out a sudden, surprising laugh. "I snapped at the bartender last night, after I was so nicely being sick all over his boots."

"What?" Anna looked both shocked and intrigued. "You were *sick*?"

"I know, I couldn't believe it. I never get sick like that. But I went outside for a bit of fresh air and the bartender was back there. I ended up spraying his shoes." Rachel closed her eyes in remembered mortification. "He was actually quite nice about it, really." In a stony sort of way.

"Wow." Anna shook her head, smiling. "I missed all the excitement."

"You had enough of your own." Rachel pulled the pad of paper back towards her. She needed to get on with things. And she didn't really want to dwell on her unfortunate vomiting episode.

"On an entirely separate subject," Anna said, "I have a solution for you and Miriam."

Rachel looked up, surprised. "A solution for what?"

"Your living arrangements. I've talked to Simon and he thinks it's a great idea."

Anna's beaming smile made Rachel feel a little wary. *Simon* did? "What's this idea, then?"

"You and Miriam can both be lodgers here at the vicarage. Simon will charge you a nominal fee so it's all above board."

"Lodgers?" Rachel rolled the idea around in her mind. It was better than freeloading, but…a lodger in her own home? Except of course it wouldn't be her own home anymore, would it? Not after her parents left in just three days. "Don't you think people in the village would gossip, the vicar living with two single women?"

"Oh, people are more relaxed than that, surely," Anna protested. "In any case, it wouldn't be just the three of you. Simon's old school friend is coming to stay as well."

"Who's that?"

"I don't really know. I've never met him. Someone from his days at Cambridge. He's fallen on something of a hard time, apparently, and wanted to get away for a bit."

"Hmm." Rachel doodled a few flowers on the corner of her paper. "Well, it's very kind of Simon. I'll certainly have a think about it. What about you, Anna? You're going to be moving into the vicarage come Christmas."

"Well, yes." Anna blushed, her eyes sparkling like the ring on her finger. She looked, Rachel thought with only a hint of envy, like she was the happiest woman in the world. And of all her sisters, perhaps Anna deserved that the most. She'd always been so quiet, content to stick to the shadows. It was good and right for her to have a bit of the limelight now.

"But what about before then?" Rachel pressed. "Will you chuck your job in? Move up here to get things ready?"

Anna twisted the ring on her finger as she answered, "Yes, eventually. My work has never been something I've been desperate to do. I more or less fell into it."

"But it's a good job." Anna worked as a legal librarian in Manchester, and had since her uni days.

"Yes, but I'm ready for something else."

"Including being a vicar's wife?" With a jolt Rachel realised just what this could mean. Anna would take over Ruth's role—she'd be the one bustling about the kitchen, baking for coffee mornings, leading the toddler times and Sunday School. "Are you going to be like Mum?"

"I don't know, to be honest." Anna looked away. "I don't think I could ever fill Mum's shoes, and I hate being in front of people." She looked down, nibbling her lip. "I *really* hate it."

Anna had always been shy, with a stammer that had improved over the years but which she still tried to hide. Rachel could understand how the public role of vicar's wife, unofficial as it was, would be daunting for her.

"But you're so warm and empathetic," Rachel said with a smile. "Which are surely good qualities in a vicar's wife."

"Thanks." Anna sighed. "If I'm honest, I almost wish Simon was going to be the vicar somewhere else, where we could start fresh. Where people hadn't known me in nappies and will no doubt constantly compare me to my mum."

Which seemed like a reasonable request. Now that Rachel thought about it, Anna had a hard course set ahead of her. Comparisons would be inevitable, no matter who was making them. "Everyone will support you, though," she said. "You know that, don't you?"

"Yes, in theory. But you know what support looks like sometimes, in a place like this. You've lived here your whole life, except for uni. People think they know you better than they do. And they have *so* much well-meaning advice, whether you want to hear it or not."

"Yes, true enough." When Rachel had started teaching at Thornthwaite Primary, it had seemed idyllic. She'd never wanted anything more than to settle down and raise a load of kids in a lovely village, just as her parents had. But living in the village where you grew up, especially when you were the vicar's kid, could be tough. More than one parent had marched into her classroom, bristling with indignation, recalling how Rachel had once nicked a sweet from the post office, so how *dare* she tell off their child?

Yes, she'd nicked a sweet when she was six, and her mother had promptly marched her back and made her give it back and apologise. It had been a lesson Rachel hadn't forgotten, and no one else seemed to have forgotten it, either.

"You'll find your way, Anna," she said. "You and Simon together. He adores you, you know." She saw in every word he spoke, every time he looked at her. The man wasn't just smitten, he was *dedicated*—and deeply in love.

"I adore him," Anna answered simply. "And that makes

it all worth it."

Yes, it would, wouldn't it? Ten days on from the debacle of her big day, Rachel could acknowledge that she hadn't felt quite that way about Dan. But she'd loved him—and whether you needed that level of mushy emotion was another matter entirely. She was still sure they could have been happy together, but perhaps not since Dan hadn't thought so. In any case, it no longer mattered. She needed to look forward to her future…whatever that was going to look like.

Chapter Seven

THE NEXT FEW days seemed to pass in hyper-speed, with everything going faster and faster, until it all was a dizzying blur. With only three days until their move, Ruth and Roger Holley had gone into imminent departure mode, with suitcases crowding the front hall and people from the parish coming and going for yet more final farewells.

Rachel realised just how much she, as well as her three sisters, had been trying to pretend her parents weren't really leaving, until now. They'd talked around it, accepted her mother's gifts of china and furniture as she emptied the vicarage, but it still, amazingly, hadn't felt real or imminent. Now there was no way to avoid the fact.

Simon spent a lot of time with Roger, going over various parish matters. Roger was leaving his study as it was, which was both comforting and strange. Instead of her dad, it would be Simon sitting behind the old leather-inlaid desk, Simon relaxing in one of the squashy armchairs by the woodstove, beckoning people in for an amicable chat.

Rachel was glad Simon was taking over; she knew and

liked him, as did many in the village. Her father had done some fancy footwork in the diocese to arrange for his curate to take his position without a waiting period or formal interview. It was all going to work out well—it just felt so *strange*.

The last Sunday the church was packed out with parishioners wanting to pay their respects to both Roger and Ruth. As Rachel stepped inside the dim, soaring space, light filtering through the stained-glass windows and impressive flower arrangements bursting from every available space, she felt a twist of bittersweet finality. This was it. Her father's last Sunday, after a lifetime of them. She couldn't remember a Sunday where he hadn't been at the front of the church, smiling in welcome, as cheerful as ever.

This morning he was dressed in his usual suit, having foregone the priestly robes years ago except for the most formal of services, and smiling as cheerfully as ever, greeting everyone at the door. He reached out and gave Rachel's hand a quick squeeze as she went by, which nearly sent her hurling into the emotional abyss she'd been hovering on since the breakup.

Blinking back tears, she took her seat in the second pew, next to her mother, as well as Esther and Will, where she'd sat since she was two years old, kicking the pew in front of her, riffling through the dusty hymnals, her mother's placating hand on one shoulder.

"You okay, Mum?" she whispered and Ruth nodded, her

chin tilted at a determined angle as she stared straight ahead, blinking rapidly even as she smiled.

"I'm fine, Rachel. Really."

Rachel glanced around at the packed pews, taking in all the different people from various walks of life who had come to say goodbye. The Tamworths who ran the village post office; the Lewises, the proprietors of The Winter Hare; Sarah Wilkes, the head teacher of the village school where she taught; and countless other people besides.

Then Rachel's wandering gaze snagged on a familiar face—those piercing blue eyes, that stern, unsmiling mouth. The bartender from The Bell, whose boots she'd been sick all over. His gaze met hers and an electric current of awareness and embarrassment zinged through her. What on earth was he doing here? She was sure he'd never come to church before.

The organ music began with a momentous swell, and everyone rose to their feet as her father strode purposefully down the aisle. The service had started.

The hymns and readings were a blur as Rachel struggled to keep hold of her composure throughout. It all felt so poignant and raw, seeing her father where she'd always seen him for so many years. She'd taken him for granted, she realised, even as she'd appreciated him, or thought she had: his steady, stabilising presence, his ready good humour, his willingness to listen even when he was busy with a thousand other cares.

And her mother, always ready with a cup of tea, a listening ear, and something delicious to eat. How many times had Rachel flung herself into a chair at the kitchen table—the one that wasn't even there anymore—to moan to her mum about her latest drama, whether it was a mean girl in secondary school, a doomed relationship in uni, or the trials and tribulations of being a primary school teacher? Her mother had always listened, offering compassion and wise advice mixed with humour and hugs. Skype just wasn't going to be the same.

As her father took the pulpit for the last time there was a rustling among the pews, and someone blew their nose rather loudly. It was clearly an emotional moment for everybody.

Her father's friendly gaze scanned the crowded pews before he smiled, a smile that was full of sympathy and sadness, happiness and hope.

"This is a hard moment," he said, and his voice choked a little, shocking Rachel, because her father never seemed sad. Next to her Anna's eyes shone with tears and Esther was looking particularly stony. Ruth's smile wavered, and Rachel reached for her hand, sensing her mum needed some strength. Ruth shot her a grateful look, her eyes as wet as Anna's, and then resumed looking ahead.

"But it's also a good moment," Roger continued. "To see you all here, to know God's work will continue to be done in this village that I and my family have called home for thirty years. Today's text is John 17, Jesus's prayer for all believers, and while I cannot put myself directly in the place of Christ, it is my prayer as well for all of you." He smiled before looking down at his notes. "Now let us take the passage verse by verse…"

Rachel had heard enough of her father's sermons to know he would do what he always did, go faithfully through whatever text he had chosen, never mind the import of the day. Her mind was in such a tumult that she could barely take in what her father was saying; it just felt so *final*.

She focused her energy on not breaking down, especially when, as her gaze wandered yet again, she saw Dan sitting in a pew across the aisle. Her heart lurched with emotion, one she didn't think she could name. Loss and love mixed together, along with the sad realisation that she didn't miss him—the man rather than the dream—as much as she should have.

After the service, everyone milled around the church, enjoying cake and champagne, the last of several celebrations that had been thrown for the Holleys. Rachel was just debating whether she wanted a glass of champagne when she bumped into someone standing next to her and saw, with a ripple of shock, that it Bartender Man.

"Oh, sorry." She blushed as he regarded her in his usual unsmiling way. "I've been meaning to say thank you for— well, for being so kind the other night. I really am sorry—"

"Don't worry about it." He sounded gruff. "Trust me, I've seen worse."

"I'm sure you have." She eyed him uncertainly. "It's nice to see you here, anyway. Have you—have you come to church before?" She'd meant simply to be friendly, but somehow the question came out sounding a little patronising. The man continued with his stony appraisal.

"Yes."

"Oh, I don't think I've seen you."

He shrugged. "Well, I've been here."

The conversation stalled out and Rachel wondered how she could get away without appearing rude. "What's your name?" she asked a bit desperately.

"Sam West."

"I'm Rachel—"

"Holley. I know."

She shouldn't be surprised, since most people in the village knew her, yet somehow she was. "How did you—"

"I grew up here. In fact, we went to school together." She couldn't keep from goggling a bit and he let out a short laugh. "You don't remember me obviously, but we were in the same chemistry class for GCSE."

"We were?"

"Yes, but you wouldn't have noticed me. I played rugby."

"Ah." Well, that made sense, then. She'd been into music and art, and the rugby players had been a bunch of loudmouth jocks she had strenuously avoided. Yet he seemed to have had taken notice of *her*, which was odd. "Well, it's nice to meet you properly," she said awkwardly. "And I promise not to be sick on your shoes ever again."

"Then you'd better avoid that," Sam said, with a nod towards the row of plastic flutes lined up on a table. It took Rachel a few seconds to realise he was joking. At least, she thought he was. She smiled back uncertainly, and then she drifted away, grateful for her escape yet also feeling weirdly energised by the interaction. There was no doubt Sam was good-looking, in his own way, and he was also kind of...*intriguing*. But she'd probably never see him again, Rachel acknowledged, especially since she intended never to set foot in The Bell ever again.

All too soon people were trickling away, and the church's self-appointed hospitality committee was cleaning up the empty flutes and crumb-scattered paper plates. Her parents were spending the night in Manchester before flying out early in the morning, and Simon was driving them to the airport.

Roger had wanted their goodbyes to be said here. It was a perfect afternoon for farewells—golden sunlight, hazy blue sky, a few sheep bleating mournfully in the distance. Their suitcases were lined up by the Passat estate they'd had for at least ten years, and which they'd given to Anna for when she moved back to Thornthwaite. Now there was nothing left but to say the actual words, and yet Rachel found her throat closing as they all stood in the foyer of the vicarage, her parents ready to go, Simon with keys in hand.

"I can't believe this is really happening," she said as her father checked he had their passports and her mother slipped on her coat.

"We'll be back for Christmas," Ruth said briskly. "And of course we'll Skype as often as we can."

"But still…" Rachel drew a shaky breath. She shouldn't make a scene, not now, when everyone was just about keeping it together. This morning before church she'd seen her mother walking slowly through all the rooms, saying her own private goodbye to each one. Rachel had watched from the top of the stairs as Ruth had gone into Jamie's old room. She still hadn't come out when Rachel had tiptoed away, not wanting to intrude on such a private moment.

"Skype will be good," she said now, and Ruth smiled in relief, grateful Rachel was going to keep it together so she could, as well.

"Yes, it will. We'll have so much to tell you!" Quickly and tightly, she hugged each sister in turn, and then Will as well. "You know how much we'll miss you all. I don't need to say it—"

"And we'll miss you—"

"Anna, I want to know all the wedding plans, all right? Every little thing—"

"Of course, Mum."

"Esther, keep me posted on the job front—"

"When there's something to say, I'll tell you," Esther said with a wry smile.

"And Miriam, you're still looking peaky. Do get some rest, darling—"

"I will, Mum. Don't worry."

"Rachel." Ruth's forehead wrinkled with concern as she hugged her. "This is just a blip, my darling. You know that, don't you?"

It was a heck of a blip. "Yes, I know."

Then it was Roger's turn to hug them all, cracking jokes to hide his emotion, and with far too many tears shimmering and lumps forming in throats, they finally got in the car and then with a honk of the horn and the crunch of gravel they were gone. *Gone.*

Rachel, Esther, Anna, and Miriam all stood there, Will alongside, silent and slightly shell-shocked as they watched the car disappear down the lane, past the church, over the bridge, and then out of the village. It felt like the aftermath of a tornado, everything battered and still.

"Well," Esther announced finally, "I brought wine." She gave Rachel a knowing glance. "I would have brought champagne, but I didn't want you puking."

"Oh, for heaven's sake." Rachel threw Anna an exasperated look. "You told her about that?"

"Sorry." Anna didn't sound remotely repentant. "It kind of slipped out."

"Sure it did."

"Come on." Esther headed back into the house. "A final farewell, just for us. Will's going to get us all a takeaway from Keswick."

"Right-o." Will saluted and then headed to his battered Rover. The four sisters trooped inside the vicarage, which felt weirdly empty and silent, already a shell of itself, a husk of a house.

"Where to?"

"The kitchen's just not the same without the table," Rachel said rather mournfully.

"Yes, why did Simon get rid of that?" Miriam demanded. "That table's a legend."

"It wasn't Simon," Anna answered. "It was me. It didn't feel right, him just taking it on, somehow. It was our family's—"

"It belongs here," Miriam cut across her, her tone stubbornly final. "Doesn't it?" She looked at her sisters for support and both Rachel and Esther nodded.

"Yes, have him bring it back, Anna. The universe feels a bit off-kilter without it in the middle of the kitchen."

Anna gave a wobbly smile. "All right, then. I just didn't want to presume…"

"Of course, when you get married, you're going to have to make this place your own." They'd all drifted into the dining room with mutual, silent accord, and now Esther unscrewed the cap on the bottle of the wine and started to pour. "You don't want us complaining about the new drapes or the fact that you painted the kitchen blue. We'd be like the worst sort of nosy parker parishioners."

"You aren't really going to paint the kitchen blue, though, are you?" Rachel couldn't keep from asking. The kitchen had been yellow for as long as she could remember.

"I—I don't know." Anna looked flustered. "Truthfully, I can't imagine changing anything. It's quite daunting, you know, to—to think of moving in here. Taking Mum's place, even though I know I couldn't, not even a little bit."

"You must make your own place," Miriam said firmly. "I know it's all raw and new now, but we'll get over it. We'll have to. Life moves on." She sounded both resigned and determined, making Rachel wonder yet again what was going on with her sister. What did she have to move on from?

"So tell us about this new man in your life," Esther said as she passed Rachel a glass of wine, and Rachel's mouth dropped open in shock.

"New man…" There was no new man, not remotely.

"The bloke you were talking to at church. Sam West, isn't he?"

"How do you know him?"

"He was a mate of Will's from a long time ago. Is he the one you puked on?"

"On his *shoes*. I was sick only on his shoes."

"Not the best way to impress someone," Miriam remarked dryly.

"I don't want to impress him!" Rachel practically squeaked. "I barely know him. And, in case you can't remember, I only just had a very bad breakup a little over two weeks ago. I'm hardly ready even to think about dating someone else."

"It wasn't that bad a breakup," Esther said, and Rachel spluttered into her wine.

"Wasn't that bad…! Esther, do I really need to remind you, that Dan jilted me the *day* before our wedding?"

"He was doing you a favour," Esther said bluntly. "You know he was, even if you won't admit it yet. You didn't love him, Rachel."

"Esther," Anna murmured. "That—that seems a bit harsh, even for you."

"Can you deny it?" Esther's laser-like gaze met Rachel's. "Really?"

"I did love him," she said stubbornly. "How would you know, anyway?"

"Because I saw the two of you together and you looked miserable half the time, as if you were only there on sufferance."

"*Sufferance…* Come on, Esther. I wasn't that bad."

Esther cocked a knowing finger at her. "Ah, but you admit it was something like that."

"Perhaps a little." Rachel blew out a breath. "Look, I get it, okay? Something wasn't right between us. I accept that. But I was still planning on marrying him, and I still think we could have been happy if we'd tried. So. I'm not jumping back into the dating pool anytime soon, all right?"

"What about you?" Miriam asked, nodding towards Esther. "If we're going to give each other a grilling. When are you going to get a real job? That community garden out back is up and running, isn't it?"

For the last few months Esther had been organising a community area in the Victorian walled garden that was part of the vicarage property. Now, in the height of summer, it was bursting with allotments, a fish pond was being dug out, and fruit trees had been planted. Several villagers had come forward eager to do the work, leaving Esther with only a little paperwork to manage.

"When are you?" she shot back, and then laughed. "Oh, we're a handful, aren't we? Do you remember how, when we used to bicker as children, Mum would make us hold hands afterwards?"

"I hated that," Rachel exclaimed with a laugh. "It always felt so forced and fake."

"And yet it made us get along, eventually." Anna smiled sadly. "Mum always had a lot of good ideas like that."

"She did." Esther gave herself a little shake. "Goodness, we're talking about them as if they've died."

"It feels a bit that way though, doesn't it?" Rachel said quietly. "I just can't believe they're not here anymore."

"I know." Esther was silent for a long moment. "What do you think Jamie would be like, if he were here?"

A ripple of sorrow seemed to pass through each sister as they remembered the brother who had been born smack in the middle of them, and who had died twenty-one years ago now. Rachel could still remember that torturous moment in all its hideous clarity. She'd been racing ahead, eager to get to school and tell her best friend Chloe about some ridiculous piece of Year Six gossip. Jamie had been running to keep up with her, and so had Anna, who had only been eight. Ruth had been behind them, with Miriam in the pushchair, calling out to take care.

It had all happened so fast, and yet at the same time so slowly. Rachel had darted across the road, and then skipped on ahead. Jamie had followed; the car had come out of nowhere, or so it had seemed. She'd racked and racked her memory, trying to determine whether she'd seen the car, when she'd gone across. She must have, surely, even if it had been no more than a blur in the distance?

What she could recall in perfect detail was the loud squeal of brakes as the driver of the car, going far too fast to begin with, tried to stop, and then the far worse sound of the thud of Jamie's body flying through the air and then falling to the ground.

"I—I think he'd be cracking jokes the whole time," Anna ventured. "He always had such a great sense of humour, didn't he? He'd be telling us not to be so mopey and stupid."

"Mum would tell him not to say stupid," Rachel said with a smile, and Esther laughed softly.

"Yes, although perhaps he would have grown out of calling things stupid. He's been frozen at just ten years old. Who knows what kind of man he might have become."

They were all silent, considering that, and then Esther raised her glass, her expression solemn.

"To Jamie," she said, and the other sisters all raised their glasses.

"To Jamie," they echoed, and they all drank as the room filled with twilight shadows, the sun setting on the world that had once been loved and known.

Chapter Eight

TWO WEEKS ON life without her parents was starting to feel both utterly strange and weirdly normal. She, Miriam, and Simon had found a halting routine of sharing the same space; Simon kept semi-apologising for living in what was essentially his own house, and Rachel and Miriam kept semi-apologising for being there.

None of them, unfortunately, could cook beyond scrambled eggs and pasta, and so they ended up having a lot of both, as well as the occasional takeaway.

All in all, Rachel reflected, it was a far cry from the cosy, busy home the vicarage had been mere weeks ago; now it felt more like an enormous and rather barren bachelor pad, if a friendly enough place. Simon was lovely, always affable and smiling, and no one seemed to have raised an eyebrow at two Holley sisters lodging in the vicarage.

As the weeks went on, Rachel found herself healing and getting stronger; it seemed her heart just couldn't help it. She held her head up in the village and didn't cringe quite as much when people gave her such blatantly sympathetic looks.

She saw Dan twice, both in passing, both brief meetings friendly enough, which Rachel counted as progress. Really, it was all good, even if she felt restless inside, as if she were waiting for something, although what she had no idea. Everything she had been expecting to happen, hadn't. What else could there be?

Two weeks after her parents' departure they Skyped for the first time, the four Holley sisters crowded around Rachel's laptop in the vicarage kitchen.

"How *is* it?" Rachel burst out, realising belatedly she'd made it sound as if they were in an endurance test rather than a new vocation.

"It's amazing," Ruth said, her voice full of surprising enthusiasm. "Everyone is so friendly. There's so much to do."

"I'm not sure about the food, though," Roger joked, smiling. He was notorious for preferring stodgy British food to anything remotely exotic.

"We're taking a crash course in Mandarin," Ruth continued. "Which is manic, but I'm enjoying using my brain for the first time in ages."

"Mum, you've used your brain—"

"Oh, not really," she dismissed. "This is something completely different."

As they continued to chat, Rachel realised with a dawning wonder that her parents really were having a good time. She'd been half-expecting her mum to be putting a brave face on it all, stiff upper lip and all that, but she could see plainly that there was no need. Ruth seemed exuberant, full of energy and excitement.

"Well," Esther said when the call had finished and they all sat around the blank-faced laptop, silent. "They seem to be doing well."

"Yes." Miriam sounded a little dazed.

"It's good, isn't it?" Anna said, her tone just a little bit uncertain. "I thought they might have trouble settling in…"

"It appears not." Rachel didn't know how she felt about it all. Of *course* she was glad her parents were having a good time; Jinan was clearly where they belonged now. And yet…

"They could have acted as if they missed us a little more," Miriam said dryly, and then she laughed. "Cheer up, everyone. You all look so gloomy. It's a good thing Mum and Dad are doing well. They deserve it."

"Yes, of course they do," Rachel said, and gave herself a little shake. She was being ridiculous. Everyone needed to get on with their lives, her parents included. "Right. It's my turn to make tea. Scrambled eggs or pasta with sauce from a jar?"

Esther gave a little shudder. "Thanks, but I'm heading back home. Will's making a ragout."

"A ragout?" Miriam raised her eyebrows. "Fancy, fancy. I didn't think Will was that domesticated."

Esther shrugged, blushing a little. "We're both changing."

"Ah, marital bliss," Rachel teased, only to have an ominous silence descend. Belatedly she realised how it had sounded. "Oh, relax, everyone," she said, rolling her eyes. "I was not being catty or bitter. Although speaking of catty, I might get one. Company in my old age." She smiled to show she was joking. Sort of.

"Simon's allergic," Anna said apologetically. "If you were serious."

"Ah, well that's it, then. I'll have to settle for a goldfish." Everyone smiled dutifully. Rachel wondered when they would start seeing her as simply a sister, a person, rather than the wounded soul she seemed to have become. And yes, she was wounded. Of course she was. But she was getting over it. At least, she was trying to.

The next morning Rachel walked to the post box and posted sixty letters to various relatives and guests. She'd looked up the etiquette online, and spent several painful hours trying to word the missive, attempting to make it apologetic, grateful, and pragmatic all at once. She'd already texted, Skyped, and emailed various friends, including two bridesmaids who had come all the way from Newcastle. Everyone had been remarkably understanding, which Rachel supposed was to be expected. No matter what Dan had said, it was clear to everyone that he'd been the one to call it off. At least everyone, except for Esther, had had the delicacy not to ask why.

As she walked back down the lane to the vicarage, she halted midstride at the sight of the BMW convertible parked in the drive, looking rather incongruous next to Simon's beat-up Volvo estate.

Then a man climbed out of the car, raking a hand through his wavy, honey-blond hair. He glanced up at the vicarage, and then turning, smiled and waved to Rachel.

"I say," he asked in an upper-class drawl, the poshest accent Rachel had heard outside of an episode of *Downton Abbey*. "Is this the vicarage, do you know?"

The man wore a pair of brick-red chinos and leather loafers, with a pale blue button-down shirt and a yellow polo jumper tossed over his shoulders; he looked like he should be in the royal box at Wimbledon.

"It is," Rachel said. "Are you looking for the curate—sorry, the vicar?"

"Simon Truesdell?"

"That would be him."

"Yes, I am." He stuck out a hand. "I'm Jasper Edgington-Jones."

"Oh, right." This was Simon's new lodger, his friend from Cambridge, and clearly quite the toff. "I'm Rachel Holley, one of Simon's lodgers." She thought about explaining how she used to live in the vicarage, but it seemed sadly unimportant. "Come on in. I think Simon's out at some meeting or other, but he should be back soon."

"Thanks very much." Jasper followed her into the vicarage, and then around the back to the kitchen. All was quiet; Anna was back in Manchester, and Miriam was closeted in her bedroom, as she seemed to be most days. Rachel switched on the kettle.

"So what's brought you to Thornthwaite?" she asked.

Jasper made a bit of a face as he untied his sweater and draped it over a chair. "Seems like a nice place. Always meant to visit the Lake District, you know."

"Right." She eyed him with a kind of bemused fascination, noting the signet ring on one well-manicured finger. There were plenty of well-to-do people in Thornthwaite, Londoners who made the Lake District their holiday destination or second home, but Jasper Edgington-Jones seemed like another species entirely. "How do you take your tea?"

"Do you have Darjeeling?"

She suppressed a smile. "Sorry, just everyday builder's brew."

"Right, then, just a splash of milk, please."

He sat at the table, looking around him with interest. "Simon's landed pretty well, hasn't he?"

"It's a nice house," Rachel answered diplomatically. "And I think he suits village life."

"So you lodge here?"

"Yes, for the time being. I'm hoping to rent a place shortly." Staying at the vicarage felt too much like being stalled in neutral. She needed to move forward with her life, although when she'd gone on Rightmove there had been exactly one place to rent in Thornthwaite, and it was a six-bedroom holiday home on the edge of the village, for three thousand pounds a week. Not exactly what she had in mind.

"Right, this kind of arrangement is temporary, isn't it?" Jasper gave a little grimace and Rachel recalled that Anna had said he'd been at a loose end.

"So do you think you'll be staying here long?" she asked.

"Hopefully not too long. I'm between jobs at the moment, but I'm going to start sending my CVs out again as soon as I work up the enthusiasm." He let out a little laugh. "It's not always easy, is it?"

"No, it isn't." Rachel felt a flicker of sympathy, as well as of curiosity, for him. He'd clearly fallen on some hard times, although not too hard by the looks of him. Still, what was money? Someone with a signet ring and a BMW could be just as unhappy, or even more so, than someone with a lot less.

"Here you are." Rachel put a cup of tea on the table in front of Jasper, and then, with nothing better to do, sat opposite him. She should have made one for herself, because now it felt a bit awkward to simply sit there and watch him sip his drink.

"Thanks for this," he said. "What do you do, then?"

"I'm a primary school teacher in the village—Year Three. But I'm on summer holiday now." Although she was looking forward to getting back to work. All this waiting around, mulling over her life or lack of it, was getting to her. Still, she only had two more weeks of holiday before she needed to get back into the classroom.

"Right." Jasper took a sip of tea. "Lovely brew, thank you."

"Even though it's not Darjeeling?" she said with a smile, and he smiled back.

"Was that terribly snobby of me, to ask?"

"No, of course not." She laughed. "But you do seem…" How to put it diplomatically? "Like you have a title or something."

Jasper hung his head with mock sheepishness. "Only a viscount."

"Pardon?" Rachel started. "You mean, you really are titled? I was actually joking."

"My father's an earl, which makes me a courtesy viscount. Sorry."

"You don't have to apologise—" She felt embarrassed for her apparent gaucheness. "So should I call you Lord Jasper or something?"

"No, please don't. Just Jasper is fine. Although actually, if you were going to call me by my title, which I really would rather you didn't, it would be Lord Hartleigh."

"Right, I suppose I'd better get a copy of Debrett's."

"Don't, please. It really is just Jasper."

"Okay."

He smiled boyishly, and with a little ripple of awareness Rachel realised how good-looking he was, with his floppy, honey-coloured hair, glinting green eyes, and teeth that looked like they belonged in a toothpaste advert. She stood up suddenly.

"Sorry, but I should be getting on. Simon will be back soon—I think he was visiting a baptism couple. I'm sure he'll tell you which room you should have."

"Oh, right." Jasper looked a little startled, and then a little disappointed. Rachel felt guilty for abandoning him so abruptly, but she wasn't remotely ready to feel attracted to someone yet. Not that she was attracted to *Lord Hartleigh*. He wasn't her type at all. He was just very handsome.

"I'll see you around," she said brightly, and then went upstairs to hide in her room, because she didn't actually have anything better to do.

Fortunately, Simon returned home a few minutes later, and Rachel listened from behind the closed door of her room while Simon showed Jasper the bedroom across the hall. He had, with characteristic sensitivity, left Jamie's old room untouched, the door closed.

Still, it all felt a little too close for comfort, living in her old house with Simon, Miriam, and now Jasper. Too many memories, too much awkwardness. It really would be far better for her to get her own place as soon as possible, and start looking towards the future.

"Aren't you worried parishioners are going to think this is a den of iniquity?" Miriam asked with some of her old acerbic wit as the four of them ate dinner around the little table that night—beans on toast, courtesy of Simon.

"A den of iniquity?" Simon looked startled. "Sorry?"

"Two men and two women living under one roof and none of us married," Miriam clarified. "Really, Simon, don't you know how gossip flies in a village?"

"Oh, but…" A blush started on his cheeks. "It's not like that."

"Of *course* it's not like that." Miriam rolled her eyes. "But that doesn't really matter, does it? When we were teenagers Dad was always going on about the appearance of evil, and causing your weaker brother to stumble, and all that. I wouldn't want tongues to start wagging." She pressed her lips together, her humour suddenly vanishing as a look of desolation came over her face. "Although they will anyway."

Rachel looked at her sister askance. *When* was Miriam going to tell her what was going on?

"Well," Simon said after a moment. "If you really think it's going to be a problem…"

"Oh, I think any gossip will die down soon enough," Rachel said quickly. "But the truth is, Miriam and I really should be looking for our own place anyway, Simon, as kind as it is for you to let us live here. We need to move on from the memories."

Jasper looked confused. "Memories…?"

"Rachel and Miriam grew up here," Simon explained. "I took over as vicar from their father."

"Oh how wonderfully Austenesque," Jasper exclaimed. "Two vicar's daughters! Shall we play whist after supper?" Rachel couldn't tell if he was joking or not.

It turned out he wasn't; they played three pleasant hands of the card game before Miriam pleaded tiredness and went upstairs. Sensing that Simon and Jasper wanted a catch-up, Rachel went up as well. She paused by Miriam's room; her sister was staring out the window at the darkened night, looking lost.

"Miriam…?" Rachel tapped gently on the door. "I wish you would tell me what was going on." Because it was painfully obvious that something was.

Miriam's shoulders slumped. "Maybe you don't want to know."

Rachel's insides lurched with alarm but she kept her voice steady. "I do. Whatever it is, it would surely help telling someone?" Miriam didn't answer and she pressed, "You're not ill, are you?" Her sister let out a huff of humourless laughter. "It's just you've been so tired and you look a bit…washed out."

"No, I'm not *ill*," Miriam said, with savage emphasis.

"Then…"

"Leave it, Rachel, please." Miriam turned to her tiredly. "What do you think of Jasper?"

"He seems nice enough."

"Yes." She sighed, shaking her head as she glanced out the window once more, at the dark night. "It feels so weird being here though, doesn't it? Now, I mean, without Mum and Dad. Last night I dreamed of Jamie. I haven't done that in ages."

"What was the dream about?" Rachel asked. She'd dreamed of Jamie several times over the years, always a bittersweet experience. He was alive in the dream, which was wonderful, but then she woke up and reality flooded in, usually leaving her feeling down for hours, if not days.

"I can't really remember," Miriam answered. "He was just *in* it. And I've been feeling as if I'm a little in that dream all day—like I can't shake it, you know?"

"Yes," Rachel said quietly. "I know."

"It's been so kind of Simon to let us live here, but I'm starting to feel like Miss Havisham. All I need is a moth-eaten wedding dress…" Her horrified gaze flew up to meet Rachel's. "Sorry…"

"Don't be sorry, for heaven's sake. I can handle it, I assure you. And if you want a wedding dress, not moth-eaten quite yet…" She smiled, inviting her sister to share the joke, and to her relief, Miriam smiled back. Rachel really didn't think she could take any more pity.

"I'll bear it in mind."

"Okay, then. You're sure you don't want to tell me what's going on?" Miriam shook her head, and Rachel relented, stepping back. One thing she was certain of now, though; something *was* going on. She just didn't know what.

The next morning, with fresh zeal and determination, Rachel decided to see if she could find her and Miriam new accommodation. If the realtor websites didn't have anything to offer, maybe she could find something on a stroll through the village. It was perfectly possible someone local might have propped a sign in the window or staked in the garden rather than going the official route of putting it on the Internet.

She had nothing better to do, anyway, and it was a lovely day, if a bit nippy. Mid-August was the start of autumn in the Lake District, whether you liked it or not. Already the leaves were turning, the air decidedly chilly as Rachel headed out.

She walked slowly across the bridge, St John's Beck burbling merrily underneath, and then up the high street, past The Bell, looking away from its frosted windows as she remembered the whole sick-on-the-boots episode afresh. Up past the post office shop, and then the primary school, tucked down its own narrow lane, and then to the top of the village, where the once-new housing estate had sublime views of the rolling fells, Derwentwater glinting in the distance.

Rachel wasn't exactly sure what she was looking for—a smiling granny to invite her in for tea and mention the flat out back she had? A sign in a window reading 'To Let—cheap and cheerful, immediate occupancy'? Whatever it was, she didn't find it. The village was quiet, only a few people out in their gardens, and while they waved as she went past nobody had a room or flat to let. Rachel asked, ignoring the looks of sympathy she got in return. Even strangers seemed to know of her plight. Thornthwaite really was a small place.

Eventually she turned back down the lane, her steps

coming more slowly now, the zeal she had started out with beginning to flag. She *really* didn't want to live in the vicarage anymore. As kind as Simon was, as friendly as Jasper seemed, it just felt too strange. Her parents weren't there. It wasn't home.

She'd almost reached the bridge when she saw the sign propped in the corner of a dusty window of The Bell. *Flat to Let—See Proprietor.*

Her heart flip-flopped in her chest as she hesitated, wondering if she really wanted to follow that particular lead. Living above The Bell would be a noisy business, and she wasn't sure she wanted to run into Sam West on a regular basis, although surely he wouldn't be working now? It was eleven o'clock in the morning. This flat seemed like the only thing going in Thornthwaite; she should at least see if it was at all suitable.

Taking a deep breath, Rachel marched towards the door of The Bell, flung it open, and went inside.

Chapter Nine

RACHEL BLINKED IN the gloom of the pub's interior, which was virtually empty on a Monday mid-morning. A few stony-faced farmers were at the bar, nursing pints, but the rest of the tables were empty, the floor swept clean of its usual drift of empty crisp packets and spills of beer. And Sam West was behind the bar, giving her one of his unsmiling looks.

Rachel nearly took a step back at the sight of him, but then managed to stop herself. What was it about the man that put her on such an edge? Was it simply that she'd been sick on his shoes, which was certainly embarrassing, or was it the fact that he looked like he could quite easily win a fistfight without breaking a sweat? The close-cropped blond hair, the narrowed blue eyes, the bulging biceps, the tattoo. She couldn't deny he was good-looking, but it was in a way that made her feel…uneasy.

"May I help you?" he asked when the silence had stretched on for several taut seconds.

"Um, yes. I wanted to speak to the…manager? Owner?"

She shrugged helplessly. "About the flat to let." She was starting to seriously regret her impulse to come into the pub. If she lived above it, she'd almost certainly come into regular contact with Sam West, a prospect that made her feel…uneasy. Yes, that really was how she felt.

"I'm the manager and the owner," Sam replied, and Rachel tried her best not to look surprised. She'd assumed he just worked the bar; although now, with a guilty pang, she realised she shouldn't have made that assumption at all. "You want to look at the flat?"

Rachel swallowed. "Yes, if that's okay. It's still available?"

"Yes." He glanced at the farmers sitting silently at the bar and then nodded at Rachel. "I can show it to you now, if you like."

"All right." She could simply say it wasn't suitable, and then that would be that. She'd never come into The Bell again. Ever.

"Follow me."

Sam came around the bar and then Rachel followed him down the back corridor, towards the courtyard where the unfortunate vomiting episode had taken place. Instead of going outside, he opened a door that led to a set of narrow stairs.

"There's a separate outside entrance to the upstairs on Finkle Street," he said over his shoulder. "You wouldn't have to come into the pub."

"Great, thanks," Rachel murmured. The stairs were dark

and narrow, and she felt as if the dingy walls were looming closer as she followed Sam upstairs.

"It's on the second floor, which is a bit of a climb. I live on the first floor."

Yet another reason not to take this flat. Rachel didn't reply as they came onto the top landing of the building, as dim and cramped as everything else, with dark panelled walls topped with ancient and rather hideous flocked wallpaper in green and gold.

Sam opened the door and then stepped aside so Rachel could enter first. She did so, unable to keep from giving a little exclamation of surprise at how light and airy it all was. A skylight in a vaulted ceiling opened the living area right up, and the floor was freshly sanded with varnished oak boards, the sashed windows overlooking the beck, the church and vicarage just visible beyond.

"Oh, wow. This is amazing." She glanced at the open-plan kitchen off the main living area, all with sparkling new appliances. "How many bedrooms is it?"

"Two." He nodded towards the hallway that led off the other side. "And one bathroom."

The bedrooms were small but well appointed, with built-in cupboards and spectacular views, and the bathroom was tiny but as sparkling and new as the kitchen. Really, it was practically perfect.

"How much a month?" Rachel asked, turning towards Sam and nearly bumping into him in the narrow hallway.

"Four hundred." He gazed at her impassively, his expression giving nothing away.

Four hundred was certainly reasonable, and she could manage it even if she had to carry half the mortgage on her former dream house for a few months. Really, there was absolutely no reason not to take this place, and yet…

"Is it very noisy? From the pub?"

"Occasionally you might hear a shout or something," Sam answered. "But you're high up enough that it shouldn't bother you. You'd hear just about as much at the vicarage."

Which was true enough. When one of the village's pubs had live music the residents of the vicarage were treated to the entire concert whether they wanted to listen or not; the sound carried easily across the river and sheep pasture.

"And there is double glazing," Sam added. "Which I believe the vicarage doesn't have?"

Rachel looked at him in surprise. He was right; the vicarage's ancient windows were one of the reasons the house tended to be on the freezing side.

"How do you know that?" she asked, and Sam shrugged.

"I've been in there once or twice, not that you'd remember."

"Oh." She felt as if there was a lot he wasn't saying, and it seemed he didn't want her to ask. "Okay, well. I'll think about it, if that's all right."

"Sure." Another shrug. "I haven't had any offers, so take as much time as you like."

"Haven't you? It seems so nice and new."

"I renovated it just a couple of months ago."

"You did it yourself?" He nodded. Somehow Rachel could see that. Sam West looked like a man who did things himself. "It's really nice. You did a great job."

"Thanks."

A silence lengthened between them, sunlight spilling onto the floor through the skylight. Rachel wondered what Sam was thinking, and how much he knew about her situation. She couldn't tell anything from his expression, which was as inscrutable as ever.

"Have you owned The Bell for long?" she finally asked, more to break the silence than anything else.

"For about a year. The last owners sold up to me and moved to Portugal."

"I didn't know them," Rachel admitted, and Sam's mouth kicked up at the corner.

"No," he agreed dryly. "You wouldn't have."

"Right, well I'll have a think." Was she just putting off saying no? Rachel glanced around the room again, admiring the skylight, the fresh paint, the surprising spacious airiness of the place. It was a lovely flat, and she could see herself and Miriam there. And she couldn't live in the vicarage forever. She certainly didn't want to.

Sam held the door open for her and with a quick smile of thanks that he didn't return she headed back downstairs, promising to let him know her decision in a few days, before she headed back out to the street.

Back at the vicarage Jasper had set up an office of sorts in the dining room, with his laptop open and papers scattered about.

"You look hard at work," Rachel remarked as she poked her head in the doorway.

"Looks can be deceiving." He stretched his arms above his head, giving her a sunny smile. "Really, I'm just faffing about on the Internet. Fancy a drive and a pub lunch?"

Startled, Rachel blurted, "Oh, I've just got in—"

"And you can go back out again, can't you?" Jasper's smile widened. "I heard about a cosy place towards Windermere that I'd love to see. Take pity on a poor tourist, you being local and all that."

"Windermere…" Was ages away. Still, Rachel was tempted. All she was going to do around here was mope and maybe read a book. "All right," she said impulsively. "What about Miriam? She might like to come, as well—" And it would keep their outing from feeling like some sort of date, which she certainly didn't want.

"She's at the doctor's surgery," Jasper replied breezily. "But I'll leave a note to let her know where we are, just in case."

Miriam was at the doctor's? Anxiety clenched in her stomach at the thought, but it was hard to hold on to it when Jasper put the top down on his BMW and they tootled down the narrow, hedge-lined lanes on the way to the pub he'd heard about.

With the sun shining and the wind blowing through her hair, Rachel gave herself up to the sheer enjoyment of such a moment. Jasper grinned at her from the driver's seat.

"Have I converted you?"

"Converted me…?"

"To convertibles."

"Ha, no." She shook her head. "You'd have to either be insane or deluded to have a convertible in a place where it rains three hundred days a year."

"I prefer eternal optimist," Jasper returned, and Rachel nodded at the few greyish clouds on the horizon.

"Watch those," she warned. "You'll be putting the top up on the way back—I guarantee it."

"Is that a bet?" Jasper said, and Rachel looked away. It almost sounded as if he were flirting, but maybe it was just the way he operated.

The pub was every bit as atmospheric and welcoming as Jasper could have hoped, with a slate floor and low beams, and a huge fireplace that was filled with an arrangement of dried flowers thanks to the warmish weather.

A waitress led to them a secluded table in the back, and Rachel glanced at the Michelin-worthy menu with a slight sinking sensation. With the mortgage to think of and wedding bills still to pay, she wasn't exactly skint but she was close.

"My treat," Jasper said firmly, as if he'd read her

thoughts, or perhaps just seen the horror on her face.

A gourmet burger cost twenty-two pounds.

"If you insist." Although Rachel supposed that made it feel more like a date. And truth be told, Jasper Edgington-Jones was a very appealing proposition—handsome, charming, affable, and wealthy. All things that would matter to her if she were shallow, as Dan seemed to think she was, which she was not. Rachel looked away, trying to curb the resentment that still bubbled up at inopportune moments.

"What's up?" Jasper asked lightly. "You look as if you just bit into a lemon."

"Sorry." Rachel smiled guiltily. "I was just thinking about something unpleasant." Hurtful, really, but she didn't want to go that far with someone who was little more than a stranger. "Has Simon told you my sordid past?"

Jasper's eyebrows rose. "No, but it sounds most intriguing. Do share."

"Oh, it's not, really. It's quite dull and pedestrian." She sighed, deciding it was better the news came from her than Thornthwaite's ever-flourishing grapevine. "A few weeks ago I was going to get married, but my fiancé broke it off the night before. Well," she amended, wanting to be fair to Dan, "we both agreed to call it off, but it was his suggestion."

"Ah." Jasper nodded, his face full of sympathy that somehow seemed less difficult to bear, coming from someone she didn't really know. "And were you thinking of him now? Did you come here before, as a couple?"

"No, I've never been here before in my life." Rachel willed herself not to blush as she remembered why she'd thought of Dan—because she'd been thinking of Jasper as a potential romantic interest, which he most certainly wasn't. "I just think about it in unexpected moments, I suppose."

"Ah, easily understandable. Let's have a bottle of champagne with lunch to banish the memories."

"Ugh, no, sorry, no champagne."

Jasper raised his eyebrows. "Is there a story there?"

"Same story, really, but anyway. I'll just have sparkling water, please."

Jasper sighed theatrically. "How utterly boring, but very well. At least let's both have dessert."

Rachel smiled. "Now that I can agree to."

They ordered their meals and as the waitress left with their menus Jasper leaned back in his seat and looked around the cosy and quaint pub. "You know, I could see myself running a place like this. Master of the house, all bustling bonhomie, that sort of thing."

"I could see that, too, actually," Rachel said. "You'd be good at it."

"Why, thank you. There we are, then. My life sorted."

"Does it need sorting?"

"Oh, yes. Terribly. Why do you think I'm here?" His tone was so light Rachel didn't know whether to take him seriously. He gave a breezy smile. "What about you, Rachel? Why did this loser of a fiancé break it off with you, if you don't mind me asking?"

"He's not a loser," Rachel replied quickly. "And the more I think about it, the more I think he was right to break it off. But it still hurts."

"Of course it does. I'm sorry. I didn't mean to be unkind."

"No, I'm the one who is being unkind. Even though I'm coming round to believing it was right of him to have ended it, I still keep trying to feel like the victim." She made a face. "Not a very attractive quality."

"But completely understandable. Personally, I think he must have been mad." He smiled, and Rachel felt a twinge of unease. This was starting to feel too much like flirting.

"No, not mad. He just wanted more from me than I suppose I was able to give."

"And what did you want?"

"The fairy tale, I suppose." The husband, the house, the kids, the puppy. The life she'd always dreamed of having. *The puppy...*

"Oh, no." Her eyes widened as she stared at Jasper who looked at her, smilingly nonplussed. "I just remembered that I'm supposed to be picking up a puppy next week."

"A puppy?"

"My fiancé and I…we were getting a dog."

"Maybe he should get the dog, then."

"Actually, I want the dog. At least, I did." But she could hardly ask Simon to have a puppy at the vicarage, especially when he was already taking care of Charlie. And would a puppy work in a second-floor flat above The Bell?

"You could tell the kennel or whoever that you've changed your mind," Jasper suggested. "I'm sure they have someone else on the waiting list. Good breeders always do."

"Perhaps, but…" For some reason Rachel was reluctant to let go of that dream, along with every other one she'd had to relinquish. She shrugged and took a sip of water. "We'll see."

The rest of the lunch went pleasantly enough, and Jasper was as charming and affable as ever, making her laugh at some of his witticisms as well as his over-the-top aristocrat attitude, but despite all that, something had gone a little off for her as well, and Rachel wasn't even sure what it was.

She wished she hadn't told Jasper about Dan; he'd been sympathetic, but it had made her feel worse somehow, and the whole episode seemed disloyal to Dan, which was absurd, considering, and yet…

She was relieved to get back to the vicarage, even as she fought a certain fog of poignant sorrow as she climbed up the weathered stone steps. Would that ever lift? Or would this place always feel like home-but-not?

The house was quiet and Rachel went in search of Miriam, determined to get to the bottom of whatever was troubling her sister. She found her curled up on her bed, a pillow tucked to her middle, looking far too woebegone.

"Miriam, what did the doctor say?" Rachel blurted. She

was filled with alarm at the sight of her sister looking so despairing. "Are you ill?"

"No," Miriam returned dully. "Not ill."

"Then what?" Rachel sat on the edge of the bed. "I wish you'd tell me, Miri. Put at least one of us out of our misery."

Miriam rolled over onto her back and gazed up at her sister, her face full of misery. "You really want to know, Rachel?"

"Yes, of course I do—"

"All right, then, I'll tell you. I'm pregnant."

Chapter Ten

FOR A MOMENT Rachel could only stare at her sister blankly, as the foolish thought *but you're not married* went through her head. Thankfully she did not point out the obvious.

"Oh," she finally said, and left it at that. Her mind was spinning.

"Won't Dad be so ashamed of me?" Miriam said, and then her face crumpled.

"Oh, Miriam." Rachel leaned forward to put her arms around her sister and gave her a tight hug. "Don't think like that. Mum and Dad love you, love all of us, no matter what. That's one thing I'm sure of. They would never be *ashamed*."

"Maybe so." She sniffed, her cheek pressed against Rachel's shoulder. "But they'll still be disappointed. They'd never want this for one of their daughters. I'm glad they're not here to see this, to hear all the village gossip about me— coming home knocked up, with no man in sight, never mind an actual ring."

"People won't talk…" Rachel began, only to stop because she knew they would. But it wouldn't be *mean*; people were sympathetic and well meaning, if anything, in their own nosy way.

Miriam eased away from her to lie flat on her back as she stared up at the ceiling. "It's not going to be easy, living here. Maybe I should have stayed in Australia."

Rachel had so many questions she didn't know where to begin. *Who? How? Why?* She swallowed them all down, because now really didn't seem the time to grill Miriam for details.

"Is that why you went to the doctor's? To have a—a pregnancy test?"

"Yes, to have it confirmed. I'd already taken a couple of over the counter ones but I wanted to make sure." She let out a shuddery sigh. "And now I'm sure."

"Oh, Miriam." Rachel patted her sister's shoulder, wishing she could offer more comfort.

"I've really messed up this time, haven't I?" Miriam said grimly as she stared at the ceiling, one hand resting lightly on her still-flat belly. "I know I've always been a bit of a rebel, but…" She trailed off, shaking her head.

It was true that of all them Miriam had been the wildest—the only one to get suspended from school for smoking behind the bike sheds, or to be grounded for coming home drunk from a party in sixth form. With two thousand well-meaning and beady-eyed villagers ready to run to her parents with tales of her misdeeds, it couldn't have been easy to be the youngest Holley.

Rachel had sometimes wondered if that was why Miriam had gone backpacking as soon as she'd received her admittedly mediocre A Level results. It was hard to grow up in the fishbowl of Thornthwaite, even if both Rachel and Esther and soon Anna had all gone happily back to it. It definitely wasn't easy, but it was also wonderful, always having neighbours and parishioners and friends looking out for you. Even in the midst of her own ongoing jilted wedding drama, Rachel wouldn't want to live anywhere else. But she wasn't Miriam.

"So." Rachel took a deep breath. "What are you thinking, Miriam? I mean, what are you going to do?"

"How many options do I have?"

"Well…" Rachel hesitated, not wanting to verbalise the possibilities.

"Rachel, I couldn't do *that*." Miriam looked genuinely shocked. "If that's even what you're suggesting—"

"I'm not suggesting anything. I just want to know what your thoughts are right now."

"I don't know. I've been feeling so rough and trying not to think about any of it." Miriam let out a long, gusty sigh. "But I know I need to."

"What about…the father?"

"No." The one word was flat, final.

"Shouldn't you tell him?"

"He wouldn't want to know, Rachel. Sorry, but that's

the sad truth." Miriam closed her eyes, her face starting to crumple again. "It all sounds so horrible, doesn't it? It *is* horrible."

"It's a baby, Miri," Rachel said gently. "Mum and Dad's first grandchild. Even in the midst of...everything, that's something to celebrate."

"Is it?"

"Yes, it most certainly is. Babies are wonderful." She'd intended to have five herself, once upon a dream. "There's no doubt about that, even if the timing or circumstances aren't right. I believe that with all my heart."

"Yeah, sure." Miriam smiled tiredly. "They're always a miracle."

"They are," Rachel insisted, and then decided to stop. Miriam didn't need a lecture. Not now, anyway. "Have you told anyone else yet?"

"Nope. I haven't done anything, Rach. I haven't even sorted out where I'm going to live, because I can't stay here, especially not if I'm pregnant, and I *am* pregnant." She let out a weary laugh. "Imagine the gossip: the vicar with the former vicar's pregnant daughter, no father in sight."

"Forget the gossip. People in Thornthwaite aren't as judgemental as you think. But I agree with you, it would be better not to live here. I feel the same. We both need fresh starts, Miriam, away from the vicarage and what it once was."

"Yes, but where?"

Rachel thought of the sunny flat, the skylight, the two bedrooms. It was perfect. All right, maybe not *perfect*—two flights up wasn't ideal for a baby or a pregnant woman. But the price was right and it was big enough for them both. And as much as she loved this dear old house, she knew she didn't belong here anymore. Simon needed his fresh start, and so would Anna after their wedding in just a few months. She and Miriam needed to move on, even if it was just down the road.

"I might have a place," she told Miriam. "A flat in the village. It's not Keswick, but it's somewhere a bit different."

"A flat?" For the first time in what felt like forever Miriam looked a bit interested and lively, a faint reminder of her old self. "Where?"

"Above The Bell." Which really wasn't ideal for a baby, but still. It was a place to live that wasn't here.

"The Bell? You seem to have a history with that place."

Rachel grimaced. "Not really. But there is a flat available, and the rent is cheap."

Now Miriam was the one to grimace. "I don't have any money, Rach. I've been living on pocket change."

"Don't worry about that—"

"What am I going to do?" Miriam cried, covering her eyes with her hand. "Twenty-three years old, penniless, homeless, and pregnant, with no qualifications. Why didn't I go to uni? Not that it would even matter now."

"Let's tackle one thing at a time, Miriam, shall we?" Rachel said in her best, briskest teacher's voice. "First, a place to stay. We'll deal with the other things as they come along."

"One of them has already come along," Miriam retorted, patting her still-bumpless stomach.

"We have time," Rachel returned. "Do you know how far along you are?"

"The nurse thought ten weeks or so. I'll have a scan in a couple of weeks to determine my due date."

"Well, that's exciting."

"Yes." Miriam sounded unconvinced, and Rachel felt a rush of sympathy for her sister. Both of their lives had become derailed, albeit in different ways. "We'll get through this," Rachel said. "Trust me. I'm not saying it's going to be easy or even fun, but we'll get through it."

That night she talked to Simon privately about her and Miriam's plan to move. Simon managed to seem disappointed as well as relieved, both reactions that Rachel understood. He had his own life to think of, but she knew he had wanted to help her and Miriam out.

"Are you sure, Rachel? I do have acres of space…"

"Yes, but you and Anna will need your own place once you're married, and Miriam and I need to find our own." She smiled wryly. "Also, it makes me feel like even more of a saddo, to be living at my parents' old house when my wedding has been called off."

"I never meant—"

"It's not you, Simon. It just is. It's better if Miriam and I have our own place. Fresh start and all that."

"Is Miriam all right?" Simon's forehead crinkled in concern. "She's seemed to be a bit a down lately…"

"She'll be all right." Her sister's secret was not Rachel's to divulge. "In time."

Simon nodded sympathetically. "Broken heart?"

"Something like that." Rachel had no idea if poor Miriam had her heart broken by some uncaring Australian, but the very fact that she insisted the father of her baby wouldn't want to know about it was a cause for deep concern and sadness.

Jasper was much less accepting of Rachel's decision to move out of the vicarage. "You mean it's just going to be me and Simon rattling about in this place?" he exclaimed in not-so-mock horror. "We'll be a pair of grumpy old bachelors, driving each other absolutely batty."

"I'm not going to be a bachelor for much longer," Simon reminded him.

"Exactly." Jasper shuddered. "It'll just be me. Rachel, really, you're abandoning me here." He gazed at her with his puppy-dog eyes, hands outstretched dramatically. "Don't you feel guilty?"

"No," Rachel answered with a smile. Jasper was charming, almost too much so, and she was not as immune as she would like to be. The further away she got from his brand of affable attractiveness, the better. She was most definitely not ready for that kind of complication in her life.

"You will visit, though?" Jasper pressed. "Sunday dinners every week. I insist."

"Who's cooking?" Rachel challenged. They were all deplorable cooks.

"I will, if you'll come. Both of you." Jasper turned to Miriam, smiling. "I'll make a roast dinner every Sunday evening."

"Sounds like a good deal to me," Simon chimed in and Rachel relented.

"All right, that's a very kind offer. We'll be there on Sunday. But in any case, we're only moving down the road, so I'm sure we'll bump into each other on a regular basis." Although not too regular, if she could help it. Jasper's twinkling eyes promised differently.

"What have you got against Jasper?" Miriam asked later, when they were alone upstairs. Rachel looked at her in surprise.

"Nothing. He's lovably charming."

"Then why were you acting as if having dinner here once a week was akin to torture?"

"I wasn't," Rachel retorted indignantly. "And it wouldn't be torture. That's the problem."

"Ah." Miriam nodded wisely. "It's like that, is it?"

"It's *not* like that. I just don't need that kind of distraction right now."

"So he is a distraction?"

"No." Rachel rolled her eyes. "I mean, he *could* be, but

the last thing I want is to even think about dating someone right now. Not that I would date him," she added hurriedly, noting Miriam's sceptical expression, "or that he'd even want to date me. But he's a bit of a temptation as well as a flirt and I just don't want to deal with that now."

"I suppose I can understand that," Miriam answered on a sigh. "I certainly don't want to deal with anyone of the opposite sex in just about forever."

Which begged so many more questions, but Rachel chose not to ask them. They would have time later to sort through the detritus of their decision-making.

The only thing left to do to sort their new accommodation was, in fact, inform Sam West—something Rachel knew she should have done before telling Simon of her plans, but for some reason Sam West made her feel apprehensive, in an entirely different way from Jasper.

She went into The Bell on Wednesday afternoon, a day of sleeting rain and chill wind, reminding everyone yet again that autumn in the Lake District really began in August, or if it was a particularly unlucky year, at the start of the summer holidays.

"Hi, Sam," she said brightly, causing two farmers at the bar to look up from their pints at her with baleful stares. "I wonder if I could talk to you about the flat?"

"You can." He regarded her in his stony way, and Rachel wondered what it would take to make the man smile properly.

"I was hoping it was still available—"

"It is."

"And that my sister and I could move in as soon as possible."

"You can."

"Would you like a deposit?"

He shrugged. "I trust you."

For some reason that made Rachel feel rather pleased. "Oh, well. Thank you—"

"It's a small village," he explained, which made her feel a little less pleased, but why on earth should he trust her, especially considering how they first met?

"The only other matter I wanted to ask about was…" She paused, and Sam arched an eyebrow, his arms folded across his impressive chest. "I'm meant to be getting a puppy next week," Rachel continued in a rush. "A darling little Golden Retriever. I thought I'd be living somewhere else, which is why—well, anyway. I don't have to get the puppy, of course. I mean, I could tell them I've changed my mind. But I really wanted a dog and if you thought it was okay then I wondered if maybe, just maybe, I could bring the puppy as well?" Her words had jumbled together so fast Rachel wasn't sure he understood. He didn't reply for a few seconds, at any rate.

"A flat's not really a place for a puppy."

"No, I know, but I've got time to walk her, and…I'll be really careful, honestly. Promise." She tried not to think about how puppies chewed things, and yipped and barked and did wees everywhere. She certainly tried not to let all that show in her face.

A full minute ticked by while Sam just looked at her. Then he nodded. "All right, you can bring the puppy."

"Oh, thank you—"

"Do you need help moving your stuff?" She blinked in surprise. "I'm only asking because I've got a van."

"Oh, well…" All her stuff was piled in the garage of the dream house—and she couldn't afford to hire a mover. "That would be kind of you, thanks." Sam just nodded, and with a little jolt Rachel realised how tangled her life was becoming with his. He was her landlord, her neighbour, and now he was acting like her friend. Yet she still felt as if she barely knew him at all.

"Just let me know when you want it."

"Is tomorrow too soon?"

His mouth quirked—was that actually a smile? "In a hurry?"

"Just want to get on with things," she said a little stiffly, and Sam nodded.

"Right, then. Tomorrow it is. Nine o'clock areet? I'll need to open up the pub at eleven."

"Perfect." She gave a little nod of farewell, followed by an uncertain smile, and then, not knowing what else to do, she left.

That afternoon she decided to drive to Will and Esther's

to tell her sister of her plans. Pulling up in front of the long, low farmhouse of white stone, smoke coming from the chimney, the black shutters newly painted, Rachel felt a little twist of envy she tried to suppress.

Esther and Will had had a hard time of it lately, first with Esther's miscarriage and then an ensuing bump on their road to marital bliss, but they certainly seemed solid together now, and Esther looked happier than she had in months, if not years. Considering the state of Rachel's own life, it was hard for her not to feel the teeniest pinprick of envy—or maybe not so teensy.

"You're what?" Esther exclaimed as soon as she'd banged the kettle on the Aga and nudged their five-month-old black Lab, Lola, from in front of the range's warmth. She turned around to face Rachel, her arms folded. "You're leaving the vicarage to live in some grotty flat above The Bell?"

"Did I say that? The flat is not grotty. It's actually really nice. Sam's done it up—"

"Sam, is it?"

"Oh, please. He's my landlord now, and he's helping me move tomorrow."

"Hmm."

Rachel rolled her eyes at her sister's predictable reaction. "What exactly are you objecting to, Esther? Or is it just that you don't like to be the last to know?"

"It has nothing to do with knowing or not knowing. I just don't want you to do something stupid on the rebound."

"Ouch." Rachel shook her head slowly, absorbing this bluntly made statement. "Trust me, Sam West is not my type. In fact, if you really want to know, part of the reason I'm leaving the vicarage is because of Jasper."

"You mean Lord Hartleigh?" Esther retorted sardonically. "Tell me something hasn't happened with *him*."

"No, of course nothing has!" Rachel exclaimed. "I was about to get married three weeks ago, remember? I'm not about to rush into a relationship, but I don't really feel like dealing with that kind of complication right now."

"And Jasper tempts you? I suppose he is a bit of a flirt, but he seems so shallow, Rach."

"Shallow! Just because he's rich?"

"I don't know. He tootles about in his BMW and pretends to work on his CV... He's a bit of a waste of space, if you ask me."

"Well, I didn't ask you." Rachel felt a bit stung on Jasper's behalf over Esther's cutting assessment. Jasper was nice enough, certainly, and in any case Esther barely knew him. "Anyway, he's a friend only. Besides, he's not the main reason why I'm leaving the vicarage. The truth is, I need a new start, not living out of my old childhood bedroom." She sighed. "I know a flat above The Bell might not seem like much, but at least it's something that's mine."

"I can understand that." Esther nodded slowly. "And Miriam is going with you?"

"Yes, it's better all around, isn't it? The vicarage isn't our home anymore. Simon's lovely, but I don't want to try to hold on to the past."

"Good thing, since you can't," Esther answered with a brisk nod. "All right, then. I approve."

"I didn't realise I needed your approval," Rachel teased, and Esther gave her a stern look.

"Since Mum and Dad are out of the country, I'm the matriarch of this family now. Of course you need my approval."

Rachel laughed as the kettle began to whistle.

The next morning Sam's van pulled up in front of the vicarage at five minutes to nine. Rachel was glad she hadn't overslept; she'd envisioned strolling up to The Bell rather than Sam coming to her, striding purposefully up the front steps as if he was on the clock, which perhaps he was.

"You ready?" he asked as she opened the door, her hair damp from the shower and her feet still bare. He was dressed in his seeming uniform of white T-shirt and jeans, battered work boots on his feet and the usual grim expression on his face.

"Just about. Do you want to come in, have a coffee?"

"No, best we just get going."

"Right." As ever, he wasn't the friendliest person, yet there was nothing precisely *unfriendly* about him, either. He just…was.

Rachel clambered into the passenger seat of the surprisingly neat van; it smelled of air freshener and there were two travel cups of coffee in the drink holders between the seats. Sam nodded to them as he turned the key in the ignition. "One's yours, if you want it."

"Oh…" His refusal of coffee made sense now, and his thoughtfulness disarmed her. "Thanks."

"Some sugar packets, as well." He nodded towards the cups. "I didn't know how you took it."

"With plenty of sugar," Rachel confessed, and opened one of the packets. "Thanks."

"So where's your stuff, then?"

"It's in the garage of a house outside of the village. If you drive through to the top end, I'll give you directions."

Rachel's heart flip-flopped at the thought of seeing her dream house again; she hadn't been there since the wedding had been called off. She didn't know how she'd feel when she did lay eyes on the place where she'd expected to live out the rest of her life, and she wasn't sure she wanted to experience that moment in front of Sam West. Unfortunately, she had no choice.

They drove in silence through the village and then up a narrow lane that cut through the fells, Rachel only speaking to give directions, and Sam merely nodding in reply.

"Here it is," she said at last, as they entered a hamlet that was no more than three or four houses. "Fellview, on the right."

He turned into the driveway of the hulking house of slate-grey Lakeland stone perched on its lofty hill. Rachel swallowed hard as Sam stared at the place impassively.

"My stuff is in the garage," she said. "I don't have all that much, to be honest. I gave a lot of it away when—well, when." She decided to stop there.

"All right, then," Sam said, and started towards the garage. As he opened the door, it gave a groaning squeak. Sam glanced at her jumbled boxes and bins, a few pieces of battered furniture, and a dead houseplant she'd forgotten about. "Let's get started," he said, and heaved a coffee table onto his shoulder.

Chapter Eleven

THEY WORKED IN silence for several minutes, hauling and heaving, as the sum total of Rachel's possessions were loaded into the back of his beat-up van. She tried not to think about how different everything was to how she'd expected, how she'd hoped and prayed and wished for, but it was hard with her dream house looming above them, its windows blank and staring.

"Is that the lot?" Sam asked when the garage was emptied. The van was only half-full.

"Yes, that's everything." Rachel glanced at the house again and swallowed. "Would you mind waiting for a bit? Just a minute or so. I want to check on the house."

Sam nodded in his impassive way. "Go ahead."

"Thanks."

She walked on slightly unsteady legs up to the shiny red front door, a door, a life, that had promised so much. Fumbling with the key, she fit it into the lock and then pushed the door open.

The house smelled empty. Lonely. Rachel stepped into

the soaring foyer, breathing in the smell of dust and emptiness and remembering how she'd imagined it all—the smell of freshly baked cookies, or ground coffee, or apple wood from the open fireplace in the sitting room. So many good smells to accompany the life she'd planned on having, the one she'd hoped to share with Dan.

Her footsteps echoed through the hall, as she walked back to the kitchen, the heart of the home with its big red Aga, the French windows overlooking a garden that led right up into the fells. She pictured where the table would have gone, with a dog bed beside it, a highchair one day…

Then she thought of her parents' table, with its lovable scars and chips and even teeth marks, still stuck somewhere in storage, and her eyes started to sting, a huge lump forming in her throat, the kind she knew she couldn't just swallow back down. She sniffed loudly, willing it all back, but that wasn't happening. She hadn't cried, not properly, since the wedding had been called off and her body was finally calling time on her lack of emotion.

"Oh, help," she muttered, barely managing to get the words out before the lump took over and her eyes started streaming.

She wiped at them desperately, half wanting to give in and half really *not* wanting to, because now certainly was not the time. Sam was waiting. Her stuff needed to be unloaded. She couldn't have a breakdown now.

"Rachel…?" Sam's voice echoed through the empty

house, and then Rachel heard his footsteps coming towards the kitchen. She drew a shuddering breath, wiping at her eyes, but it was hopeless. She was a snivelling wreck.

"Sorry to disturb you," he said as he came into the kitchen. "But your phone was ringing and I didn't know if it was important." He held out her smartphone, which she'd left on the front seat of his van.

"Thanks." Rachel's voice sounded clogged as she attempted to clear her throat. She reached for the phone and Sam gave it to her, frowning as he noticed her tears, or rather, her blubbering mess.

"What's wrong?"

"Sorry, I'm just having a moment." She tried to laugh but it came out as a sob and then she was starting all over again with the streaming eyes and the wretched lump in her throat that made speaking nearly impossible. She shook her head as she kept wiping her eyes. "Sorry, sorry."

"You don't need to be sorry." Sam took a step closer to her, so she caught a whiff of his aftershave. "Is there anything I can do?"

"Turn back time?" Rachel tried to joke, but she really shouldn't have attempted another laugh, because that clearly wasn't working. "No, sorry. There's nothing." She drew a shuddering breath, willing her body to behave itself. "Coming back here was harder than I thought." Obviously.

Clumsily Sam patted her shoulder once, and that small gesture touched Rachel more than anything else he could have done.

"You were going to live here, weren't you?"

She managed a smile through her tears. "How much do you know about me, Sam?"

He shrugged. "Word gets around."

"So you know I was supposed to get married three weeks ago."

He paused, his intent gaze scanning her face. "Yes."

She sighed. Of course he knew. Everyone knew. "Well, it didn't work out. Obviously. But this house..." She flung an arm out, gesturing to the huge kitchen. "This was meant to be our dream home, where we raised our children, where we all sat around the dining room table for cosy suppers, where we lived our life together..."

"Where you had your puppy," Sam added and Rachel nodded.

"Yes, that too. It was all going to happen here. The life I've always wanted—the home, the happiness, the togetherness and joy...and now none of it is happening. It really is all just dreams. Maybe it will always be just dreams."

"Life sucks sometimes," Sam offered, and Rachel let out a wobbly laugh.

"Thank you for saying that, because no one else has. And yes, it does. Sometimes it really sucks." She made a face. "We were never allowed to say that word at home. My mum thought it was rude."

"Sometimes it's the right word, though."

"Yes." She smiled at him, thankful the steady stream of tears was finally abating. "Thank you for understanding that."

"It's all right." He glanced around the empty kitchen. "So are you selling this place?"

"Yes, we have to. Neither of us can afford it on our own. In fact, we couldn't really afford it together. It's best if it's sold, but unfortunately there haven't been any offers yet."

"Early days, still."

"Yes, I suppose." She drew in a shuddery breath and nodded towards the door. "Should we get a move on?"

"Do you want to see more of the house?"

She gazed around the empty kitchen with its marble counters and expertly distressed oak cupboards, the archway into the just-as-large family room. The kitchen alone was probably bigger than the flat above The Bell. Really, the place was huge—and it had been out of their budget. Way out of their budget.

Perhaps Dan was right, at least a little bit, about how she'd cared more about the trappings of their future life—the house, the dog, the kids who would come along—than she had about him. She'd certainly been set on this house, and now it seemed foolish of her, to have wanted something so badly. In the end, it was only a house. A very big house.

Sighing, Rachel shook her head. "I don't need to see any more."

They walked in silence back to the van, but it felt companionable rather than tense. Having a cry had been embarrassing but it had also felt good, healing. Rachel took a deep breath and let it out in a rush as she glanced at the jumble of her belongings in the back and straightened her shoulders. *Onwards.*

Back in Thornthwaite, Sam parked in front of The Bell and they started emptying the van, carrying boxes and bins up the narrow steps to the flat above. Sam hefted the furniture while Rachel kept to the little stuff, and soon the cosy living area of the flat was nearly full of her belongings. With each load Rachel felt something bloom inside her, something fragile and small but *there*—a tiny seed of hope, burrowing its roots down into the tender soil of her soul.

"So," Sam said when they'd finished, as he'd wiped his brow with his forearm. "Do you need anything else?"

Rachel glanced at the pile of her things. "I don't know," she admitted. "I'll have to sort through it all." When she'd been packing up, she'd been in a rush, and she'd assumed they would use Dan's furniture, which was far nicer than hers, at least until they could buy new things together. Her stuff, as was painfully obvious right now, was charity shop tat and castoffs from her parents, and she was missing quite a lot of essential items, such as a bed, because she'd given it away.

"All right, then. Well, just let me know." Sam turned to go and impulsively Rachel reached for his hand, startling him so he tensed, his eyes narrowed.

"Thank you, Sam. You've been really kind."

"It's all right." She was still holding his hand, clinging to it like a limpet in fact, and so with a self-conscious smile Rachel released it and stepped back.

"I haven't even signed a contract or anything. Are you sure you can trust me?"

"Pretty sure," Sam answered. He handed her a set of keys. "Rent's due on the first of the month. Since it's halfway through this month, you can pay me half whenever, if that suits you."

"Sure, fine—"

"Good." He gave her a quick nod and then he left. Rachel stood in the middle of her new home, hardly able to believe how quickly everything had happened. Miriam hadn't even seen the place yet! As usual, Rachel had rushed into something head first, impetuous, impulsive, but it had felt right. Yet how many times had she thought that?

Dan had felt right when they'd started together—although, upon further reflection, she knew he hadn't, not completely. What he'd represented had felt right, so right—the home, the family, the life. But Dan himself? Rachel had liked him, loved him even, but she could acknowledge now that he had never felt like her soulmate, if she was even going to believe in that rather romanticised concept. But in truth he hadn't even come close to such a thing. They'd been friends more than anything else, and Dan had known it.

Rachel gazed out the flat's windows at the steep rooftops of the village, the fells beyond, and then turned to the other side to catch sight of the church and the vicarage. Past and future.

Taking a deep breath, she turned from the windows and started back to tell Miriam of their new plans.

THEY WERE MOVED into the new flat by sundown, with both Jasper and Simon helping haul over the last of Rachel's stuff from the vicarage as well as Miriam's two suitcases. All in all, it wasn't that much; the only furniture they had was a tiny table, a single armchair, and one bureau.

Simon insisted that he and Jasper bring over two beds from one of the spare rooms, although Rachel initially resisted.

"You can't sleep on the floor," Simon pointed out reasonably. "And I don't need them."

Rachel relented, mostly for Miriam's sake, who was looking decidedly nonplussed at sleeping on the floor in her still-undisclosed condition.

"We'll do it up slowly," Rachel told her, conscious she had said the same thing to Dan when they'd been in the enormous kitchen of the dream house. He'd been so sceptical; he'd wanted her to move in with him after the wedding, which Rachel realised now would have been far more sensible. But she'd wanted to get started on the fairy tale right away. Looking back, she realised, with a guilty pang, that she should have just moved in with Dan after the wedding. Why couldn't she have been happy with that? Why had she insisted on over-the-top everything?

Because you thought it would make you happy. She'd been determined it would, and now she wondered why. She'd never thought herself shallow; she was a simple girl at heart, a girl who just wanted a home and husband and a couple of kids. She loved teaching, she adored village life, and she didn't have grand aspirations to, well, anything. And yet somehow she'd let herself get caught up in fairy-tale pretensions without even realising she was doing it.

She needed to be different now. She would be, living life as it was rather than how she longed for it to be. Providence had put her here, and here she would stay. For now, at least.

After Simon and Jasper had finished bringing over everything, Rachel opened a bottle of wine and they sat in the sitting room with the windows wide open to the night air, which wasn't as warm as she'd initially thought, and so she ended up closing the windows after a few minutes. Typical Cumbria.

Still, it felt like a minor achievement to be sitting in her own flat, having navigated the recent bumps in her road, her sister and friends around her. She'd considered asking Sam if he wanted to join them, but he was manning the bar in the pub as usual. Rachel wondered if he had any help; he always seemed to be there.

"To the future," Rachel said grandly, and everyone

heaved their plastic tumblers aloft.

"To the future!"

"I hope you'll be happy here," Simon said after they'd had a sip of what was quite cheap plonk—with Miriam sticking to sparkling water—"but if it doesn't work out, you know you're always welcome back at the vicarage."

"Thank you, Simon." Rachel was touched by his kindness. "I think we'll be all right here. But I do appreciate the open door."

"And you're coming on Sunday," Jasper reminded her. "I'm doing a leg of lamb."

"Are you? I'm impressed. A man who cooks."

"Don't be impressed until you've tried it," Simon warned her with a laugh. "Back at Cambridge, Jasper couldn't even make beans on toast. In fact, his mother sent him these ridiculous hampers from Fortnum and Mason to make sure he wouldn't starve, and that was with full catering at college."

Jasper shrugged as he downed the last of his wine. "I was a growing boy."

Rachel shook her head, glimpses into Jasper's unashamedly privileged life always managing to both amuse and awe her. What did he really think of this poky little flat? Not that it really mattered.

After Simon and Jasper had left, Rachel set about unpacking the last of the boxes while Miriam sat in their one armchair, watching her.

"I'm sorry, I know I should help, but I'm absolutely shattered. When is this going to get better, do you think?"

"I'm afraid I'm not an expert on pregnancy-related matters. End of the first trimester, perhaps?" Rachel placed the dead houseplant on the windowsill. She'd watered it and it was starting to perk up a little, so now it only looked mostly dead. It seemed apt.

"A few more weeks, then."

"When are you going to tell people, Miriam? Esther and Anna? And Mum and Dad?"

"Soon, I suppose. I'll have to, won't I?"

"You're still thin as a stick," Rachel acknowledged wryly. She'd always struggled to keep her curves under control. "Where do you think my *Casablanca* poster should go?"

"In your bedroom?"

"You never were a fan of old films, were you?"

"I'm more of an action flick girl."

"Right." Rachel stopped bustling about and perched on top of a packing crate that would have to serve as their other chair. "But seriously, Miriam. You should tell family, at least. People will be supportive, and you'll feel better for it. Mum and Dad will want to help you."

"From China?"

"They're good listeners. Good advice-givers, too."

"I know." Miriam sighed. "I just dread disappointing them, and I know I will. Even if they're really, really nice about it, which they most certainly will be, I'll still feel like

I've let them down."

"You have to live your own life—"

"And getting pregnant was not the way I wanted to do that."

"What about the father?" Rachel asked cautiously. "Do you want to talk about him?"

"Not really." Miriam sighed. "I don't want you to be disappointed in me either, Rachel."

"I wouldn't—"

"The truth is, I didn't really know him that well." Rachel tried to school her face into an unshocked expression but she must have failed because Miriam let out a huff of humourless laughter. "I know, I know, it sounds so sordid, and I guess it is. It was a party on the beach and we got to talking because he was—is—English and I'd had too much to drink... The only thing I know about him is his name. Rory." She cringed, shaking her head. "Isn't that awful? How can I tell Mum and Dad or anyone *that*? Now you will look at me differently, like I'm some—"

"No, I won't, Miriam. I never will." Rachel leaned over to hug her. "In any case, I'm hardly one to talk to you about being impulsive—"

"But you've never done anything like this."

"'There but for the grace of God, go I,'" Rachel quoted with a sad smile. "It could happen to anyone, Miriam. Well, any woman. We're all fallible. All susceptible."

"Still." Miriam shook her head. "I'm so mad at myself,

for being so stupid and reckless. For not thinking—"

"You were carried away. It does happen. Is there any way you could get in touch with this bloke?"

"I don't know. Is he really going to want to know? He was travelling after finishing uni." She grimaced. "His whole life is in front of him."

"So is yours."

Miriam shook her head. "I don't want to drag him into this, Rachel. And I don't even know what he's like, not really. He's basically a complete stranger."

Rachel bit her tongue against the urge to tell her sister that a man should know if he'd fathered a child, even a virtual stranger. They could talk about that later.

"Well, that's all in the past," she said with determined brightness. "And this is our future."

Miriam looked around at the jumble of boxes, the few bits of furniture. "Hooray," she said dryly, as a peal of raucous laughter floated up from the pub two storeys below.

Chapter Twelve

IT WAS THE week before school started, and Rachel was in her classroom, taking down the faded summer reports and decorations, to replace them with all her new autumn kit. It was one of her favourite parts of the year, when everything felt shiny and new—freshly sharpened pencils, brand-new crayons, and plenty of optimism and determination. September felt like a much better time for new year's resolutions, rather than January.

It was now four weeks since her wedding had been called off, and the wound was definitely healing, or at least scabbing over. She'd had several conversations with Dan, mostly about the house—they'd had three showings and were hoping to have an offer soon—but she felt as if they were moving back into friendship territory, and it felt surprisingly natural. Maybe they really had worked better as friends, after all.

She'd also gone to dinner at the vicarage twice; Jasper's roast lamb had been a disaster, charred on the outside, raw on the inside, with mint sauce so strong it had tasted like toothpaste. He'd been abject, but in typical Jasper-style he'd rallied wryly, giving Charlie the dinner of his life and ordering a curry from Keswick for everyone.

"I'll do better next week," he'd promised. "I'll try a roast chicken."

"Please don't," Simon joked. At least Rachel thought he was joking. "Stick to takeaways."

"That hurts, Simon." Jasper looked comically wounded before turning to Rachel in appeal. "You believe in me, don't you?"

"You could always try again," Rachel said, ignoring the flirtatious way Jasper always seemed to address her. She didn't think he really meant anything by it; he was just that way. At least that's what she kept telling herself.

Now, after she'd set up her classroom, she was going to drive to a farm near Carlisle to pick up her Golden Retriever puppy, and she could hardly wait. She was so ready to retrieve a little piece of the dream life she'd constructed for herself. Miriam had been dubious about bringing a dog into their lives, but Rachel was determined.

She'd already bought a crate, and feeding bowls, a lead and a collar with a heart-shaped tag, and a book on puppy training. All she needed now was the puppy.

With a smile Rachel stapled several leaf-shaped cut-outs in various autumnal colours to her new noticeboard. Twenty-four new children to greet next week, another favourite part of her school year—all that possibility and potential in those shining, freshly washed faces. She was ready to get back to work, to feel busy again.

"Rachel!" Another teacher at the school, Diane Cross, popped her head in the Year Three classroom. "How are you? How's married life?"

Diane, Rachel recalled, lived outside the village and had spent the summer teaching at a summer school outside London. She steeled herself for one of undoubtedly many awkward conversations.

"I wouldn't know, actually, Diane."

Diane frowned. "What…?"

"I didn't get married." Rachel waggled her ringless finger, trying to pitch her tone between pragmatic and cheerful. "We called it off at the last minute. Shocker, I know."

"Oh, Rachel…" Diane looked aghast.

"It's all right," Rachel said firmly. "I'm getting over it. Naturally I was devastated, but I'm moving on, and really, it's better this way." She kept her smile in place with less effort than it had taken even a week ago. She really was speaking the truth, amazingly. "How was your summer?"

Diane stammered through some description of her month and a half at summer school, and Rachel murmured the right replies, but she could tell Diane was still uncomfortable. How long would it take her colleagues to see her just as herself, and not the jilted fiancée? Rachel supposed it hadn't helped that she'd bored for England about her wedding for the last six months.

"Let's talk soon," Diane said as she edged out of the classroom. "We'll go out for a drink."

"Why not at The Bell?" Rachel suggested. "I'm living above it now."

Which made Diane look even more startled and somewhat horrified, so much so that Rachel almost laughed. She liked living above The Bell. It was central to the village's main offerings, which admittedly were only the school and the post office shop, but still. The flat was bright and cosy and quaint, especially now Esther had given them their old sofa, and Will and Sam together had managed to lug it up the narrow stairs, getting it stuck only once.

Beyond that, Rachel hadn't actually seen much of Sam; he seemed to work all the time, and when he wasn't at work, he was out. She'd paused several times on the way up to her flat in front of his, and considered knocking on his door to say hello, but she'd never quite been able to work up the courage.

She had a feeling Sam would open the door with that flatly unimpressed look on his face, clearly wondering what she wanted. It would have been nice to have seen a bit more of him; he seemed like a decent guy, even if he was one who kept his distance.

"Right, The Bell," Diane said, and scooted out of the room. Rachel watched her go with a flicker of regret, as well as one of relief. One day these conversations would be easier. Hopefully.

It was a lovely evening for a drive to Carlisle, and Rachel rolled the windows down and let the breeze blow over her as she drove up the A595, enjoying the way the sun spread its honeyed light across the fells, colouring them in gold. She'd asked Miriam if she wanted to come along, but although she was starting to feel a bit better, her sister had declined. Miriam wasn't nearly as sold on the puppy as Rachel was.

Half an hour later she pulled into a cosy farm, a sprawl of whitewashed buildings around a central courtyard, dogs barking happily as Rachel got out of the car, and then was lovingly mauled by a pair of Golden Retrievers.

"Duke, Sorcha! Down!" a woman barked, and the dogs immediately sat down, tongues lolling and tails wagging.

"Wow, they're well trained," Rachel said.

"They're scamps, but very lovable." The woman, smiling and grey-haired, came forward to give Rachel a brisk hand-shake. "Rachel, yes? I'm Evelyn." She raised her eyebrows. "Your husband didn't want to meet your new family member? He's a vet, isn't he?"

Not again. Rachel decided this was one awkward conversation she could avoid. "He's working, I'm afraid," she said, which as far as she knew was true. "But I'm very excited to meet her."

"Come through, then." Rachel wended her way through a cosily cluttered kitchen, admiring the colourful, mismatched pottery, the various jumpers drying over the Aga rail, the jumble of wellies by the cloakroom door. It all looked so lovably lived in, exactly the kind of house she'd wanted, the kind of home she'd grown up in. It felt more elusive now than ever, and so she focused on the one good thing coming her way—an adorable ball of golden fluff with chocolate-button eyes. Her puppy.

"This one's yours," Evelyn said cheerfully as she scooped up the squirming ball of cuteness with expert ease. "She's lovely. Has a very gentle temperament."

"I can't wait." Rachel held out on her arms and Evelyn put the puppy into them; she squirmed and wriggled and licked Rachel's face, making her let out a little yelp of happy surprise.

"A match made in heaven," Evelyn said with satisfaction.

"She's perfect," Rachel exclaimed. She was in love already, her arms holding fast to her wriggling bundle of affection. "Absolutely perfect."

On the ride home Rachel kept glancing at her puppy, who after a vigorous sniff and a little wee, had settled down in a corner of the blanket-lined box Rachel had placed in the footwell of the passenger seat. She really was the cutest thing Rachel had ever seen. Miriam might not be convinced about having a dog, but she'd fall in love with this puppy. She wouldn't be able to help herself.

It didn't, however, quite work out the way Rachel had hoped. She carried a beautifully sleeping puppy nestled in the box inside and up the stairs, only to have her wake up as soon as Rachel had set the box down to open the door to the flat.

Before she could blink, the puppy had scrambled out of her box, her bottom landing with a thump, and was trying to get down the stairs, half-tumbling, half-crawling down each step.

"Oh, no, you don't," Rachel exclaimed, and scooped her up, cradling her to her chest. "You're not ready for stairs, little one."

The puppy gave her an adoring look and weed all over her shirt. Rachel yelped and held the puppy away from her; she looked scared and ashamed, and Rachel's heart melted all over again. Her shirt was sopping. How did such a little thing have so much wee?

"Rachel?" Miriam opened the door, taking in the sight of the cowering puppy and the blossoming yellow stain on Rachel's shirt. "Ah. Just as I expected."

"Isn't she adorable?"

"Umm. Sure."

"Oh, come on." Rachel nudged the empty box inside with her foot and then, with the door closed firmly behind her, let the puppy down on the floor. She sniffed, turned in a circle, and did a little wee—and a poo.

"Ugh!" Miriam backed away. "Seriously, Rachel…"

"Come on, it's not that bad. Puppy poo is rather innocuous." She grabbed a paper towel and disposed of the offending faeces. "She needs to be housetrained, obviously."

"Obviously."

Rachel gave her sister a mock glare. "You like dogs, Miriam. You loved Charlie when we were growing up. I have a vivid memory of you lying next to him, your arms wrapped around him, after school. There is even a photo of you together—your hair is dyed pink."

"I remember. A mistake in Year Twelve." Miriam retreated to the sofa, hugging a cushion to her chest.

"So why aren't you in love with this puppy?" Rachel asked as they both watched the puppy sniff around and then curl up into a ball by Rachel's feet. *Bless.*

She looked up, smiling, waiting for Miriam's answer, only to see her sister's face crumple.

"Miriam—"

"I'm scared," Miriam said, her voice coming out in something between a whisper and a whimper.

"Scared…?"

"Of taking care of something. Loving something—someone."

Rachel's heart twisted as she realised they were no longer talking about the puppy—or at least not just the puppy.

"I'm no good at it, Rach," Miriam continued, her voice wobbling all over the place. "I never have been. I've been so selfish my whole life—living for myself, travelling where I like, dropping a job as soon as I feel like it. I didn't study in school—do you remember how Mum and Dad despaired of me? How on earth can someone like me raise a child? I'll be a horrible mum."

"Miriam, don't say that." Gently Rachel scooped up the puppy and placed her in the box, where she curled into a corner. "You don't know what kind of mother you'll be. The maternal instinct is pretty strong—"

"In some people, maybe."

"And why not in you? You have a lot of love to give, Miri, and I think you'll be a dead cool mum." Rachel was gratified to see a smile flicker across Miriam's face. "The past doesn't have to define you, though, Miriam. Yes, we've all lived a certain way, made plenty of mistakes. But it doesn't mean we have to be that way in the future. That's what Mum or Dad would tell us, and it's what I've had to tell myself. Repeatedly."

"What mistakes have you made, Rachel?"

"Well, becoming engaged to the wrong man, for starters."

"Do you really think Dan was the wrong man?"

"Yes, I do. And it hurts to realise that, because I was so consumed with constructing my dream life that I didn't even realise the foundation wasn't solid."

"Dan seems like such a good guy."

"He is a good guy, a wonderful guy." Rachel's voice trembled. "And he's a great friend…but that's all he ever really was. A friend. I thought it was enough for a marriage, and sometimes I think it can be. Love can grow…but Dan didn't agree with me, and I'm coming to see that he probably was right. We weren't suited…not in that way." She tried to smile. "So here I am, for better or for worse." Words she'd never got to say, and now never might. She was thirty-two after all, and the dating pool in Thornthwaite was more like an evaporating puddle. "But we're talking about you now. Are you going to talk to Mum and Dad?"

"Yes, I'm Skyping them tomorrow. Dreading it."

Rachel nodded, relieved that Miriam was at least taking some positive action. "Do you want the place to yourself, or would you rather have some moral support nearby?"

"Place to myself, I think." She made a face. "Sorry…"

"Don't be sorry. Whatever you want." The puppy stirred, raising her head to gaze at them balefully over the rim of the box, her chocolate eyes mournful and appealing. "What do you think we should name her?"

"Did you already have a name in mind?"

"I had a couple. Daisy, because she's yellow, or Bailey, after my favourite liqueur, since that's kind of yellow, as well. Or at least beige."

They grinned at each other, and then Miriam nodded. "I like the sound of Bailey, especially since I won't be able to drink any for about seven months."

"And it's fitting, since we're above the pub. Have you seen Sam around?"

Miriam's eyebrows rose. "No, should I have done?"

"No, I just wondered where he was. I thought I'd let him know about the puppy." Rachel didn't know why she'd automatically adopted a pseudo-insouciant tone. It was a sure giveaway of…something. "Anyway, I'm sure I'll see him around sometime."

"And he'll hear the puppy soon enough. Don't they bark all night long?"

"Only in rom-coms," Rachel promised. "She'll be as good as gold, I promise."

As it turned out, Bailey wasn't quite that good—but almost. Rachel took her out several times over the course of the evening, and then finally settled her around eleven, as the pub's custom was starting to empty out. She barked and whined for about an hour and then thankfully settled to sleep.

Rachel was just dropping off herself when she woke suddenly to what she thought was a pounding on the door. She sat bolt upright in bed, her heart thudding in time with the pounds on the door.

Bailey started howling and Rachel threw on a dressing gown and rushed to the door, sure someone had a bullet wound at least, as Miriam stumbled out of her own bedroom, bleary-eyed and tousle-haired.

"Who is that…?" she mumbled as Rachel unlocked the door, a split second later realising that might not have been the wisest idea. What if some drunken lout from the pub had stumbled upstairs?

But it only took her a few stunned seconds to realise that no one was actually knocking on her door. Someone was knocking on Sam's door downstairs.

"Sam." The woman's voice was wild, desperate, and drunken. "*Sam!* Open up, please. Come on, please, Sammy."

Miriam came to the door, exchanging an uneasy look with Rachel. "Who is that?" she whispered.

"I have no idea." Rachel listened to the continued pounding with a horrified fascination. *Sammy?* It couldn't be some random customer from the pub. It was someone he knew.

"Sammy!" The woman bellowed again, her voice seeming to fill the hallway and ring in their ears. "Open the bloody door!"

Finally, Rachel heard the door being unbolted and then Sam's low voice. "Tiffany, what are you doing here?"

"Let me in, Sam."

"Tiff—"

"It's Nathan, Sam. They've taken him."

"*Taken* him—"

"Earlier tonight." The woman, Tiffany, started to cry.

"Ssh, ssh." Sam's voice was low and comforting. "Come inside, Tiffany. I'll sort it, don't worry." Still crying, Tiffany went inside, and the door clicked softly shut behind her.

Miriam and Rachel exchanged a silent, wondering look; they'd been transfixed, listening to the whole conversation, but now Rachel felt guilty for eavesdropping, even as she was dying to know who Tiffany was, and where'd they'd taken poor Nathan.

"A man of mystery," Miriam murmured as they closed

their own door. Bailey was running around in circles, barking, clearly wide awake again. "Who do you think that is? A girlfriend?"

"I don't know." It was nonsensical, but she didn't like the thought of that woman, drunken and sobbing, being Sam's girlfriend. "I suppose it's none of our business."

"No, but I'm still curious, aren't you?" Miriam stretched and yawned. "I'd just finally got to sleep, as well."

"Me too." Rachel glanced at Bailey. "I might as well take her down for another wee since I'm up."

"All right. I'm going to head back to bed."

Rachel scooped up Bailey and crept down the stairs, pausing only for a few seconds on the landing outside Sam's door. All was silent.

She went out to the patch of grass across from the pub, the late night—or rather, early morning—air damp and chilly, the whole village utterly quiet and still. Bailey had her wee and Rachel picked her up again, hurrying back indoors. This time she didn't pause by Sam's landing, wanting only to get back to bed.

She woke the next morning to a chilly, grey overcast day—hello to September. Miriam was still asleep when Rachel stumbled out of bed to brew some much-needed coffee. As the kettle was boiling, she threw on her dressing gown to take Bailey downstairs; she was already starting to regret having a puppy on a second-floor flat.

She headed back inside, Bailey tucked under one arm,

only nearly to smack into Sam's chest halfway up the first flight of the stairs.

"Oh…!" Even though there had been no impact, she was still breathless. Bailey squirmed and Rachel grabbed her with her other arm. "Sorry, I didn't see you."

"Sorry," Sam said gruffly. "And sorry for the disturbance last night that I'm sure you heard."

"Well…yes." Rachel regarded him uncertainly. He looked exhausted—unshaven, with bloodshot eyes and a stale smell of beer on him from spending the night serving pints. But then she probably didn't look that great, either, with her hair in a bird's nest and wearing a ratty dressing gown that she normally didn't even let her sisters see, yet she'd thoughtlessly gone outside in it because it was so early and she was exhausted. "Is…everything okay?"

"Not really." Sam raked a hand through his hair. "But I'm trying to sort it."

"If there's anything I can do…" Rachel began, although she couldn't imagine that there was.

Sam stared at her for a moment, his eyes penetratingly blue even when they were bloodshot. "Actually," he said. "There might be."

Chapter Thirteen

RACHEL STARED AT him, startled. She hadn't actually expected him to take her up on her nebulous offer, even though she was willing. "Oh, okay. Well, how can I help?"

"I need to be out this afternoon, and I'd rather not have to close the pub. It shouldn't be too busy, if you wouldn't mind manning the bar for a few hours?"

"Manning the bar?" Now she was even more startled. He was trusting her with his entire operation? "I mean, sure. Fab. It's only... I've never actually pulled a pint." Or operated a till, for that matter.

Sam cracked a tiny smile, making Rachel's spirits lift. "It's not all that difficult, but I can show you, if you like, take you around the place."

"Okay." Bailey squirmed and Rachel transferred her to her other arm. Sam glanced down at the puppy and gently patted her head.

"She's sweet."

"I hope she didn't keep you up with her whimpering—"

"I think I was the one who kept you up."

"Sam, is everything okay?" she blurted. She'd already asked him that but she didn't know what else to say. Something was wrong, and she wanted to help. And so she would be, although in a rather unlikely way...but she wanted to help in another way, as well. She wanted to listen, even to comfort...if Sam would let her.

He sighed heavily. "It's not okay, but like I said, I'm working on it. Do you want to meet downstairs in an hour or so?"

"Sure." Of course Sam wasn't going to unburden his soul to her. She barely knew him, and he didn't seem like the type of person who unburdened his soul to anyone.

Upstairs Rachel deposited Bailey on the floor before reaching for the coffee. She definitely needed a cup, or three.

Miriam still wasn't awake by the time Rachel had showered and dressed and was heading downstairs, but since Bailey was curled up in her crate asleep, Rachel figured she could leave her for a short while. Hopefully Miriam wouldn't mind taking the puppy out a couple of times this afternoon while Rachel was—rather unbelievably—pulling pints.

Sam stepped outside his flat as Rachel came down from hers. He must have been listening for the click of her door, the creak of the stairs. He looked a lot better, freshly showered and shaved, smelling of soap, his hair damp and spiky.

"Thanks for doing this," he said as they headed down to the pub. "I really appreciate it."

"It's no problem." Rachel glanced around the empty, darkened pub as Sam flipped on the lights. The floor was cleanly swept, the top of the bar shining and polished. Sam must clean up every night before he closed—it was a lot of late nights. "Do you have any paid help?" she asked. "It seems a lot to manage on your own."

"I have a few part-timers but they're not people I'd like to leave alone in the pub on their own."

"And I am?" Rachel said with a little laugh. "Are you sure about that? I'm a bit scatty, Sam."

He shrugged one shoulder. "You're a teacher. You must be organised."

"If you'd like a display board on autumn colours, I'm your woman." She gestured to a blank space of white plaster by the front door. "It could go right there."

"I'll think about it." Sam gave her one of those infinitesimally small smiles, making Rachel's stomach do a strange little flip. It almost felt as if they were flirting, but of course they weren't.

"So how does one pull a pint?"

"Come here and I'll show you."

Rachel came around to the back of the bar, and Sam directed her to the row of taps. He reached above her head for a clean pint glass and handed it to her. She breathed in the smell of his soap as his hand brushed hers and she told herself not to be so ridiculous.

"Hold the glass at forty-five degrees," Sam instructed as

he stood behind her. "And aim to pour at the midpoint of the glass, tilting it as it fills up." He reached across and flipped the tap.

Rachel concentrated on holding the glass at the correct angle; she was stupidly conscious of Sam standing right behind her. This really was ridiculous. She needed to get a grip. Why was she so disconcerted, so *aware*?

"Watch it." Sam righted the glass she had actually managed not to watch, and the foam spilled over both their hands. Rachel jerked back.

"Sorry." She flushed in embarrassment, both at her reaction to him and her inability even to pour a pint. "I'm not very good at this, am I?"

"All you need is a little practice." He emptied the glass down the drain and handed it back to her. "Try again."

This time Rachel gave the process her entire focus and managed it successfully, if rather slowly.

"Much better."

She turned around, only to bump into Sam's chest. He stepped back quickly, but it was too late. Her face was now officially scarlet.

"So how about the till?" she asked unsteadily. "How does that work?"

"It's pretty basic." Sam walked over to the cash register and Rachel followed, keeping her gaze trained on the machine rather than the man. Fortunately, she could grasp the mechanics of it quickly, and she practised ringing an order up and giving change, before Sam deemed her ready.

"It shouldn't be crowded in the afternoon, just a few old codgers who sit at the bar for an age over their pint. I don't do food yet, and the soft drinks are in the chilling cabinet down there." He nodded to below the bar. "I doubt you'll get any orders for cocktails, but if you do just say you can't do them. Unless you know how to make a whisky sour?"

"I can make a decent gin and tonic," Rachel offered. "Plenty of experience."

"Well, you know your capabilities then. As for wine…again, it probably won't be an issue, but if it is, the glass sizes and prices are there." He pointed to a blackboard sign propped against the frosted mirror behind the bar. "There's a house red and white, your basic plonk." Rachel nodded. It seemed simple enough.

"Fab," she said brightly. "It all seems rather straightforward."

"I hope so. Thanks for doing this."

"It's not a problem. You've helped me out. It's my turn to help you."

Sam nodded, looking as if he wasn't entirely comfortable with that idea; Rachel got the sense that he was not a man who willingly accepted help or shared personal details with anyone. At least she'd won a few smiles from him this morning. Each one had pleased her a rather absurd amount.

"I should be back after an hour or two," he said. "Hopefully."

"I don't have any plans for the day, so no worries."

And so it was, at one o'clock, Rachel found herself positioned behind the bar, smiling cheerfully at the flat-capped farmer who gave her a stony look in response. He was the only customer, thankfully; she'd been half-fearing some deluge of summer ramblers demanding difficult drinks.

Miriam had promised to take Bailey outside, and Rachel had sensed in her sister a slight thawing towards the puppy. Perhaps it would be good for her sister to have something to take care of for a little while. At least Bailey didn't need nappies, although on second thought that wasn't a bad idea.

"What are *you* doing behind the bar?" Another farmer had clumped in through the door, scowling at her rather ferociously.

"Just standing in for a bit," Rachel answered as cheerfully as she could. "What can I get you?"

"Aren't you the vicar's daughter?"

"The former vicar, yes. One of them, anyway."

The man let out a harrumph as he plonked himself onto a bar stool. "That'll be the day, when the vicar's daughter is serving at the pub!"

"I suppose it is the day, then," Rachel chirped, smile firmly in place. "Now what can I get you?"

It wasn't too hard, once she'd got the hang of it, serving up pints and ringing the till. The farmers who came in weren't a chatty bunch, although Rachel did her best. She asked about the sheep, and whether the price of wool had gone up, to which she received a snort of disgust.

"Wool? *Wool?* You don't raise sheep for wool," one man said, shaking his head. "I'd almost think you were an off-comer." Rachel supposed she should be gratified that after thirty years in Cumbria, she wasn't considered an offcom-er—just close to one.

"Is no one buying wool jumpers anymore?" Rachel asked innocently, knowing the answer, and the man snorted.

"Wool jumpers, with all this fancy Neoprene and Lycra about? No one wants a proper jumper anymore, I tell you. The only reason to raise sheep is for the meat."

"I do enjoy a nice lamb chop." Esther had already told Rachel many times about the state of farming in Cumbria, and she knew that most farmers survived on the subsidies given to them for keeping their land in 'Good Agricultural and Environmental Condition'. The result was a way of life that wasn't sustainable, even if it made the rolling hills and dales dotted with fluffy sheep and drystone walls look appealing, the England that everyone knew and loved.

By three o'clock, having served all of four customers, Rachel was starting to feel restless, wondering where Sam was, and what he was doing. Had he sorted out whatever problem he'd had? And who was the woman who had been banging on his door in the early hours of the morning?

At a quarter to four Sam finally walked into the empty pub where Rachel was mindlessly wiping counters, and he looked so tired and rumpled that Rachel wanted to hug him.

She didn't, of course. She took in the crooked tie and button-down shirt that looked a bit incongruous on his muscular form, and the shadows both in and beneath his eyes, and gave him a sympathetic smile instead.

"How are you?"

"In need of a strong cup of coffee." He rubbed a hand over his face. "Or two."

"Shall I make you one?" The pub, Rachel now knew, did basic teas and coffees, no cappuccinos or lattes on offer.

"Yes, please." He slid onto a stool, his elbows resting on the bar, his head in his hands. Rachel flipped on the kettle and regarded him silently, unsure if she should ask, well, anything.

"I owe you an explanation," Sam said after a moment.

"You don't, not really. Not if you don't want to tell me anything."

"The woman who was knocking on my door last night was—is—my sister Tiffany." He paused, and Rachel wondered if he was going to say more. "She's had a history of alcohol and drug abuse, bad boyfriends, the lot. She also has a son Nathan, who is seven." His voice thickened a little, and Rachel felt a lump forming in her throat. Already she felt sympathy for that poor, vulnerable boy.

"I…I overheard her saying last night that they'd taken Nathan away…?"

"Yes, social services put him in temporary care last night. Apparently, she had one of her boyfriends round, shouting the place down. He knocked her around, and he scared Nathan. There had been complaints... It's not the first time something like that has happened, but it looks like this time it might be for good, or at least for a long while. She has too much bad history."

With just a few bleak words he painted such a grim and desolate picture. "I'm sorry, Sam," Rachel said quietly.

"So am I. He's not a bad kid. He's no angel, either, I know that, but he's had a raw deal and I know what that's like."

Did he? Rachel decided not to ask, even though she was rather desperately curious. "Is there something you can do to help?" she asked instead.

"I met with his caseworker this afternoon and I put in an application to take care of him myself." He looked up then, bleary-eyed and haggard. "Not that I'm the ideal candidate by any stretch. In fact, I'll be surprised if they let me have him."

"Why? You seem like a decent prospect to me. You have your own place, you run your own business..."

"Yes, but it's a pub, not exactly a place for a child to grow up in." He sighed and shook his head. "And I have my own chequered past." He pressed his lips together, clearly keen not to say any more on that subject, although Rachel was even more curious now.

"When will you find out if you were successful?"

"Today or tomorrow. The case is urgent, because they

haven't got enough foster carers in the region. He's with a respite worker but it's only temporary—they don't take kids for more than forty-eight hours."

Rachel frowned. "That sounds kind of cold and clinical."

"Sometimes it is. The foster system is a good idea in theory, but basically it sucks."

He sounded almost as if he had personal experience of it. Another question not to ask, and one that made Rachel realise how little she knew of this man—and yet how much she wanted to know.

"If they haven't got the carers," she asked, "then surely they'd approve him coming to you? You're a close relative—"

"It's not always that simple." He looked away, his expression grim. "How about that coffee?"

"All right." Rachel made the coffee, her mind whirling. What was Sam hiding? And realistically, how would he take care of a seven-year-old boy, when he worked all hours at the pub? When she thought about it a bit more, she could understand how a social worker might be reluctant to entrust Nathan to his uncle, no matter how good Sam's intentions were.

"What's your sister doing now?" she asked as she set a cup of black coffee in front of him. "Is she still with you?"

"No, she took off this morning. It's what she always does. Comes round in a bad way and then buggers off." He sighed wearily. "I'm used to it."

"It sounds tough."

"It is. But you've got your own problems. Thanks for this." He raised the cup and then downed it in one steaming go.

"If I can help…"

"You have helped." Sam's voice took on a stubborn note. "I'm sorry to have had to ask you, but thanks. I'll take over from here."

Rachel felt dismissed, and a little stung by it. Weren't they friends now? Yet even so, she understood Sam's self-protective instinct; hadn't she felt the same? It wasn't particularly pleasant, having someone pore over your wounds and probe your weaknesses. She was already tired of several weeks of how-are-you-coping conversations; Sam had probably had years of them in relation to his sister and her son—and who even knew what else.

"Well, if you do need any help," she said as she took off her apron and hung it on a hook, "do let me know. I'm right upstairs."

"I know. Thanks, Rachel." He gave her a fleeting smile that didn't reach his eyes before turning back to the bar. Rachel nodded, wishing there was more she could say or do, but Sam wasn't interested and so after a second's pause she headed upstairs.

When she got into the flat Miriam was sprawled on the sofa with Bailey asleep on her chest like a furry baby.

"I'm in love," she admitted. "She's adorable, even if she wees everywhere, including on me. Twice."

"She *is* a puppy." Rachel smiled at the sight of the pair of them. It was good to see her sister looking more cheerful, and Bailey was as cute as ever, eyes closed tight as she snored softly.

"How was the pub?" Miriam asked as she stroked Bailey's golden fur.

"Fine. Quiet, actually."

"And Sam?" Miriam's eyebrows rose in expectation.

"The same, really."

"Still waters run deep and all that," Miriam mused. "Who do you think that woman was last night?"

"It was his sister." Rachel wasn't sure how much information about Sam she should share with Miriam. He hadn't told her not to say anything, but he seemed such an intensely private person she felt reluctant to part with any more details than necessary.

"His sister? Now that's unexpected."

"Who did you think it was?"

"A girlfriend, obvs." Miriam shrugged, and Bailey let out a little whimper of protest at the movement. "He's quite good-looking, isn't he, in a rough and ready sort of way?"

"Oh Miriam, honestly." Rachel tried to sound dismissive but she was remembering the way her stomach had flipped when Sam had stood so close to her, and she started to blush just as she had back then.

"You're blushing," Miriam crowed. "Oh, Rachel, have you got a crush on our hunky landlord?"

"Of course not. And why are you sounding like an episode of *Barbie*?" Rachel retorted. "Obvs and hunky? Seriously, Miriam."

Miriam just grinned, and then Rachel started to laugh. It was nice to see her sister seeming a little bit back to her sassy self.

"Hey, aren't you Skyping Mum and Dad today?"

"Already did it."

"Oh." Rachel sank into an armchair opposite Miriam, surprised. It must have gone well, based on Miriam's mood. "And?"

"And they were really lovely about it all," Miriam said quietly. She looked away, blinking rapidly. "Completely gobsmacked, of course. Dad looked a bit…dazed. But they said they'd support me and my baby—it feels so weird saying that!—and they would do whatever they could to help, no question."

"I bet Mum wanted to get on the next plane back here."

"A bit, but I think she knows I need to sort this out myself. She said she'd be here when the baby is born, in January. She might stay on after Anna's wedding."

"Oh, right. Well, that's something, then."

"Yes." Miriam nodded slowly. "It just feels so unreal, Rach. I *can't* be a mum. I'm so not mum material. I've never held down a proper job, never even lived in a proper home besides the vicarage…"

"Hey, what about our flat?" Rachel exclaimed in mock

indignation. "This seems quite homey to me."

"Yes, but you know what I mean. I just don't know how I'm going to *do* any of this."

It did seem quite daunting—Miriam had no job, no training, no money. But if she wanted to keep her baby, Rachel would do all that she could to help with that. "You'll figure out a way. Together, we will. And we have time, you know. About six months to figure it all out."

Miriam nodded, still looking unconvinced, and Rachel found herself thinking of Sam, and his hope to take care of his nephew, not in six months, but in the next two days. How was he going to do any of that—and how much help and support would he have? Not a lot, by the looks of it, but it didn't seem as if he wanted help from her. But perhaps she would give it anyway, no matter what he wanted, because life was too hard to try to manage on your own. That much Rachel knew; she was blessed to have both family and friends nearby, even if she sometimes resented their well-meaning interference. Sam didn't seem to have anyone…and goodness knew he'd need someone now.

Chapter Fourteen

OVER THE NEXT few days Rachel kept an eye out for Sam, but she didn't catch so much as a glimpse of him. She'd have almost thought he was avoiding her, except she knew he was busy in the pub, which she hadn't gone into. She hadn't wanted to seem aggressively helpful, especially since Sam had been reluctant to ask for help in the first place. But she was curious, and something more than that. She cared. Sam West seemed like he could use a friend, even if he didn't want one.

In any case, she was busy herself, getting ready for school and then enduring two inset days where they had to listen to the long-suffering head teacher Sarah drone on about all the new government policies that seemed to herald every single year of teaching. Rachel loved the beginning of every school year, the possibility and promise of each one, but she hated the boring bureaucracy.

Miriam, at least, had perked up a bit, taking responsibility for Bailey and going on several walks around the village, a camera slung about her neck. Rachel had forgotten how much her sister liked photography; she'd set up a website ages ago, documenting her travels. Rachel was glad she was taking an interest in something again, and perhaps it could even lead to some sort of job at some point. She knew Miriam needed to start earning money, but she was reluctant to push her sister into anything when she was still feeling so battered and fragile.

The Saturday before school started, all four sisters converged on the vicarage for a family meal and Skype session with their parents. Miriam had promised to tell the others about her pregnancy, something Rachel knew she would find incredibly difficult.

Even though she'd only been living in the flat above The Bell for a few weeks, it already felt strange to be back in the vicarage with her sisters, the place foreign yet familiar, both achingly so.

"You put the table back!" Esther said in approval as they all congregated in the kitchen.

"It seemed right," Anna said shyly. "As long as none of you want it…?"

"It wouldn't fit in our flat," Miriam said, and Rachel nodded her agreement.

"It belongs here," Esther declared. "I'm glad it's back." They all took a moment to gaze in bittersweet memory at the table of scarred oak with its cheerfully mismatched chairs.

"How are the wedding plans coming along?" Rachel asked finally, because someone had to and it might as well be her. Break that dreaded ice. Anna had come back for the weekend to start planning, and she was staying with Esther and Will.

"We've booked the church, of course—"

"Not difficult to do, when your groom is the vicar," Esther interjected dryly.

"I did have to check with the parish secretary," Simon half-joked.

"And we've decided to have the reception in the parish hall. I know it's simple—" this with a strangely apologetic look at Rachel "—but it felt right. We're not fancy people."

"With flowers and decorations you could do the hall up quite nicely," Esther said. "And hopefully cover the smell of sweaty socks from having the Scouts meet there every week."

"Plus the price is right," Miriam chipped in, and Rachel tried not to feel slightly accused by it at all. *She* hadn't been happy with the parish hall, clearly, or a reception in the vicarage garden the way Esther and Will had had.

She'd insisted on the posh hotel in Keswick, a three-course meal, linen napkins and crystal goblets, the works. She'd wanted something special, but she felt shallow now for caring about those things. Did it *have* to be shallow, to want things to be nice? Had her sisters, and her parents even, felt she was over the top with her wedding preparations, with her whole life? In the aftermath of her cancelled wedding, she felt as if she were starting to question everything...not just about her relationship with Dan, but about herself.

"Something smells delicious," Esther remarked as she nodded towards the cast-iron pot on top of the Aga. "I gather Anna has been cooking, rather than Simon?"

"You gathered right."

"Beef bourguignon. I've made enough for Simon and Jasper to eat it all week."

"Thank heavens," Jasper added with a theatrical shudder that made everyone smile.

It was all so cheerful, the seven of them gathered around the table as Anna doled out the beef, Charlie sniffing underneath for scraps, and yet there was something poignant and even sad about it too. Rachel felt her parents' absence keenly; she could almost hear the ghostly remnant of their voices— her father's jovial comments, her mother's insistence that everyone have second helpings.

"I have an announcement," Miriam said in the middle of the meal, her voice loud and abrupt. Rachel tensed as Esther and Anna looked on in surprise, Simon, Will, and Jasper all nonplussed.

"This sounds serious," Esther remarked.

"It is, rather." Miriam placed both hands flat on the table; Rachel saw her fingers tremble and realised how nervous she was. Miriam, the boldest and sassiest of them all, looked terrified, and she longed to reach over and give her sister a hug, but she didn't think Miriam would appreciate it in this moment.

"Well, spit it out then," Esther said not unkindly. "We're

all ears."

"I know you are." Miriam's voice trembled along with her fingers. "All right, here goes." She took a deep breath and then expelled it slowly. "I'm pregnant."

The silence in the cosy kitchen felt like a thunderclap. No one said anything for far too long. Jasper glanced questioningly at Rachel, and then looked away. Esther and Anna both looked completely gobsmacked. Miriam pressed her lips together and tried to smile.

"Well, there you have it," she said. "I've managed to silence even Esther. That's quite a feat."

Esther took a sip of water, still looking dazed. "Sorry," she said after a moment. "I wasn't expecting that one."

"No, I'm the one expecting," Miriam joked feebly, and Anna gave her a sympathetic smile.

"How...how far along are you, Miriam?" she asked.

"Twelve weeks, due in January." Miriam glanced down. "I have a scan next week, to confirm. The dates, not the pregnancy. That's definite." She tried for a laugh, but it wobbled and she stopped, looking down at her plate.

The silence stretched on as everyone struggled with what to say. Miriam was starting to look near tears but she blinked them back, her gaze still fixed on her meal.

"Well, you know what Dad would say," Rachel jumped in with determined cheer. "Babies are always miracles."

"In fact, he did say that, when I Skyped him and Mum a few days ago," Miriam said, the threat of tears now audible in her voice. "He said they were always a gift from God."

"Oh, Miriam." Anna's voice choked and she scraped her chair back, rushing to her sister to throw her arms around her. "I'm sss…sorry we're all a bit stunned. We should be happy for you, that is—" She trailed off uncertainly, and then just ended up clasping her tightly in a hug that Miriam returned.

"Thanks, Anna."

Esther was looking at Miriam thoughtfully, her eyes narrowed, and Will rose from his seat. "I think this might be my cue to bring out the whisky," he said. "Simon? Jasper? Join me in the other room?" He nodded meaningfully towards the four women huddled around the table, and Simon and Jasper jumped up with alacrity.

"Right, yes. Sounds like a capital idea," Jasper said. He clapped Miriam on the shoulder awkwardly. "Congratulations and all that."

"So what about the father?" Esther asked bluntly as soon as the men were gone.

Miriam's expression turned closed. "Not in the picture."

"Not now, but he obviously was, at one point. Have you told him?"

"No."

"Esther—" Rachel said warningly, and her sister gave her a quelling look.

"No matter what kind of tosser he is, he deserves to know."

"He's not a tosser," Miriam said with a sniff. "Not exactly."

"What is that supposed to mean?"

"Do we have to do this right now?" Anna pleaded. "We've only just heard…"

"Esther is just being Esther." Miriam sniffed again and wiped her eyes. "Good grief, these hormones. I will tell him, Esther, at some point. At least I'll try to."

"*Try* to? What does that mean?"

"Enough," Rachel commanded. "You're badgering her, Esther."

"Sorry, it's just…" Esther shook her head. "And you told Mum and Dad?"

"Yes." She sniffed again. "They said they'd support me."

"Of course they'd support you. Oh, Miriam." Esther shook her head sadly. "Babies are miracles, but they're bloody hard ones. Are you sure you want to do this?"

Miriam looked shocked. "What's the alternative?"

"You could give it up for adoption."

"I suppose…" Miriam looked uncertain. "I might think about it."

"But you should keep the baby if that's what you really want," Rachel added. She didn't want Miriam to feel pressured either way. "Whichever decision you make, we'll support you, Miriam."

"Of course we'll support you," Esther interjected impatiently. "She knows *that*."

Miriam managed a little laugh. "Cheers, Esther."

The tension eased a little, as everyone looked around at each other with wry smiles. This was really happening.

A few minutes later, Will and Simon poked their heads back in the kitchen, followed by Jasper.

"All clear?"

"If you mean are all threats of tears or other excess emotion passed, then yes."

"Phew." Will came into the room, smiling good-naturedly, followed by Simon and Jasper. A few minutes later the four sisters headed to the sitting room to Skype Ruth and Roger, the laptop in pride of place on the coffee table as they huddled around it. It was a relief to Rachel that her sisters knew about Miriam's blessed state; she'd been feeling a bit anxious, being the only one to know, and yet…

It was also strange that everyone knew, that it had already become part of the fabric of their family life, woven into its colourful, complicated strands; as they Skyped their parents after dinner, Ruth asked after Miriam's health, and reminded her to take prenatal vitamins, and then reminded Rachel to remind her to take them. This was the new normal—Anna getting married, Miriam having a baby, Esther and Will trying for one. At least Rachel had a puppy.

She was not going to feel sorry for herself, she decided as she took Bailey out for a wee that evening. Bailey cavorted around the sheep pasture, sniffing excitedly, while Rachel perched on top of the drystone wall and tried not to shiver in the damp night air. No, she was not going to feel left out or left behind or whatever, simply because it felt as if everyone else had exciting things going on in their lives except for her.

It was ridiculous to feel that way, anyway, because obviously Miriam's news was mixed, and her little sister was still feeling decidedly ambivalent about becoming a mother. Esther might be feeling prickly about not being pregnant, and Anna was worried about becoming a vicar's wife. No one's life was perfect or untroubled. Rachel knew that, but the hurt rushed in anyway, along with the sorrow. Why, Dan? Why, God? Why had this happened to her?

Rachel could almost hear her father's calm voice telling her that trust was easy when things were going fine. *The point to trust,* he'd say with a smile, *is when things aren't. That's when you put your faith where your mouth is.*

Rachel had always had a faith, had counted on it, even taken it for granted. It was simply part of who she was. She'd wrestled with it when Jamie had died, but somehow that had been not easier, but simpler—what else could you do when faced with such tragedy *but* trust? The alternative was too grim to contemplate.

And yet now it felt harder, because she'd lined everything up so perfectly and it felt as if God had simply smacked the chessboard of her life and sent all the pieces spinning. Why? *Why?*

Rachel sighed heavily, and then gave herself both a literal and mental shake. She was hardly the first person in the world to have her life go off course. It didn't mean she had to wallow. She hadn't wanted anyone else to feel sorry for her, so why should she feel sorry for herself?

She glanced back at the vicarage, a darkened hulk against the night sky, and then at The Bell, lit up, with boisterous laughter coming from inside. A few drunken lads stumbled out of the front door. Slowly she turned towards home.

By Monday morning, the first day of the new school year, Rachel had managed to shake off the sorry-for-herself mood that she didn't have time for anyway. She left Miriam in charge of Bailey and headed towards the primary school, aiming to be at her desk before eight. Although she loved a lie-in, Rachel was always an early riser on the first day of school.

The school smelled of cleaning fluid and new paint—just about the only time it would smell fresh—as Rachel stepped in her classroom, appraising the colourful noticeboards, the laminated nametags for the cubbyholes, with a smile of satisfaction.

She shed her jacket and hung up her bag, pulling her laptop towards her for the register, when Sarah Wilkes, the head teacher, walked into her room.

"Morning, Rachel. Ready for another year?"

"Absolutely." Rachel smiled extra brightly, just in case Sarah had come in for a little pitying check-in. *If you're finding you can't manage... If you need a few days off...*

No, she did not want to have that conversation.

"There is a new addition to Year Three," Sarah said, surprising and also relieving Rachel. So she wasn't here to offer pity, thank goodness. "A young boy who is new to the village."

"Oh? A new family?" Since she had only twenty-four in her class and was legally allowed to take thirty, Rachel couldn't foresee any problem. Sarah seemed to, however, for she was regarding Rachel with a frown settled between her straight brows.

"Not quite a new family. I'm afraid this child has somewhat of a difficult background. He was in care, and he's now living with a relative, temporarily at least."

Rachel stilled, schooling her expression to one of professional interest. Sarah had to be talking about Sam's nephew.

"What's his name?"

"Nathan. Nathan West."

Rachel nodded. So, Sam must have been granted at least temporary custody of his nephew. Why hadn't he told her? Although, really, why was she surprised he hadn't? Sam was a man of few words and fewer feelings, or so it seemed to Rachel. Still, it stung a little that he had his nephew living with him, the boy was even in Rachel's class, and Sam hadn't said a word.

"Anyway," Sarah resumed, "let me know if you run into problems. I've had his report from his previous school—one of them, anyway, and there have been a few issues."

Rachel recalled what Sam had said about Nathan being

no angel, due to his difficult background. "I'm sure I can handle it," she said with confidence. She could deal with one troubled little boy. She could show him both the affection and discipline he might have been lacking in his short life.

"Well, keep me updated," Sarah said. "I know you're experienced." With a smile of farewell, she left the room; already the junior children were arriving in the playground, their uniforms looking September-smart, with pristine cardigans and pinafores, crisp polo shirts and flannel shorts.

The Year Threes always looked titchy in September, having just moved up from the Infants building for children up to the age of seven, especially compared to the gangling Year Sixes who would soon be bursting to head to the comprehensive secondary school in Keswick.

Rachel straightened a cut-out leaf on the noticeboard, and then a laminated nametag on one of the cubbyholes. Her heart raced with excitement and a touch of apprehension, as it always did on the first day of school, today perhaps more than other first days. She was curious to meet Nathan West.

A few minutes later the bell rang and the children formed semi-orderly queues outside for each year group. Rachel stepped outside, glad it was sunny for this start, and stood in front of her line of Year Threes.

"My brother said you're the nicest teacher in the school, Miss Holley!" a girl with beribboned plaits called from the middle of the queue.

"That's very kind of him to say so."

"My mum said you were supposed to be Mrs Taylor," a boy shouted, and Rachel kept her expression pleasantly neutral.

"I'm Miss Holley to all of you," she said briskly. "Now look smart. It's time to go inside and hang up your coats."

She scanned the line of children but she didn't know all the children from Infants, and she didn't recognise Nathan West, not that she'd know what to look for.

The next few minutes were taken up with the cloakroom scuffle of finding cubbyholes, shedding bags and coats, and stowing lunch boxes.

Rachel scanned the register as the children began to trickle into the classroom, looking slightly awed at the chairs and desks that were bigger than the ones in the Year Two classroom—it was a significant step up to Juniors.

"Take a seat on the area rug in the story corner, please," Rachel called out, "and sit criss-cross apple sauce. I'll call the register and then we'll assign tables." The children began to sit down, and Rachel took her seat, the register on her lap, when a sudden wailing came from the cloakroom.

Quickly she rose and went to see what was going on; a boy was sobbing, one hand pressed to his cheek, which sported a red welt. Another boy was glaring at him.

"What's going on here?" Rachel asked in her sternest teacher's voice.

"He hit me!" The boy sounded disbelieving even as he

continued to cry, tears running down his plump cheeks. "He hit me right in the face!"

Rachel turned to the other boy, who glared at her, his blue eyes glinting with defiance. "Did you hit him?" she asked calmly.

"He put his coat on my hook."

"I didn't mean to! I thought it was my hook."

The boy said nothing, and Rachel took a deep, careful breath. "What's your name?" she asked the injured boy gently.

"Henry," he said with a hiccup.

"We'll get some ice to put on your cheek." She turned to the other boy, who still wasn't looking at her, his arms folded, his lower lip jutting out stubbornly.

"And what's your name, young man?"

He threw her a sullen look. "Nathan," he said, making her heart sink with the inevitability of it. "Nathan West."

Chapter Fifteen

I T HAD BEEN the longest first day Rachel could ever remember in her ten-year teaching career. Her body ached, and she longed for a bubble bath, except the flat didn't have a tub, just a shower. She half-wondered if she could ask Simon to use the vicarage bathroom for a nice long soak, and then decided that wouldn't be a good idea.

But for once she wasn't looking forward to going back to her flat at The Bell. For once she didn't want to pause on the first-floor landing, to see if Sam was about. At that moment, feeling decidedly tired and fed up, she wished she'd never heard of Sam West. She certainly wished she'd never heard of his nephew Nathan.

Guilt rushed in at that uncharitable thought, and Rachel let out a heavy sigh as she started down the high street towards home. She knew Nathan couldn't help being difficult, considering his turbulent upbringing, but it hadn't made dealing with him all day any easier.

In retrospect, Rachel realised she'd been imagining a quiet, contained little boy—a mini-Sam, maybe, who was stony and silent but essentially good-hearted, waiting for someone to understand him. She'd fantasised, just a little bit, about being that person, the inspirational teacher who brought a quiet, misunderstood child out of himself. Or not.

What she'd got instead was a total terror who challenged or defied her at every possible opportunity. She'd spent the entire day dealing almost solely with Nathan, whether he was arguing with another child, talking when he shouldn't, scribbling on the table, throwing his pencil on the floor… Whatever he was doing, he was always too loud, too rough, too *much*.

If she told everyone to write their names on their books, he wrote a rude word instead. If she asked them to do a simple page of maths, he scribbled silly answers all over it, and then tore the page in two. At snack time he spilled someone else's milk, and then purposely dumped his on the floor. And every time she disciplined him, trying to pitch her tone between kind and firm, he gave her a look of such blatant defiance she wanted to scream. At one point he called her a silly cow.

When she'd finally sent them all to lunch and playtime she'd collapsed at her desk, her head resting on her arms. In all her years of teaching she'd never come across a child who was so contrary, so *impossible*. It was as if Nathan West had no self-control at all.

He tried, challenged, and tormented her at every turn. She had no idea how she was going to deal with him all year.

In fact, she was quite sure she couldn't. But it felt intrinsically wrong to write off a child on the first day, as much as she was, at the end of it, tempted to do so. Sam had said Nathan was no angel, but that now seemed like a vast and unfortunate understatement.

She'd had difficult children before—children with learning disabilities, emotional issues, ADHD, autism. She'd considered herself somewhat a veteran in that regard, but now she felt like the worst kind of know-nothing. She didn't know how to handle Nathan West. So far he hadn't responded to any of her attempts—being kind, being firm, sitting him by himself, sitting him with others, sending him outside of the room, having him sit with her. She'd tried it all and nothing dented his defiance, his determination to be as difficult as possible.

The Bell loomed ahead of her, relatively quiet on a Monday night. Rachel paused by the front door, wondering if she should duck inside the pub and face Sam. But what could she say? And how was he handling his nephew, now that she knew how challenging Nathan was?

How on earth could a single man who worked all hours of the day and night give the emotional support such a troubled little boy needed? Rachel appreciated the social caseworker's dilemma even more now. And she wondered just how Sam was managing with Nathan.

Even though she would have rather kicked back with Netflix and a glass of wine, Rachel resolutely squared her shoulders and headed into the pub. Sam looked up the instant she came through the door, and something shivered in the air between them, although Rachel had no idea what.

A handful of men were sat at the bar, and a group of lads who had clearly just got off their shifts were sprawled around a table in the back, already becoming boisterous.

"Rachel." Sam nodded once, alert, waiting.

He knew, Rachel realised with a pang. He knew Nathan was in her class, and he knew what a terror he was. How could he not? He was clearly bracing himself for bad news— and suddenly she couldn't give it, not that that's what she'd been going to do, exactly. She hadn't known what she was going to do.

But she knew now, looking at his wary expression and slightly slumped shoulders, that Sam already had a tremendously challenging job, taking care of his nephew on his own, and she couldn't possibly make it any harder.

"I haven't seen you in a while," she said. "I just wanted to say hello."

Sam nodded tersely. "Hello."

"Everything all right?"

"Yes, I think so."

"I'm glad you have Nathan with you." She glanced around the pub. "He's here, isn't he? Afterschool club is over…"

"He's in the back." Sam nodded towards a swinging door. "In my office."

"Is he going to be there every night while you work?" That seemed both impractical and unfair, not to mention unwise.

"Until bedtime, and then I'll nip upstairs with him to tuck him in. It's not ideal, but..." He shrugged defensively, spreading his hands. What else he could do?

What could *she* do?

Rachel knew she didn't want to do anything. She'd just had six hours of Nathan West; she really, really didn't want to offer another three or four. And yet she couldn't stomach the thought of a seven-year-old stuck in the dreary backroom of a pub for hours on end.

"It's not very nice for him back there," she said. "He could always come up to ours, you know. Have tea with us and play with Bailey." Boys liked puppies, didn't they? Although Rachel wasn't sure she wanted to unleash Nathan on poor Bailey.

Something flickered across Sam's face and then was gone. "You don't have to do that."

"I know I don't," Rachel said lightly. "It's called being nice, Sam. Being neighbourly, friendly."

"You've had a long day—"

"Trust me, I know that, as well. But it's not fair to Nathan to leave him in a backroom for hours on end, and I think your caseworker would agree with me."

His eyes narrowed. "Are you *blackmailing* me?"

Startled, she drew back. "No, of course not. I'm just

209

pointing out the obvious." Why was Sam so suspicious? What was in his past to make him so unwilling to accept help? "Look, I won't fight you over it, because like you said I've had a long day, and your nephew was part of that. But he's a little boy and I believe you want the best for him and I don't think that involves sticking him in a corner." Sam didn't reply and Rachel sighed, too tired to argue the point any longer. "But you're his guardian so you do what you think is best." Without waiting for an answer, she started back towards the stairs to the flats.

"Rachel, wait." Sam came out from behind the bar. "I'm sorry. I should be more grateful. You're being very kind and generous."

"I'm already starting to regret it," she only half-joked.

"It's just…I'm not used to accepting help."

Her heart melted a little at the reluctant admission. "I gathered that."

Sam nodded slowly. "But you're right. It's not fair on Nathan. But it's not fair on you, either. I can't ask you to do my job for me every evening—"

"Maybe not every evening, but once in a while, surely." *Definitely* not every evening. She'd go insane. "And maybe you could hire more help so you could be here for him, because that's why you took him in, isn't it?"

Sam's jaw tightened and bunched. "Yes," he agreed tersely. "It is."

"Well, then. Let's make this work…for Nathan's sake."

And for Sam's, because he clearly needed help. Rachel just hoped she had the strength to give it, because she knew, with a surprising and unexpected ferocity, that she wanted to.

"I'll go talk to him," Sam said, and started down the hallway. After a moment, Rachel followed.

Nathan was sitting in a swivel chair, watching Minecraft videos on Sam's computer and munching his way through several packets of barbecue crisps. Hardly the most edifying way for a seven-year-old to spend an entire evening.

"Hey, Nath." The smile Sam gave his nephew was so tender Rachel had to look away; she felt as if she'd seen something she shouldn't have, something that made her both melt and yearn.

"What's she doing here?" Nathan gave her a blatantly unfriendly look, one she already recognised. Great start.

"You know your teacher, Miss Holley, hey?" Sam said in an attempt at cheerfulness. "She lives in the flat above us." Nathan looked decidedly unenthused by this information. "She's offered to have you come up there, have your tea and that. And play with her puppy, as well. He's really sweet."

"I don't want to." Nathan jutted out his lower lip.

Rachel didn't want to either, but she stayed silent, sensing the fear and vulnerability behind the boy's attitude, or at least hoping it was there, underneath the blatant aggression.

"There's a puppy, Nath."

"And sausages for tea," Rachel chipped in. It was just about the only thing in the fridge.

"And chips?" Nathan asked suspiciously, and she nodded, relieved that somewhat miraculously she had those in the freezer.

"You can't have sausages without chips."

"Try it once, maybe?" Sam suggested. "See how you get on? You can always come back down here if you like."

Nathan glanced at his uncle and then at Rachel, looking unconvinced. She smiled encouragingly, but it seemed to bounce off him. "I'll *try* it," he finally said, sliding off the stool. "But if I don't like it, I'm coming back." He glared at Rachel for good measure. "Areet?" He sounded far too tough for a little boy, and it made her ache—and feel a little bit afraid.

"All right," she agreed.

She should have warned Miriam about their unexpected guest, Rachel realised as she unlocked the door and stepped into the flat. Miriam was on the sofa, scrolling through photos on her camera, Bailey snoring softly in her lap. She straightened, startled at the sight of Nathan, and tipped poor Bailey right out onto the floor.

"Oh, hi—"

"Miriam, this is Nathan," Rachel said cheerfully. "Nathan West. He's staying for tea."

"Maybe," Nathan said, and then dropped to his knees, holding his arms out towards Bailey.

Bailey came towards him with a curious sniff, and Nathan stroked the dog with surprising and gratifying gentleness. Maybe this was all it would take—a boy, a dog. Simple pleasures.

With a small sigh of relief, Rachel kicked off her shoes and headed towards the kitchen.

Of course it wasn't that easy. Nothing ever was. Within five minutes of coming home, Nathan had tugged too hard on Bailey's tail and sent the poor puppy scampering to hide under the sofa.

"Nathan, you need to be gentle with her," Rachel said as kindly as she could. "She's only little. If you're rough, she won't want to play with you."

"I don't want to play with her," Nathan retorted, and then started kicking the legs of the sofa. Hard. Miriam gave Rachel a startled, beseeching look, clearly having no idea how to handle this. And despite her ten years' teaching experience, Rachel wasn't sure she did, either.

"Nathan." She placed one hand on his shoulder, the movement deliberate and careful. He tensed underneath her touch, and she was suddenly struck by how small he was. How *little*. He was just a little, angry, frightened boy. "Why don't you come help me with the sausages?" she suggested. "And the chips."

He glared at her with the same overt hostility she'd been faced with all day—blue eyes like Sam's narrowed in suspicion and dislike. She kept her smile in place, her gaze steady on him. "Please?"

It seemed an age before Nathan finally shrugged off her

hand and stomped over to the kitchen. It was a victory, whether it felt like one or not.

The evening was interminable. As patient as Rachel tried to be with Nathan, he resisted and defied her at every turn. He refused to eat his sausage, and he deliberately squirted ketchup all over the floor, even aiming the bottle at poor Bailey, who whimpered and hid under the table. He refused to clear his plate, lounging back in his chair instead, arms folded in direct challenge as he glared at her.

After tea, he demanded to watch television, and grabbed the remote from her when Rachel had tuned it to the innocuous CBBC, choosing a game show instead, which he watched with surprising avidity, giving Rachel and Miriam a few minutes' peace.

"I am so not ready to have a child," Miriam whispered as Rachel stooped to wipe the blobs of ketchup from the floor with a paper towel. "Seriously, Rachel." She looked panicked and Rachel sighed.

"Trust me, they're not all like this," she said in a low voice. She was so tired her teeth ached. It was seven o'clock at night and she still had a full day's lessons to prepare.

As soon as the game show was over, Rachel turned off the television and gave Nathan a briskly cheerful look. At least, she hoped it was, and not the simmering glare of resentment she felt inside.

"Right, Nathan. Time for bed."

He looked at her uncertainly. "Where am I sleeping?"

Rachel gazed at him, seeing the way his shoulders hunched, his eyes darted. It was moments like this that she remembered how absolutely impossible his life must have been—in and out of care, the adults in his life letting him down again and again. And now he wasn't even sure where he was sleeping.

"At your uncle's, of course," she said gently. "You have a bedroom there?"

"Yes…"

"Then why don't we go down together, and you can get ready for bed."

Fortunately, for once, Nathan didn't resist or answer rudely. He slunk from the room, and Rachel followed. She was, she admitted to herself, curious about Sam's flat. What would it look like? What might it reveal about him?

In the end, not much. Nathan flung open the door and Rachel followed, glancing around the nondescript lounge with its bland furnishing and military neatness. Nothing was out of place, not that there was much to be in place—no photos, no books, no pictures or mementoes or knickknacks. The place looked like an especially boring hotel room.

"My room's in here," Nathan said, and Rachel peeked in the doorway of the second bedroom. The flat had the same layout as hers upstairs, but without all the new fittings and fixtures. Clearly Sam had done up the rental before his own place, although as she looked in the bedroom, Rachel saw he'd made an effort here—there was a starchy new duvet and curtains in blue plaid, a model of the solar system hanging from the ceiling. The little touches made her smile even as she felt strangely saddened by them.

"What a lovely room, Nathan."

"It's all my own." He spoke proudly before turning away from her, as if afraid he'd revealed too much.

"I like it a lot," Rachel said. "Why don't you get changed and brush your teeth? I'll wait in the lounge, and then we can have a story."

"A story?"

"Do you have any story books?" He shook his head. "All right, I'll just have to make one up, then. Even better."

As Nathan got ready for bed, Rachel prowled around the flat, feeling restless and sad. She could feel herself getting tangled up in Sam and Nathan's lives, wanting to help their loneliness, assuage their need, and yet already she suspected she was in over her head. What help could she really give them, two hurting people with so much against them, especially when she was still hurting herself?

"What kind of story?"

Nathan's words, spoken sulkily, startled her out of her thoughts and she turned to him with a smile. "Whatever kind you like. You know what my mum used to do, for stories?" Nathan shook his head, still looking sceptical. "She'd tell me to name three things, whatever I wanted, and she'd put them into the story." Rachel sat down on the sofa and patted the empty space next to her.

"Why don't you do the same?"

"Three things."

"Yes."

"Can I have five?"

Rachel almost laughed at that bit of brashness. "Let's start with three."

Slowly Nathan edged towards her and then sat on the sofa, a little bit away from her, his arms folded, his expression turning sulky again. "This is stupid."

"Is it? But you haven't tried it out yet," Rachel returned lightly. "Why don't you wait and see?"

Nathan drummed his heels against the sofa. "What kind of things?"

"Whatever you like." She thought of the solar system model in his room. "A rocket or an alien or a spaceship…"

He looked at her scornfully. "Those are stupid."

Rachel held on to her patience. "Then why don't you choose?"

More drumming. His arms were folded, his shoulders hunched. Maybe this had been a bad idea. Still, Rachel waited. Hoped.

"A monster," he finally said, the words practically a growl. "Two monsters." He glanced at her to see if she would object, and Rachel just waited some more, smiling. "And…a poo."

Of course. "Fab, let's get started, then." Rachel settled back into the sofa as she began to weave a tale of the two monsters and the very big, messy, monster poo.

It was after eight o'clock by the time Rachel finished; to say Nathan had been spellbound would have been optimistic in the extreme. He tolerated her storytelling, at least somewhat; halfway through he got up and started circling the room like some caged predator. Towards the end he started hitting himself rhythmically in the face with one of the sofa cushions. At least he was relatively quiet. By the time Rachel managed to get him into bed, it was half past and she was even more shattered than she'd been previously, which she hadn't actually thought possible.

"Now I'll be right upstairs," she promised. "And Sam is right downstairs, if you need anything." *But please don't get out of bed.*

"You're going?" Nathan's voice wavered before he rolled over so his back was to her, thin shoulders hunched. "Fine."

Rachel stared at him wretchedly, feeling all the more out of her depth. "I don't have to go, Nathan," she said after a moment. "I can bring my books and things down here if you like. I'll stay in the lounge while you go to sleep."

Nathan just hunched his shoulders all the more, a small, sad hump under his duvet.

"I'll go get them," Rachel said quietly.

"You're going back down?" Miriam exclaimed when Rachel went back upstairs to get her school bag. "Rachel, you must be exhausted—"

"He's only little."

"He's a holy terror."

"He'd had a rough start to life."

"I'll grant you that, but you can't spend every evening in Sam's place while he works downstairs, can you?"

Could she? Rachel was too tired to think about it. "I'm just focused on tonight," she said. "Sam will figure something out eventually."

Back downstairs Nathan was settled in bed, if not asleep, and Rachel spread her papers on the coffee table as she started planning for the next day. The flat was quiet save for the occasional bout of raucous laughter from downstairs, and suddenly Rachel felt quite unbearably lonely. She was a people person, always had been, and she wanted to be with Miriam, the TV on in the background, a glass of wine by her elbow, planning her lessons while chatting and watching TV all the while. That was how she operated, how she thrived.

A whimper sounded from the bedroom, and Rachel tiptoed over to check on Nathan. He was muttering in his sleep, and as she gazed down at him her heart contracted with pity. It wasn't a bad emotion, she realised, even though she'd resisted being the object of it herself. It was borne of care and compassion rather than any sense of smug superiority. She only wished there was more she could do. She touched his hair gently and then tiptoed back out to the lounge to wait for Sam's return.

Chapter Sixteen

"RACHEL... RACHEL?"

The low voice and gentle prodding of her shoulder had Rachel coming out of a deep, dreamless sleep with a complete sense of disorientation. She sat bolt upright, blinking the sleep out of her eyes, having no idea where or even who she was. What day was it? What on earth was happening?

"Rachel, it's okay. It's me. Sam."

Rachel blinked again, registering the warm hands on her shoulders, the face peering intently into her own. *Sam.* She was in Sam's flat, and she must have fallen asleep on his sofa.

"I fell asleep," she said, and Sam's mouth kicked up at the corner.

"So you did."

"What time is it?" She felt completely out of sorts, distantly conscious of how dazed she must look, her hair in tangles about her face. She fought an urge to curl up on the sofa and go back to sleep. She was still so *tired.*

"It's a little bit after one in the morning." Sam rose from

his crouched position to sit on the opposite end of the sofa. "Thank you, Rachel."

"It's okay." She just needed to get to bed. Now. Rachel stumbled up from the sofa, nearly losing her balance, and Sam rose quickly, reaching out a hand to steady her. Her body collided with his for a millisecond, but it still sent a scorching wave of—something—through her, shocking her awake.

Sam stepped back immediately, dropping his hands, and Rachel righted herself. Had she just imagined that moment? Was she that crazy tired?

"I should go to bed."

"Let me see you upstairs."

"You don't—"

"I will."

Since it seemed he would brook no argument, Rachel just shrugged and headed for the door. Her body tingled and her head felt fuzzy, a completely disconcerting combination.

The corridor felt very dark and narrow as she headed upstairs with Sam right behind her. She paused on the second landing, fumbling with her doorknob, and then Sam placed one hand flat on the door, staying her.

"Rachel." His voice was low, warm, intent. Rachel stilled.

"Yes?" Her voice came out in little more than a whisper as she waited for who only knew what. If she didn't feel so disorientated, she could navigate this moment more certainly, she was sure of it. As it was, her emotions were in a ferment, her thoughts a tangle. She half-turned, only to come into contact with Sam's chest, more closely than she ever had before, so she could feel his pectoral muscles pressed against her, his hand braced by her head, everything about him so very close, and something flared white-hot inside her.

She backed up, but there was nowhere to go, and so she stood there, pressed against the door, waiting, her heart starting to thud.

"I…" Sam's gaze scanned her face, his eyes looking very blue. Very piercing. Rachel's breath caught. Was she imagining the chemistry that suddenly seemed to sizzle between them?

The moment spun out, and then suddenly it screeched to a halt. "Thank you," Sam said, and stepped back. Rachel released her breath in an audible shudder. *What had just happened?*

Nothing, obviously. Sam was already turning away. Rachel fumbled once more with the doorknob and then let herself into the flat, letting out a little cry of surprise as a ball of golden fluff tackled her legs—and then had a wee on her shoes.

Five hours later Rachel was stumbling once more, out of bed and into the shower, her head feeling as if it were full of cotton wool. Miriam was still dead asleep, and so she sat alone at the little table in the living area, cradling a cup of coffee between her hands, feeling as if she were hungover even though she hadn't had a drop to drink last night, more was the pity.

Her mind kept going round in circles, first wondering how she was going to cope today, and hoping that Nathan might be a bit better behaved, considering he knew her better, and then thinking about Sam and that odd moment last night when he'd seemed as if he'd wanted to say—or do—something important.

When it had seemed, for a split second, almost as if he wanted to kiss her.

"You are a dolt," Rachel said out loud. "A very big dolt *and* a ninny." She didn't want to be kissed by Sam West. She didn't want to be kissed at all. She wasn't ready for romance, and Sam West of all people…yes, he was attractive in his own way, but he was so *different*—and she barely knew him. No, Sam West was off the table, not up for discussion or even consideration. Friend zoned, most definitely.

Half an hour later, dressed and feeling marginally better after two cups of strong coffee, Rachel headed downstairs and then up the high street towards Thornthwaite Village School. It had rained in the night and the pavement was washed clean, everything glittering in the bright autumn sunshine, the air crisp and clear.

"How did yesterday go?" Sarah asked as she popped her head in Rachel's classroom right before the bell rung. Rachel couldn't keep from making a face.

"He's a handful."

"So I've heard."

"I'm going to spend about eighty per cent of my time on classroom management," Rachel said honestly. "Which isn't fair to the other children."

"I know." Sarah looked both tired and torn. "You know what it's like with all these budget cuts, Rachel. If we could get you a classroom assistant, I would, in a heartbeat—"

"I know, I know." As a Year Three teacher with only twenty-five pupils, she wasn't eligible for a classroom assistant, not unless one of her pupil's special needs required it— and Nathan didn't, at least not officially.

One of the government's austerity measures had been to reduce the number of children who could be given what was now called an EHC plan, or Education, Health, and Care plan for children with special needs, which would allow the school to obtain extra help and staffing. Nathan West didn't have a plan, and Rachel doubted his current behaviour would qualify him for one. He was troubled, and there were, sadly, far too many troubled children.

"We'll get there," she assured Sarah, although she felt far from such confidence herself. "Eventually. Perhaps he just needs time to settle in."

A lot of time, she decided later, as she told Nathan to sit by her for the third time that morning. He came so quickly Rachel wondered if he wanted to sit by her, and was misbehaving towards that end. Maybe she needed to think up new methods of discipline...ones that actually worked.

By three o'clock, as she dismissed the children for the

day, Rachel was glad to be finished, but also encouraged that it hadn't been *quite* as difficult as yesterday. Nathan hadn't been as openly defiant, although he still seemed to have a big problem with self-control, especially when it came to sudden movements or noises from his tablemates, whom Rachel had to continually swap out in order to achieve some degree of classroom sanity, never mind serenity.

She heaved a gusty sigh as she sat at her desk, grateful for the peace of a quiet and empty classroom. She would spend a couple of hours marking maths sheets and preparing for tomorrow, and then head home…to goodness knew what. Would she offer to take Nathan again? How could she not?

"Rachel."

Rachel looked up in surprise as someone came through the doorway of her classroom. *Sam.* Her heart flip-flopped at the sight of him—in surprise, obviously. Not anything else.

"Sam." She rose from the desk, one hand on the back of her chair. "What are you doing here? Is something wrong?"

"No, nothing's wrong. I just wanted to speak to you for a bit. How was Nathan today?"

"Better than yesterday," she admitted.

"That's not saying much, though, is it?" Sam said with a grimace, and she smiled in sympathy.

"He'll get there."

"Thanks for the vote of confidence." Sam raked a hand through his close-shorn hair. "As well as for everything else you've done for him. I know he's not easy." Rachel decided to diplomatically remain silent on that point. "Anyway," Sam resumed, "I just wanted to tell you I've sorted the evenings, for the most part. I've hired some more part-time help so I'll get off my shift at half past five, in time to pick him up from the afterschool club."

Amazingly, Rachel felt the tiniest, most treacherous flicker of disappointment at this assuredly welcome news. "Oh," she said after a second's pause. "Wonderful."

"The only thing is," Sam continued, with an unusual hesitancy in his voice, "I haven't been able to get cover yet for Friday and Saturday evenings. I will, of course, as soon as possible, but in the meantime..."

It took Rachel a few seconds to realise what he was trying to say—or rather, ask. "You want me to watch Nathan on Fridays and Saturdays?"

"Only this week," Sam said quickly. "I'll find someone by next week—"

"I don't mind," Rachel cut him off, realising she meant it. "And it's not as if I'm doing something exciting on the weekends. Really, Sam, I'm happy to help." In case she sounded too eager, which didn't really make sense considering what she was agreeing to, Rachel sat back down and needlessly shuffled a few papers. "So," she said, apropos of nothing.

"Are you sure about this?" Sam asked after a moment, his voice low. "I feel as if I'm asking a lot of you..."

"You're really not," Rachel assured him. "And anyway,

what are friends for?" The words seemed to hang in the air, holding far more import—and intent, even—than Rachel had meant them to.

Sam stared at her for a long moment, his eyes narrowed, his jaw taut. Rachel had no idea what he was thinking, and his next words floored her.

"You really don't remember, do you?"

Remember? Rachel stared at him blankly. "Sorry, remember what, exactly?"

He let out a huff of laughter, the sound a little too sad to be one of humour. "Not that I'd expect you to remember. I know your parents had loads of people coming through the vicarage."

"Coming through the vicarage? Wait, you mean…"

He nodded, affirming what she hadn't been able to voice. "I lived at the vicarage for a couple of weeks."

She goggled at him, hardly able to believe what he was saying. "You did? When? Was I at uni or something? Or…"

"No, you were seven. So was I." His mouth quirked at the corner, barely a smile. "My sister was four. We had nowhere to go so your parents said we could come live with you until something was sorted."

He spoke matter-of-factly enough, but the simple statement was enough to cause a lump to form in Rachel's throat. *Seven. Four. Nowhere to go.*

"Why?" she whispered. "Why did you have nowhere to go?"

Sam's expression hardened, his eyes turning flinty. "My parents were…well." He shrugged, shaking his head. "My dad was a drunk, and he wasn't above knocking my mum around when he'd had a few too many. Knocking us around, too. A neighbour finally called the police and we were put into care, except there were no places available. That's when your parents stepped in."

Rachel knew her parents had trained as respite foster carers a long time ago, just so they could step in as they had with Sam and his sister. But she still found it hard to believe Sam had actually lived in her house and she hadn't even realised or remembered.

"I'm a bit shocked," she admitted with a laugh. "What do you remember of that time?"

"Not all that much. Your mum's cooking stands out. She made a treacle tart and let me have three slices. I thought it was the best thing, ever."

Rachel smiled, assailed by a pang of bittersweet nostalgia. "That sounds like my mum."

"Yeah, she was great." Sam smiled and shook his head. "Sorry, I'm making it sound as if she's dead."

"No, just far away." She smiled sadly. "Do you have any others memories?"

"A few. We stayed up on the top floor, and the windowpanes rattled. It scared me but I wouldn't have wanted anyone to know."

Big brave seven-year-old. Rachel could see him, trying to

be tough, blue eyes narrowed with determination, lower lip jutted out stubbornly, thin shoulders squared. Kind of like Nathan. It sounded as if Sam had had a similar upbringing, and look how he'd made good now. Rachel was both impressed and humbled.

"So were you as challenging as Nathan back then?" she asked and Sam laughed, the sound one of genuine amusement like she'd never heard before from him, and it made her grin in response.

"I hope not, but maybe. Probably." He cocked his head, lost in memory. "I do remember your father taking me aside one time, in his study. Telling me I was a fine representative of my family. I think I'd just nicked some sweets and so I felt terrible."

"He probably knew it," Rachel rejoined. "Dad always had a wonderful way of making you want to live up to his expectations."

"He's a good man. You're lucky, you know, with your parents."

"Yes." Rachel swallowed hard. "I know."

The silence between them stretched on for a few beats, comfortable and weirdly intimate. He'd lived with her family. She must have talked with him, played with him. Rachel wished she could remember, but she'd been so young and they'd had so many people through the vicarage over the years—a parade of those in need. Perhaps Esther remembered more.

"I should go," Sam finally said. "Nathan's waiting for me outside, and by now he's most likely torn up the play equipment or started a fire."

"My bet's on the fire."

They shared a smile, adding to the sudden sense of intimacy. Rachel looked away first.

"Right, I'm off then," Sam said, turning towards the door. "I'll see you later."

It almost felt like a promise. "Yes," Rachel agreed. "Later."

After he'd gone she remained where she was, staring into space, a silly little smile on her face. After a few seconds she snapped out of it, giving herself a mental shake as well as physical one. What was she on about? She was almost acting as if...

But, no. Of course she wasn't. Rachel pulled some papers towards her and focused on them with extra concentration, yet another few minutes passed before she could take anything in.

She left school two hours later, with a mizzling drizzle falling, cloaking the village in grey mist.

"Hello there, Rachel Holley."

Rachel slowed, peering through the damp gloom, to see the wizened little woman standing in front of the gate to number fourteen on the high street, a whitewashed terraced cottage with a garden of neatly tended lavender.

"Hello, Mrs Cribbs." Fortunately Abigail Cribbs was one

of her father's elderly parishioners whom Rachel knew by name. She attended church every Sunday without fail and sat in the back pew. She was also a ferociously keen knitter, and had outfitted all four Holley sisters with white crocheted cardigans every Easter for at least ten years. She had a stern, no-nonsense manner about her, a beady-eyed, gimlet stare, and a heart of pure gold.

"How are you today?" Rachel asked, and Abigail's lips pursed.

"Oh, I'm fine," she answered with unmistakeable emphasis. "It's you I'm wondering about."

Uh-oh. Rachel's footsteps had slowed, and she now fought the urge to step up her pace once more. She didn't want yet more pity—and she soon realised she wasn't going to get it.

"So the wedding's been called off," Abigail announced, as if Rachel didn't know. "What are you going to do now?"

"Um…just keep on, really. With my job and…stuff." Not the most eloquent answer.

"There aren't many likely husbands-to-be in Thornthwaite," Abigail said, another thing Rachel knew all too well. "Have you thought about one of those dating websites? Kindling or some such…?"

"I think you mean Tinder," Rachel said, smothering a laugh, "and, no. I'm not quite ready to cast my bread upon those cyber waters."

"No, it does seem a bit risky. Never know what you

might get." Abigail Cribbs harrumphed, crossing her arms. "Of course, you could end up like me. An old maid and happy about it."

"Have you always been happy about it?" Rachel asked, and then realised that was rather an invasive question. Abigail, however, didn't seem to mind.

She chuckled, a dry, raspy sound. "Oh my heavens, no. I spent half of my twenties casting around for Mr Will-Just-About-Do but even he was difficult to find. By the time I was thirty, I was desperate. That was on the shelf in those days." She gave Rachel a significant look, and she smiled weakly in return. If she wasn't yet on the shelf, she was certainly climbing her way towards it.

"And what happened then?" she asked.

"I suppose I finally realised I was wasting my life looking for someone who may or may not exist. And as you know, God only gives you one chance at this world, although of course I have eternity to look forward to."

"Of course," Rachel murmured.

"I suppose I also thought if I stopped looking for him, he might show up. But he didn't." She shrugged philosophically. "After a while, I no longer minded."

"Well," Rachel said with an attempt at both diplomacy and cheer, "I'm not giving up hope quite yet, but I am taking a bit of a breather when it comes to the manhunt."

"A wise idea, my dear." Abigail took a step towards her, one hand on the gate. "Are you very much broken-hearted?"

Was she? Wasn't a heart either broken or whole? "A bit," Rachel finally said, because that was the truth. She was healing, but she was still hurting too, and she missed the companionship she'd had with Dan, even if it hadn't been enough to build a marriage on.

Abigail nodded sagely. "I understand completely," she said. "It was wise of you to break it off, then."

"I didn't quite mean—" Rachel began, but the drizzle was turning to a downpour, and with a cheery wave Abigail headed back inside. Rachel stared after her in bemusement. She had definitely not had the upper hand in that conversation.

A bit annoyed with herself more than with Abigail for the turn the conversation had taken, Rachel avoided her habitual loitering by the door of The Bell—a ritual she could not give a reason for—and headed upstairs.

"No Terror of Thornthwaite with you today?" Miriam asked cheerfully. To Rachel's surprise, she was standing by the stove and the flat was full of cooking smells, which were only somewhat appetising.

"He's not that bad, really." She put her bag down with a thunk. "What are you doing?"

"Making tea. I thought I should be useful, for once."

"Okay." Rachel took an exploratory sniff. "What is it?"

"Adzuki beans with kale and brown rice."

"Oh. Okay." Three foods she would never choose to eat, but at least Miriam was taking an interest. Maybe she would start looking for a job soon.

"I went to the library," Miriam explained, "and got this book called *Best Foods for Baby.* Did you know that adzuki beans are some of the most nutrient-dense foods on the planet? And one of their health benefits is fewer birth defects in a foetus."

"I suppose no birth defects would be the ideal," Rachel returned lightly. The smell of the dish Miriam was making decidedly did not make her mouth water.

"Oh, you know what I mean. I figured I need to start watching what I eat. The last few weeks I've pretty much been subsisting on pork scratchings and plain crackers, both of which have very little nutritional value."

"And the first one is absolutely revolting," Rachel answered with a shudder. "I just might take adzuki beans over pork scratchings." She sniffed again. "Maybe."

"At least try them," Miriam said. "They're almost ready. I'll dish them out while you get changed."

"All right." Rachel headed towards her bedroom, looking forward to putting on a pair of comfy yoga pants and an old T-shirt, and hanging out with her sister for a few hours. And yet…she wondered about Nathan and Sam. What they were doing. How they were doing.

"Tea's ready!" Miriam sang out, and Rachel changed quickly and headed back to the living area, where a plate of mushy red beans piled on top of brown rice awaited her. She regarded it sceptically.

"Hmm."

"At least try it, Rachel."

"I'll try it." She sat down at the table, and as she had just about every night since she was two, she recited the grace her father had taught her as a child. "For what we are about to receive, let us be truly thankful."

Miriam regarded her with a slightly funny look on her face. "I think of all of us, Mum and Dad are most proud of you."

"What?" Rachel nearly choked on the mouthful of beans she'd just unwisely shovelled in. Somehow she managed to swallow the mush. "Why do you say that?"

"Because you've followed them faith-wise. You go to church regularly—"

"So do Esther and Anna."

"Oh, is it just me, then?" Miriam let out a huff of hard laughter. "Oops."

Rachel hesitated, knowing how tricky it was to talk about these things. She didn't want to seem pushy, but Miriam was so clearly unhappy, needing an anchor in the stormy sea her life had become.

"You could try it, you know," she said as she took another, smaller bite of the beans and rice.

"Try what?"

"Church. Faith. The whole lot."

"I think it's too late for me."

"It's never too late, Miri."

Miriam sighed and pushed her plate away. "It's too late for these beans. They're horrible. How have you managed to eat two mouthfuls?"

"I wasn't going to say anything…" She had, for her sister's sake, been willing to choke the whole plate down, although it would have been a challenge as well as an act of love.

"They're horrible. Clearly I'm not a cook."

"I'm not sure anyone could make these appetising—"

Miriam whisked away the two plates, dumping the product of her hard efforts into the rubbish bin. "Right," she said briskly. "I'm ordering fish and chips."

Chapter Seventeen

OVER THE NEXT few days, Rachel started to feel as if she'd reached something of a pleasant stasis, a barely there balance, although admittedly it still felt tenuous. Nathan continued to be a challenge, and he still took far too much of her time to manage in the classroom, but she was able to get through her lessons and return home exhausted every night, grateful for Miriam's company and sometimes a glass of much-needed wine.

On Thursday afternoon, she left school as soon as she'd dismissed the children to take Miriam to her first scan at the West Cumberland Hospital in Whitehaven. Miriam was uncharacteristically quiet and understandably tense as Rachel drove her across on the A66, and then down towards Whitehaven, the steely glint of the Irish Sea visible as they travelled along the coastal road.

"This is all making it feel so much more real," Miriam said as Rachel finally pulled into the hospital's crowded car park, inching along in the hope of finding a space. "Plus I have to wee *so* badly."

"Hold it in." Biting her lip in concentration, Rachel reversed into a space that only just fit her car and forced them both to shimmy out of their seats.

"What if something is wrong with the baby?" Miriam asked as they took their seats in the waiting room. "How will I cope then?" Her hands were twisted together, her face pale. "I can barely cope now, as it is."

"Don't borrow trouble," Rachel said, patting her arm. It was something her mum said frequently, and she appreciated the sentiment now. "You're young and healthy. There's no reason the baby shouldn't be healthy, as well."

"I had a glass of wine before I realised I was pregnant," Miriam said in a low voice. "Several, actually."

"I'm sure you're not the first to have done so." Rachel had never seen her sister looking so anxious, even more so than when she'd told her sisters about her pregnancy. "Didn't women drink mead or ale or whatever back in the Middle Ages? They were probably completely soused their whole pregnancies."

"Still." Miriam looked away, nibbling her lip. "I haven't taken care of myself. I'm not even taking those prenatal vitamins you bought, because they make me throw up."

"Well, that's reasonable. Miriam, let's wait until we see what the scan tells us, okay?" Rachel patted her arm again. "Really, I think it's going to be okay."

Miriam nodded, looking unconvinced. A few minutes later, her name was called, and Rachel accompanied her into a darkened room with an examining table and an ultrasound machine.

"This will be cold," the sonographer warned as she squirted clear gel on Miriam's bare tummy. Rachel watched as Miriam flinched slightly, her stomach still nearly flat— flatter than Rachel's, anyway. She'd probably blow up like a balloon when she had kids. *If* she had kids. Rachel thought of Abigail Cribbs' years of spinsterhood and mentally shuddered. Was that going to be her one day, maybe even one day soon?

"All right, here we are," the sonographer said with a smile. "Baby's wriggling around nicely."

Rachel and Miriam both peered at the ultrasound screen, but all Rachel could make out was a bunch of black and white blobs and squiggles, kind of like a moving Rorschach test. By the look of confusion on her sister's face, she judged that Miriam was having the same problem.

The sonographer took pity on them and started to explain. "Here are the feet and legs," she said, gesturing to the screen, "and tummy and head. Looks like Baby is sucking her thumb. Or his thumb. I'm afraid I can't tell the sex at this stage."

"Oh, I see it," Miriam cried, sounding awed, and Rachel let out a laugh as she saw it too, the tiny baby coming into wondrous focus. Maybe this was what her sister needed— irrefutable prove that a baby was growing inside her, that she was going to be a mum. Maybe this would help to allay her fears.

"So Baby looks healthy," the sonographer continued. "And bang on twelve weeks' gestation." She turned to Miriam with a smile, who was still staring at the screen.

"Isn't it amazing, Miriam—" Rachel began, only to stop as her sister suddenly burst into noisy tears.

The sonographer looked taken aback, and Rachel quickly went over to put her arm around Miriam's shoulders.

"Sorry," Miriam sobbed. "It's all too much."

"Shall I give you a moment?" the sonographer murmured and quietly left the room. Rachel ripped off a few sheets of the rough paper towel and handed it to Miriam, who pressed it to her eyes.

"How completely embarrassing," she mumbled against the tissues. "That woman must think I'm an utter basket case."

"I'm sure it's not the first time she's seen something like that." Rachel squeezed her shoulders. "What's going on, Miriam?"

"It's just so terrifying," Miriam said after a moment, blowing her nose. "That's a real, live person there." She gestured to the screen. "Someone who is going to have hopes and dreams and fears and all the rest of it. And I'm responsible for them."

"Yes…" There was no denying that parenthood was a massive step.

"I just don't know if I can do it," Miriam said wretchedly. "I've never stuck with anything in my life, Rachel. I've always been about having a good time."

"I think you might be selling yourself a tiny bit short, Miri." It was true her youngest sister had lived life on the fly, enjoying the pleasures as they came, but she'd worked hard at—well, some things. She'd been a keen sportswoman, playing hockey for the school's First Eleven.

"If you're thinking of my hockey," Miriam said, reading her mind sister-style, "then come on. That's completely lame."

"It isn't," Rachel said, somewhat half-heartedly.

Miriam snorted. "Raising a child is not the same as playing right forward." She blew her nose again, loudly. "I just don't know what I'm going to do."

Rachel regarded her quietly. "What you mean?"

Miriam was silent for a long moment. "I've been thinking," she said finally, choosing each word with care, "of giving this baby up for adoption." She glanced at Rachel above her bunched tissues. "Do you think that's horrible?"

"No, of course not," Rachel said. "It's a noble thing to do, Miriam, but it needs to be the right thing. It's a huge decision, to give up your child. And you have no idea how you'll feel in a couple of weeks or months, never mind after you actually give birth."

"I know." Miriam was silent for a moment. "But does it even matter how I feel or will feel," she finally asked, "considering? Rachel, I've got *nothing*. No job, no home—"

"Hey—"

"You know what I mean. I can't freeload off you forever, and in any case that flat isn't exactly suitable for a baby long term, is it? Besides, it's not just that. I have literally no money—I withdrew my last ten pounds from my bank account this week. I can't afford anything."

"We'll help…"

"But I don't want to be the failure my family has to keep bailing out. That's hardly a way to begin as a mother."

Rachel was silent, processing all Miriam had said—and all she hadn't. "Look," she said at last. "I understand that you're scared. That's completely normal, especially in your particular situation. But you're talking about two different things here, Miriam—whether you're emotionally able to care for a child, and whether you're physically and financially able to. Now, if you've got no money, you still have six months before you give birth, and right now you spend most of your days on our sofa." Miriam flinched a little at this, but Rachel continued, determined to give her some tough love. "You could get a job, make some money. Save some. And you'd be entitled to maternity allowance once the baby is born. I know it might not be much, but it's something."

Miriam let out a shuddery sigh. "I know you're right, but who is going to employ me? There are few jobs going in Thornthwaite and I can't even drive."

"There are buses to Keswick," Rachel returned staunchly. "If you want to make it work, Miriam, you can. But you've got to want it, and you've got to try."

"I know," Miriam whispered.

"And if you decide you're not ready to be a mother, and this baby might be better with someone else, then that's okay too. But be pro-active, Miriam. Take some positive steps, even if they're just baby ones, no pun intended."

"Ha-ha." Miriam looked thoughtful for a moment, and more serious than Rachel had ever seen her. "I have a lot of thinking to do," she finally said. "And a lot of doing, too. I'll look for a job. I should have done it before now, I know. See what a waste of space I can be—"

"Don't bother about the past, just keep looking towards the future," Rachel reminded her. "And you will *never* be a waste of space."

Miriam mopped up the last of her tears and then lobbed the sodden tissues into the bin. "Thank you. I know I needed to hear all that."

"And you also needed to cry." Rachel thought of her own tears in the empty dream house, and Sam's surprising comfort. It was always hard to let go of what you thought your life was going to look like, and embrace the reality, whatever it was. "It's all part of the process."

"We'd better call the sonographer back in before she thinks I'm having a breakdown."

"Like I said, I'm sure it's not the first time she's seen something like this." Smiling, Rachel gave her sister a quick hug before she went to open the door.

The next night Rachel picked up Nathan from after-school club, smiling in sympathy at the play assistant who had clearly been dealing with his antics for the last two hours, and they walked together towards The Bell.

"I don't see why I have to go with you," he said, scuffing his shoes along the pavement. "It's so boring just sitting in your flat."

"We don't have to sit in my flat," Rachel said. It was a nice evening, not too chilly, the sun peeking from behind shreds of cloud. "We could take Bailey to the play park, if you like. She's not meant to see other dogs yet, since she hasn't had her jabs, but as long as we avoid them it should be okay."

Nathan regarded her suspiciously. "You'd take me to the park?"

He sounded so disbelieving, Rachel's heart ached. "Of course I would, Nathan. It will be fun."

Unfortunately, it wasn't that fun. Nathan in the play park was just as challenging to manage as Nathan in the classroom. He didn't seem to understand the concept of taking turns, and he pushed a boy off the swings as soon as they got there. Rachel hurried over to apologise to the irate mother and sobbing boy. When she tried to explain to Nathan that he couldn't push someone like that, he just turned away from her, kicking at the base of the climbing frame with methodical thwacks.

Rachel prayed for patience, as well as for wisdom. She

really didn't know how to reach this boy sometimes, but more and more she knew she wanted to. Somehow, she wanted to.

"Come on, Nathan," she said when one of the swings was finally free. "I'll push you, if you like."

They spent a relatively peaceful and happy twenty minutes on the swings; Nathan couldn't get enough of them, and was happy for Rachel to push him back and forth, back and forth. Rachel was just as happy to do it; the monotony of it was far better than the fraught negotiation of managing any of the other apparatus in the park.

Finally, as the sun began to sink behind the fells and the air turned decidedly nippy, Rachel suggested they head for home. Nathan shook his head, pumping his legs with even more determination as he continued to swing back and forth, and Rachel's heart sank. Of course nothing was easy.

"Come on, Nathan," she said as firmly as she could. "Bailey needs to eat her supper, and so do we. I've bought pizza dough and all the toppings—we can make our own pizzas." Yes, against all her teacher's instincts, she would resort to bribery, if that's what it took for the two of them to get home in one piece.

Still Nathan continued to swing, his legs pumping, his head tucked low, determinedly ignoring her. Rachel watched him with increasing frustration. How on earth was she going to get him off the swing?

"Nathan…" Taking a deep breath, she reached forward

and grabbed the swing's chain; the force of Nathan's motion nearly knocked her off her feet but she held on and with more effort than she knew she possessed, managed to stop the swing. "We're going home," she said firmly, and to her shock Nathan flew off the swing at her, his clenched fists connecting with whatever part of her they could find.

"Whoa…what!" Rachel's voice ended in a shriek as she brought her hands up to her face to ward off the worst of his blows. "Nathan… *Nathan!*" She was in shock, for even after a week in the classroom, she'd never seen him so out of control—or so violent, his fists hammering her body.

"Whoa there, buddy." Another parent, a burly-looking dad, put his arms around Nathan in a gentle but firm bear hug, forcing him to still. "Time to stop." His voice was kind, his manner authoritative, and after what felt like an age Nathan stopped resisting, sagging in the man's hold, the fight clearly gone out of him.

Rachel lowered her hands, dazed and shaken by the episode. "I'm sorry…" she began, and the man shook his head, smiling in sympathy.

"I have a son who is autistic."

"But Nathan isn't—" She stopped, because she didn't actually know if Nathan was autistic. Admittedly he didn't have all the typical symptoms, but then no child did. Autism was a spectrum, and it manifested itself differently in every child. One of those symptoms, Rachel knew, was an inability to tolerate disruption to routines, which Nathan had clearly just exhibited.

Her mind whirling, she reached for Nathan's hand, breathing a sigh of relief when he took it. "Come on, Nathan," she said, her voice wobbling a little from the sheer intensity of the situation. Nathan seemed oblivious to the fact that he'd just been doing his best to beat her up. "Let's go home." She managed a smile for the man. "Thank you."

Back at the flat, things settled down as Rachel got out the makings for pizzas and Nathan spent a contented ten minutes decorating his. Miriam was out at the cinema with Esther and Anna, who was back for another weekend of wedding planning. While Rachel enjoyed spending time with all her sisters, she was glad to avoid it this time; she wasn't in the mood for wedding talk or how-are-you-coping questions. But then, she never seemed to be.

As challenging as Nathan was, he was also a distraction, and that was something Rachel needed. After they made and ate their pizzas, she put on the latest Pixar film she'd borrowed from the library's small DVD collection, and made popcorn for them both to share. By eight o'clock Nathan was yawning and Rachel managed to chivvy him downstairs and into bed without too much hassle.

Along with the DVD, she'd taken out several children's stories from the library, including her favourite, *The Faraway Tree* by Enid Blyton. It might have seemed a bit young for a worldly-wise seven-year-old, but Nathan listened with surprising avidity, which made all the difficulties of the evening worth it, or at least almost.

When he was settled in bed, Rachel flopped onto the sofa

and reached for her laptop, typing *autism symptoms* into the search engine. After an hour of scrawling various websites and diagnoses, she didn't feel any the wiser; Nathan didn't have all or even most of the symptoms she'd expect, but he definitely had some. She was no doctor, but as she spent more time with him, Rachel couldn't help but wonder if Nathan was something other than just difficult. Something that required a diagnosis.

Despite her best intentions to stay awake for when Sam returned so she didn't have another awkward and disorientating wake-up, she dropped off to sleep sometime after midnight, only to startle awake when Sam opened the door to the flat.

"I wasn't asleep," she blurted, and Sam gave her a small smile.

"I don't mind, Rachel. It's late."

"How late is it?" she asked as she peered blearily at her watch.

"Half past one."

"How do you do it? Staying up that late night after night, and having to get up early with Nathan?"

Sam shrugged. "You do what you have to do."

"Still, Sam, it's awfully hard." She regarded him with both sympathy and admiration, or at least she thought she did, but whatever expression Sam saw in her face, he obviously didn't like it, because his mouth tightened and his jaw clenched.

248

"Don't feel sorry for me, Rachel," he said, and it sounded like a warning.

"I don't, but would that be so bad if I did?"

"Yes. I don't want to be your pity case."

"I felt the same, you know, with everyone feeling sorry for me after I was jilted. But I'm realising that pity doesn't have to be a bad thing, not when it's based in compassion. It means people care." The words seemed to have more meaning than she'd intended them to. *She* cared.

Sam regarded her for a few tense moments, seeming to battle some deep emotion. Then his brows pulled together in a ferocious frown. "Do you have a *black eye?*"

"What?" Rachel put one hand up to her eye, only to wince as her fingers brushed her skin. "Oh. Maybe." She hadn't actually looked in a mirror all night, but now that she thought about it, the area around her eye did feel tender.

Sam moved closer, crouching down in front of the sofa and taking her face in his hands as he examined her eye. Rachel went completely still, far more conscious of Sam's nearness, and the careful way he held her face in his hands than any pain in her eye. His palms were callused and rough and yet his touch gentle.

"You do. It's turning purple." His thumb skimmed underneath her eye and Rachel flinched a little. It did hurt, now she was aware of it, but she felt something else too. Something a far cry from hurt, something that was far more powerful. Sam grimaced. "Sorry. How did you get a black eye?"

"Ah…"

Sam's expression darkened. "Don't tell me it was Nathan?"

"He didn't mean to—"

"What happened?"

"He didn't want to get off the swings—"

"Oh." Sam nodded slowly. "I should have warned you about those. He's a bit obsessed."

So Sam knew? "You could say that," Rachel answered.

"Still, he shouldn't have hit you. I'll have to talk to him in the morning. He will apologise."

"It was as if he couldn't control himself," Rachel ventured. "As if he didn't even realise what he was doing." She hesitated, thinking of her Internet searches, but she didn't really want to get into that whole conversation at one o'clock in the morning. "Don't be too tough on him, Sam."

"Maybe he needs a little toughness." Sam took her hand and helped her to her feet. "I'm sorry, at any rate. That's clearly more than you bargained for."

All of this was more than she bargained for—Nathan's demands, Sam's nearness, the way her heart was starting to race as his fingers twined with hers.

As if suddenly aware of what he was doing, Sam dropped her hand as if it were scorched. "See you tomorrow," he said gruffly.

This time he didn't walk her to her door.

Chapter Eighteen

ON SUNDAY EVENING Rachel and Miriam headed to the vicarage for the usual family dinner, i.e. a scorched roast and subsequent takeaway alternative. Rachel was looking forward to seeing her sisters as well as Simon and Jasper; it wasn't the same as having her parents around but over the last few weeks they'd all developed a friendly, familial camaraderie that felt both comforting and fun.

The kitchen was full of laughter as the two sisters headed in, enveloped in the warmth from the Aga, the cosiness of the scene. The table was set for seven, with two places squeezed on one end, and something delicious-smelling bubbled away on the stove.

Charlie thumped his tail on the floor as they came in, and Rachel crouched down to fondle his silky ears.

"Where's your puppy, then?" Esther asked.

"Where's yours?" Rachel returned good-naturedly. "We should get them all together, see how they get on."

"I think we should wait a few weeks before we bring Bailey," Miriam chimed in. "She hasn't quite got her toilet training sorted."

"Yes, please," Jasper said with a theatrical shudder. "Definitely wait."

Sitting around the table as Anna dished out the beef stew she'd made, Rachel felt a deep-seated happiness bloom inside her. For what felt like ages now, she'd been struggling to look forward to, well, anything. Lately, since her dreams had been taken away, life had felt like a long, hard slog, and while it was still challenging in parts—a lot of parts—it was also starting to feel more hopeful. More like living. She had family, and Sunday dinners, and Anna's wedding, and weekends with Nathan, yes, even those—to look forward to.

And she'd spent a little more time with Sam... Last night she'd managed to stay awake for his arrival and they'd ended up chatting for a good hour before she'd headed downstairs. It had been surprisingly easy and companionable; they'd steered clear of any touchy topics—the past, Nathan, her responsibilities or Sam's need for help.

Instead Sam had told her some humorous horror stories of a few of his customers, and she'd shared about her one dismal experience waitressing. They'd agreed that they both loved Thornthwaite, even though it felt like a fishbowl at times. Sam hadn't said anything *too* personal, and Rachel hadn't pried, but it had felt nice, and she'd had a warm glow in her heart region when she'd stumbled up to bed at three in the morning.

"What are you smiling about?" Esther asked as she noticed Rachel's rather silly grin from across the table. "You look like the proverbial cat with the cream."

"No, no cream, no cat," Rachel said hurriedly. "I was just thinking."

"Oh, do tell," Jasper said, leaning forward. "You sound like you have a wonderful secret."

Rachel started to blush. She *didn't* have a secret, but of course now she looked as if she had one, because it was discomfiting to have everyone's speculative gazes trained on her and so her cheeks were going wretchedly scarlet.

"Honestly, there's nothing," she protested. "I live a very boring life."

"You've been spending a lot of time with Sam West," Esther remarked shrewdly, and Rachel's mouth dropped open. Sometimes it felt as if her sister could read her mind.

"I haven't," she exclaimed, because really, that was mostly true. "If anything, I've been spending time with his nephew."

"Yes, what's that about? Miriam mentioned something." Rachel glanced at Miriam, who shrugged. Esther could ferret information out from anyone.

"He's been made temporary guardian of his nephew," Rachel explained carefully. "And he hasn't any childcare coverage for Friday and Saturday nights, so I've agreed to help, just for a little while."

"That's awfully nice of you," Esther remarked in that same shrewd tone. "Considering it completely scuppers your social life."

"What social life?" Rachel joked, except she wasn't even joking. Talking to Sam last night was the extent of her social life…and she didn't actually mind.

"You need to get back out there," Esther insisted. "And if you're babysitting every weekend night, you've got limited opportunity."

"I've got limited opportunity anyway, since I live in Thornthwaite. And it's only been six weeks, Esther. Give me a break, please."

"You're not getting any younger—"

"Trust me, I know." Rachel gave her well-meaning sister as quelling a look as she could before she turned to Miriam with a determined smile. "Miriam had her scan last week—did you bring the print-out, Miriam?"

Her younger sister looked discomfited to have the spotlight swung on her, but Rachel was desperate to get out from under it herself.

"No, I didn't," she answered. "You can't see much, anyway. Just a bunch of blobs and squiggly lines."

"Everything's healthy, though?" Esther asked, sounding a tiny bit diffident. Rachel felt a pang of sympathy for her. Six months ago, Esther had been pregnant, only to discover at the first scan that the embryo had never developed. No doubt she was remembering it now.

Will put an arm around his wife's shoulders. "Exciting times, Miriam," he said easily, and gave Esther's shoulders a squeeze. She leaned in to him, her head against his shoulder.

Rachel watched them, trying not to let envy curl its vine-like tendrils around her heart. She could have had that with Dan. Nearly a month after the wedding…she could have even been pregnant by now, with her own happy news to share. And no matter how much she was trying to move on, how much she tried to accept what Dan had decided, it still hurt that she didn't have that. She might never have that.

Quite unexpectedly she caught Jasper's eye; he seemed to be regarding her with a certain, knowing sympathy that made Rachel squirm. She looked away quickly.

"We're going to have the most fabulous wedding photos," Anna said with a laugh. "With Miriam looking as if she's about to pop!"

Miriam grimaced. "And with a bridesmaid dress that will resemble a tent. I can hardly wait."

"Oh, but you've got to be a bridesmaid," Anna said quickly. "Pregnant or not, I want you all by my side."

"And of course we'll be there," Rachel assured her. "I can't wait." This was met with a predictably awkward silence that Esther even more awkwardly broke.

"How is Sam doing with his nephew, anyway?" she asked, swinging the spotlight back onto Rachel. "Sam has had a rather troubled past, hasn't he?"

"Has he?" Rachel tried to sound diffident, as if she didn't know at least some of it.

"Troubled?" Miriam asked. "How so?"

"His father was an alcoholic who ended up in jail," Esther supplied. "I don't know about his mum."

"That's awful—"

"Let's not talk about him like this," Rachel protested. "None of us would like it if—"

"And he got into trouble himself as a teenager, didn't he?" Esther looked to Will for confirmation, who shrugged.

"I knew him from rugby, but we weren't in the same year. I couldn't say."

"Really," Rachel protested. "I don't think…"

"You're sounding very protective."

Rachel shot Esther a sharp look. "No more than any of us should be—"

"It's common knowledge, anyway," Esther continued, a stubborn glint in her eye. Rachel knew the only reason her sister was pursuing this line of conversation was because she wanted to figure out what Rachel felt about Sam, which was, of course, nothing—or at least very little. Not much, at any rate. They were friends.

"Sam is a very private person," she said with quiet dignity. "I doubt very much he'd appreciate us all gossiping about him. Anyway," she continued with determined emphasis, "what about Miriam?"

"What about me?" Miriam looked startled, as well as annoyed that Rachel was throwing her under the conversational bus again.

"You need a job," Rachel declared. "We were talking

about it the other day. Maybe someone here knows if there's anything going." She sat back with a silent sigh of relief as everyone began discussing Miriam's job prospects, or lack thereof.

"I really don't have any transferrable skills," Miriam protested as the suggestions came thick and fast, and rather wild. "I could not help out at the primary school, Anna, and while The Queen's Sorrow might be looking for a sous chef, beans on toast really is the extent of my abilities." She tried to smile, reclaiming a bit of her old insouciance, even if it seemed only a thin veneer. "I'm really just an expert in having a good time."

"Don't keep selling yourself short," Rachel admonished. "What about your photography? And the website you built and managed?"

"Website?" Simon sat forward, looking alert. "Do you have experience building a website, Miriam?"

"Only a titchy one, straight out of a box," Miriam dismissed. "It was nothing, Simon."

"I'm looking for a part-time administrator for the church," Simon said. "Helen Hughes has retired after thirty-five years, claiming she could only work with your father." He smiled wryly. "Which is fine, because I really need someone who knows their way around a computer as well as a website."

"Mrs Hughes was a bit of a dinosaur when it came to technology, wasn't she?" Anna reminisced fondly. "But she made the most amazing biscuits. She brought some every time she came to the vicarage."

"Simon, that's really very kind of you, but I don't think I'm your woman," Miriam said. "My typing speed is snail-like and the website I built could be done by one of Rachel's pupils. Honestly…"

"Why are you shooting yourself in the foot?" Esther demanded. "Here's a job, and you need one. You could teach yourself what you don't know."

"And you could keep at it after the baby is born," Anna chimed in. "You'd work in Simon's office—you could put the baby down for a sleep upstairs! And lots of lovely ladies from church around for cuddles."

"The pay's not much," Simon said in apology, and Esther snorted.

"It's better than what she's making now, which is nothing."

"Still…" Miriam looked dazed by how quickly it all seemed to have been decided.

"It would be twenty hours a week," Simon said. "If that's not too much?"

"Too *much*?" Esther scoffed. "What else is she doing?"

"Fine, fine." Miriam held up her hands, laughing a little although she still looked dazed. "Thank you, Simon. Your offer is very kind. I'll accept, even though you might live to regret it."

"Never," Simon said gallantly, and the conversation

moved on, thankfully not back to Rachel and her supposed secrets.

The next week passed by with surprising speed; while things had settled down somewhat in the classroom, now that Rachel was familiar with Nathan and his ways, the days still felt challenging and on Wednesday she asked Sarah to see Nathan's educational records.

"As you can see," Sarah said, once Rachel had looked through the file, "at his last school he was given a statutory assessment, but the local authority decided not to give him an EHC plan."

"We could appeal, though," Rachel said. "Or his guardian could."

Sarah's eyebrows rose. "Do you think he's in need of a plan? You seem to be managing the class without extra help."

"Managing, yes, but Nathan's behaviours don't seem as if they come from him just being difficult."

"He has had a very challenging background—"

"I know." Rachel took a deep breath. "But for Nathan's sake, he needs more support."

Sarah regarded her for a moment. "The authority could deny the appeal, or even that he be assessed again. You know how it is these days, Rachel. It's brutal for kids who have special needs. There simply isn't the funding or support that is really required, and it's the children who suffer."

"I know, but we could try." Rachel was conscious that Nathan didn't have parents to advocate for him. She didn't even know where his mother was, and Sam was so busy, barely able to keep it all together as it was. Someone needed to fight for him, for the rights he should have, the help he might need.

"We could," Sarah said after a moment. "I won't keep you from it, certainly. But the first port of call would be communicating with his guardian."

"Yes…"

"You know him, I believe?"

"Yes…"

"Do you think he would be receptive to having Nathan assessed?"

"Yes, I think so," Rachel said, hesitation audible in her voice. How well did she know Sam, really? The answer was hardly at all, and yet she trusted him; she believed he was a good man. "I think Sam wants what's best for his nephew."

Sarah nodded slowly. "Then why don't we ask him to come into school for a meeting?"

By Friday afternoon, heading back to The Bell with Nathan, Rachel was feeling gently optimistic about, well, everything. Miriam had started work and seemed to enjoy it; Rachel had Skyped her parents, who were full of excitement about the ministry in Jinan; and Nathan, skipping along next to her, seemed in a good mood. She'd bought a thousand-piece jigsaw puzzle from a charity shop for them to tackle that evening, because during school that week Nathan had mentioned liking puzzles.

She'd just started up the stairs to the flats when Sam appeared in the corridor, looming in the doorway that led to the pub's interior like a dark shadow.

"Rachel," he said, his voice hard. "May I have a word?"

Startled, Rachel's hand flew to her chest. "Oh, you surprised me. Yes, of course." She glanced uncertainly at Nathan as she belatedly registered Sam's not-so-friendly tone.

"Nathan, go up to the flat while I talk to Miss Holley, areet?" Sam instructed. "The door's open."

"I call her Rachel when we're not in school," Nathan said a bit resentfully, but he headed upstairs while Rachel waited, her heart starting to thump in a way she didn't like.

"What's going on?" she asked, because Sam was looking at her with a cool appraisal she also didn't like.

"Are you behind the letter I received this morning, requesting a meeting with the head teacher to discuss Nathan's special education needs?" His voice was low and somehow menacing. Rachel had to keep herself from taking an instinctive step backwards. She'd never seen him like this, the blatant aggression, the powerful stance. He didn't scare her, precisely, but she was definitely alarmed.

"Well, er, yes, I suppose I am—"

"And you didn't think fit to talk to me about it first?"

"As Nathan's teacher, it was my responsibility to talk to my supervisor first." She straightened her shoulders, meeting his gaze directly. "I know we're friends, but I have to follow policy and procedures, Sam—"

"Friends?" Sam repeated disbelievingly, and Rachel flinched. That hurt a lot more than it probably should have.

"I thought we were," she answered, lifting her chin. "Perhaps I was wrong."

Sam shook his head, raking a hand through his hair. "Rachel, there's stuff you don't know. That makes things a lot more difficult than you realise."

"Then perhaps you could tell me, considering I'm Nathan's teacher and I take care of him two evenings a week."

Sam dropped his hand and gave her a look so miserable, her heart ached. "I don't want to."

Rachel swallowed hard. "Why not?"

"Because..." He blew out a breath, his gaze distant and troubled. "Because we *are* friends, and I don't want you to look at me differently."

And suddenly Rachel's aching heart was tumbling right over. "I wouldn't, Sam," she said, but he just shook his head. The moment stretched on, and then Sam let out a heavy sigh.

"I'll come up when Nath is in bed. I'll have someone cover downstairs if I can. And then we'll talk."

He turned to go back in the pub, and Rachel watched him go, her unruly heart now beating hard. *We are friends, and I don't want you to look at me differently.* In that moment, Rachel knew she already was, or at least she could if she let herself, but in an entirely different way than Sam had meant.

Chapter Nineteen

RACHEL SPENT THE whole evening in a ferment of curiosity and anxious anticipation. What on earth was Sam going to tell her? What secret could he be hiding? And what if it did change things? She'd hate to look at him differently, hate to disappoint him that way.

She tried to rush Nathan into bed, which backfired hugely as he resisted and then threw a strop, which Rachel had since learned had to be simply endured, and eventually he calmed down and she got him into bed, although it took two stories with naming five things rather than three in each, to get him there. At least he liked the stories now.

In any case, Sam ended up being late, so she sat curled up on the sofa counting the minutes until he opened the door to the flat at half past eight, giving her a tired smile that twisted her heart into knots along with her stomach.

"How is it going down there? You found someone to help?"

"Yes, Lizzie. She does weekday evenings, but she agreed to come in for an hour." He closed the door behind him with a soft click. "Sorry for all the aggro I gave you downstairs earlier. I was being..." He shook his head as he blew out a breath. "Stupid."

"It's okay, Sam. You have a lot going on."

"Yeah, but...I know you're trying to help." Something about his tone made Rachel feel like he didn't think she was helping.

"So tell me what's going on," she said quietly. "Tell me what I don't know."

Sam walked slowly to the other side of the sofa and sat down heavily, his forearms braced on his thighs. He was in his usual work uniform of white T-shirt, faded jeans, and work boots, his hair a bit spiky from raking his fingers through it, golden stubble glinting on his jaw. He didn't speak, and Rachel waited, her hands going clammy as she wondered what on earth Sam was going to say.

"You know about my parents," he said at last.

"A little..." Only what he'd told her.

"Well, after my sister and I were taken from them that first time, things got worse. After a few months we left foster care and went back to them, but then my dad skipped out and my mum went right downhill. Depressed, drinking, drugs too probably, although I don't remember. The authorities decided she couldn't care for us any longer, and so Tiffany and I ended up in foster care for good. She ran away when she was fourteen, and I stayed in until I aged out at sixteen."

"Oh, *Sam*." Rachel had to blink back tears. Nearly ten *years* in the system? She could barely begin to imagine how hard that would have been. "Did you stay with the same family, at least?"

"Nope." He gave her a wry smile. "I'm afraid I was a bit like Nathan that way, and so was Tiffany. Nobody wanted us for long. We were here and there, bounced around the county. We ended up separated in our teens, and when Tiffany ran away I didn't see her for a couple of years. When I did..." He paused, his expression snared in some memory, and as gently as she could Rachel tried to fill in the blanks.

"Was that when she started to...?"

"No, it was before." Sam seemed to come out of a reverie, giving himself a little shake. "She'd been on stuff since she was little more than a kid. She'd been living with blokes, in and out with the drugs and drink, since she ran away."

It sounded like a terrible, tragic life. "So what happened when you saw her again?"

"She came to visit me." He paused, lifting his bleak gaze to meet Rachel's as he waited, weighing his words. "In prison."

Rachel felt a jolt of shock, along with one of recognition. Hadn't she sensed Sam was hiding something like this? Hadn't she figured there was something in his past, the bad boy made good? Except that made it all sound so trite, and it *wasn't*. It was terrible and sad and so very broken.

"What happened?" she asked quietly.

Sam didn't answer for a long moment. He lowered his head, staring down at the floor, while Rachel waited. "I got into trouble in my teens. Started hanging out with a bunch of lads I shouldn't have been. We ended up stealing cars for a shady bloke up near Workington. It was stupid as well as illegal—we didn't even get much for it. The bloke kept the others in line because he supplied them with drugs; but I was never into that, or drink. Not after I saw the way my mum and dad went."

Rachel tried to swallow past the lump in her throat. She had no words, no comfort to offer, because it all sounded so awful.

"Anyway, when I was seventeen I got arrested. That was stupid, as well—the others ran but I wasn't fast enough. I could have got off if I'd named them but I didn't—misplaced loyalty if there ever was, eh?"

"It all sounds so..."

"Bad, I know." That hadn't been what she was going to say, but Sam ploughed on, his jaw set. "I was seventeen and I was given four years at Lancaster Farms. I got out in two."

"Okay." Rachel nodded slowly. Now she realised why Sam had felt taking Nathan's guardianship might not be straightforward, but she still didn't understand what it had to do with his nephew being assessed for special needs. "You've obviously moved on from all that, Sam," she said carefully. "And you've done so well for yourself, and for Nathan. Surely your past experience won't affect Nathan's assessment?"

Sam blew out a breath and straightened, giving Rachel a disconcertingly direct look. "Yes, it could, because when I was given his guardianship I didn't disclose that I had a criminal record."

Shock jolted through her. "You didn't...?"

"No, because I didn't have to," he answered steadily, and Rachel relaxed. "I was convicted as an under-eighteen and given forty-eight months' sentence in a juvenile prison, which means my conviction is spent and doesn't have to be disclosed after eleven years, which was in July. Lucky, eh?" His smile was humourless, his expression bleak.

"So if it doesn't have to be disclosed..."

"That doesn't mean people couldn't find out about it if they wanted to. Or if I was asked directly. I looked at the assessment, Rachel. They look at everything—home life, history... They dig deep. It will come out, and what do you think is going to happen then?"

She gulped, hating the thought that her good intentions might have put Sam—and Nathan—at risk. And yet surely the system was better than that? "Sam, they'll see how well you've been providing for Nathan—"

"Then you have more faith in the system than I do. I think they'll see a tough-looking bloke with a criminal conviction, who runs the roughest pub in the village."

"The roughest? That's not exactly saying much." Rachel tried to keep her voice light even though everything in her was aching. "Besides, there are only two pubs in the village."

"You know what I mean, Rachel."

"Of course I do." She gazed at him steadily, her heart filled with compassion for this man who had suffered so much and tried so hard. "And I'm sorry, so sorry, if what I've done has jeopardised your custody of Nathan. But I'm not convinced it has, Sam. Maybe that's naïve, maybe it's wrong, but…" She took a deep breath, knowing she needed to say this but afraid of Sam's reaction. "You can't run forever, Sam," she said as gently as she could. "You can't keep ducking and dodging. If not now, then something will happen later. And if they find out, they find out. Let your current record speak for itself, not what you did in the past."

Sam stared at her, his expression hardening. "Like I said, you have a lot more faith in the system than I do."

Rachel nodded slowly. "I suppose I do. I haven't experienced it the way you have, certainly. My only experience with the local authority and the foster care system is as a teacher, and I know while caseworkers are overworked and burned out, they're doing their best to put children in the safest, healthiest situations that they can. And I think, I hope, they would see that was with you."

Sam rose from the sofa, shaking his head. "Save the speech. I'm not going to change my mind."

His tough tone caught her on the raw. "But—"

He folded his arms. "I don't want Nathan assessed."

Rachel stared at him, stunned even though everything

Sam had said and done had been leading to this statement. Still, she couldn't believe a man like Sam wouldn't want the best for the child in his care, his own flesh and blood. To deny Nathan even the chance of an assessment…

"Sam, I understand why you're reluctant, honestly I do, but I think you need to think about this more carefully, for Nathan's sake—"

"Don't patronise me, Rachel."

"I'm not," she exclaimed. She rose to her feet, frustration surging through her along with the hurt. "Look, the letter you received outlined some of the school's—and my—concerns. Nathan is exhibiting behaviours that suggestion a condition, Sam, and not just a boy being difficult—"

"Now you're the expert?"

"No, I'm not, which is why I'd like him to be assessed. If Nathan does have a disability, or some special needs, then I want them to be taken care of as best as they can. And I'm not the person who can do that, as much as I wish I could. I have twenty-five children in my class—"

"So now it's about you."

Rachel closed her eyes, praying for patience. She knew Sam was feeling vulnerable, driven to the defensive, and she was trying to keep her temper because snapping at him wouldn't help anyone, least of all Nathan. "It's about Nathan," she said as steadily as she could. "And what he needs. But it's also about you. Nathan needs help, Sam, and if you refuse it, it could look worse for you—"

"Ah, and now you're threatening me?"

"*No*, I'm trying to help you," she cried. "The school can't do anything without your consent—we can't put Nathan forward for assessment, we can't discuss him with any specialists. And that will hurt him, Sam, and it will hurt you when your case comes up for review and the social worker sees that you refused consent, because that *will* go on the record. It has to."

His jaw tightened. "So you'd bollocks everything up just for this assessment?"

"I'm not trying to," Rachel protested, a pang of guilt assailing her at how she must seem to Sam—heartless, indifferent to what this could cost him. What did she really know about the system, anyway? Not nearly as much as he did. "He might not even be granted an assessment, if they don't think he's in need of another one—"

"Then what's the problem?"

"We need to give Nathan the best chance we can."

"And if he's taken away and bunged into foster care?" Sam demanded. "Is that the best chance?"

"It's a chance I believe you have to take," Rachel answered levelly, although in truth she felt torn. How could she honestly say what was best for Nathan? Sam knew him better than she did, and he knew the system better than she did. Still, it felt wrong not to try. "Not every foster care situation is like yours was, Sam—"

He swung away from her, muttering under his breath,

his shoulders hunched. "Go back to the vicarage, Rachel," he said, his back to her. "Go back to your charmed life, your big, empty house where you were going to raise all your kids. The dog, the Rover, the sub-zero fridge. All of it."

Now *that* hurt. The *fridge*…? "I'd hardly want to go back there," she said quietly. "Even if I could. I can't pretend to understand what you're going through, Sam, or what you've gone through in the past, but I really am trying to help. I know it doesn't feel like it—"

"You have no idea." His voice thrummed out low as he turned back to face her, his expression stonier than she'd ever seen it. "No. Idea."

And gazing at his bleak eyes and hard-set mouth, Rachel knew she didn't. Sam's life was a million miles from her cosy, cossetted existence—growing up in the vicarage, three fun years at university, and living her adult life as a beloved member of a small, close-knit community. Sam was right, but so was she. Nathan needed help. He deserved a chance.

"Please, Sam," she said quietly. "I know it's hard, and I can't even imagine what's at stake, but at least think about it. For both your sakes. After observing Nathan for the last few weeks, I think an assessment could really help him, if it means he can get extra learning support, a better start in life. And as for you…wouldn't it be better to have your conviction out in the open? If you were granted permanent custody of Nathan, so you'd never have to worry about this again?"

"Life isn't like that, Rachel."

His words twanged through her, because who could say that he wasn't right? Hadn't she learned that lesson over these last few weeks, as she tried to recover from Dan's breaking it off? Life *wasn't* like that. It wasn't a soft-focus fairy tale with all the lavish trimmings; happy endings were rare and definitely not guaranteed, and sometimes you simply had to carve what you could out of the crappy materials you'd been given.

"Maybe it isn't," she said finally, "but it can be. I still believe that." She wanted to believe it. "And it's worth taking the risk."

"Says you, who wouldn't be taking it." He sighed, and for a second she thought she had him, but then he shook his head. "I'm sorry. I know I must seem harsh to you, but I can't risk it." He paused, regret briefly twisting his features. "I really am sorry, Rachel."

"It's not me you should be saying sorry to," Rachel said quietly, and Sam's face closed right up. "I'm sorry. I didn't mean it like that… I understand where you're coming from, Sam, or at least I'm trying to, but—"

"I think this discussion is over," Sam answered coolly. "I need to be back downstairs."

Rachel watched him go, wishing she'd handled the conversation better. More sensitively, perhaps, because she did understand where Sam was coming from, or at least as much as she could…but did he understand what was at stake for Nathan? He seemed like he didn't even want to think about it.

As he left the flat, she realised she was feeling more than just disappointed for Nathan's sake. She was hurt for her own, because she'd thought... Oh heaven help her, she'd started to think he might have *feelings* for her. Friendly feelings, or even more than that. And she'd had them, too.

Rachel sank onto the sofa, her head in her hands. How could she have been so stupid, so *deluded*? She'd told herself all along she just wanted to help, but right now she knew it was more than that. More than a neighbourly altruism or a teacher's concern. She *cared*—about Nathan, and also about Sam. And right now she felt as if she were no more than an irritation to him, something that hurt far, far more than it should.

By the time Sam arrived back at half past one in the morning Rachel was more than ready to escape to her own flat. His voice was brusque as he thanked her, his gaze avoiding hers.

"And just so you know," he said when her hand was on the doorknob, "I've arranged cover for the weekends, so you won't have to watch Nathan any longer."

Rachel flinched, hurt even more by this coolly spoken statement. Was he trying to cut her out of his life completely? "I didn't mind, you know," she said quietly.

"Well, all the same," he answered. "It's best this way."

Was it? Rachel left without saying anything more, because she didn't trust herself to speak. She shouldn't feel so hurt; she knew that. What had she and Sam shared, anyway? A couple of conversations? She was being an absolute ninny, reading way more into their brief friendship than had ever been there, probably because of the way things had ended with Dan. Like Esther had said, she was on the rebound—and she hadn't even known it.

"What's wrong with you?" Miriam asked the next morning as Rachel lounged on the settee, unable to face an endless Saturday alone. "You look like the world's caved in."

"I'm just tired," Rachel mumbled.

"You don't look just tired."

"Who are you, Esther? What's with the inquisition?"

"I'd hardly call that an inquisition." Miriam perched on the end of the sofa. Now that she was out of the first trimester, she was looking remarkably well, still slender but with a glow that only came from pregnancy. She was also eating everything in sight, with relish. "Seriously, Rach. What's up?"

"Nothing." Rachel scooped Bailey up from the floor and buried her face in her fur. Sweet, uncomplicated, mostly housetrained puppy. Thank goodness she had Bailey.

"Did something happen with Sam?"

"Why do you ask that?" Her voice was muffled against Bailey's fur.

"Because that's the only thing I can think of—"

"The only thing I've got going on in my life, you mean?" Rachel returned with a sigh. She put Bailey down, unable to keep the sadness and disappointment she'd choked down for so long from finally spilling out. "Because I'm so sad and pathetic, the only possible thing of interest in my life is a fake friendship with our landlord who barely strings two sentences together when he sees me?"

"Whoa." Miriam held up one hand as if to stop Rachel's tirade, but she was already petering out. "Where did that come from?"

Rachel covered her face with her hands. "Nowhere," she mumbled.

"Come on, Rach." Miriam moved closer to put a hand on her shoulder. "You've seen me as a falling-apart wreck—"

"What are you saying?"

"Just that I want to help. I won't be shocked. What's going on?"

"Nothing," Rachel declared with emphasis. "And maybe that's the problem. Nothing, absolutely *nothing*, is going on." She picked up the pillow she'd been clutching to her chest and hurled it at the wall; it bounced harmlessly, soundlessly, to the floor, which was far from satisfying.

"Ah." Miriam nodded slowly. "I think I'm starting to see."

"What could you possibly be starting to see?"

"You care about Sam."

Rachel let out a sound that was half-laugh, half-moan. "I don't," she said, and she didn't even convince herself. "I can't."

"Why can't you?"

"Because…"

"Because why?"

"I barely know him, for starters." Which was true, sort of—and yet he'd shared so much about his life. He'd comforted her when she'd cried. And she couldn't deny the spark that leapt to life whenever she was close to him.

"I think you know him well enough," Miriam answered. "Although obviously I'm not one to talk."

"There are other reasons," Rachel said stubbornly. She'd already confessed to herself that she cared about Sam last night, yet now she felt a deep-seated need to convince herself otherwise. Putting herself out there again, especially for a man as closed-off as Sam, was way too risky.

"Such as?"

"He's not my type."

"Says who?"

"Me."

"Why?"

"Because…"

"Because he's a rough sort of bloke, from the wrong side of the tracks?"

"There's no railway here, Miriam."

"You know what I mean."

"Yes, but that's not it." Rachel sighed. "Maybe it would have been, once upon a time. I had an idea in my head of what Mr Husband would look like and it wasn't Sam West,

I'll admit that. But Dan ticked all the boxes and our relationship clearly didn't work, so I think I've learned my lesson there."

"Then what is it?"

"Look, Sam doesn't care about me that way, okay? He's made that clear. And after having had my life upended by a broken relationship mere months ago, I'm not quite ready to risk it all again. Loving someone hurts, and yet Dan seems to think I didn't even love him." She let out a sound somewhere between a laugh and a sob. "I just can't win."

"Oh, Rach." Miriam gave her a quick hug. "You have it bad, don't you?"

"Miriam."

"Sorry, but—"

Rachel sighed. "The truth is, we had a row."

"About…?"

"Nathan. But I can't go into it."

Miriam nodded slowly. "I imagine Sam is a bit prickly where Nathan is concerned. Anyone would be."

"Yes, but…" Rachel sighed. "It doesn't matter. None of it matters." Which was why she was lying here on the sofa, moping and feeling miserable.

"If you say so." Miriam rose and reached for her bag. "As much as I'd like to stay and keep you company in your misery, I've got to go to work. The church bulletin needs photocopying."

"How is that all going?" Rachel asked, feeling guilty that

she had not shown more of an interest in Miriam's burgeoning life recently. "Do you like working for Simon?"

"Simon is a dream. So kind and patient—honestly, the man is a saint."

"And the work itself?"

"It's not rocket science, but then I'm not a rocket scientist." Miriam smiled breezily, but Rachel saw the worry that still lurked in her eyes. Still so much was uncertain. She was in the middle trimester and taking steps towards independence, but she still didn't have much of a life plan. "I'd better go, though. You'll be okay?"

"Fine." Rachel waved her off. "I'm not going to move from this sofa all day, except to take Bailey out. Netflix is calling my name."

"Sounds like a plan."

As the door clicked shut behind Miriam, Rachel tried not to feel lonely—and horribly, unbearably lonely at that. She had Bailey, after all. This was why she'd got a puppy, for moments like these. And in the past a whole day of Netflix would have been pure bliss, the perfect way to spend a rainy Saturday. Why wasn't it now?

It could be, Rachel decided, if she just put a little effort into it. She was going to have a great day today. An absolutely wonderful, relaxing day.

Twenty minutes later the doorbell rang.

Chapter Twenty

"JASPER."

Rachel stared at him, wishing she'd thought about how she looked before she'd answered the door. It was after ten in the morning and she was still in her ratty dressing gown; her hair was a bird's nest and she hadn't brushed her teeth that morning. She wouldn't want anyone to see her like this, and certainty not the impressively turned-out Lord Hartleigh.

"I say, have you just got up?" Jasper declared sunnily. "I've been up for hours. Always was an early riser."

"I've been up for hours too," Rachel said a bit grumpily. "I just haven't got round to getting dressed." Or showering or brushing her teeth.

"Well, get round to it, because I want to go out," Jasper answered. "I've packed a picnic and I've got a perfect place to have it."

"A picnic?" Rachel was startled. "But it's raining."

"One thing I've learned is you can't wait for the sun to shine. And I mean that literally," Jasper said with an easy smile. "So get dressed, showered, whatever. I'll wait." And with deliberate nonchalance, he sat down on the sofa, one leg swinging jauntily.

Rachel stared at him, both disconcerted and nonplussed by this sudden turn of events. Jasper smiled, and something in her both lightened and eased. Why shouldn't she go out? Jasper had gone to some trouble, and it certainly was better than moping around here by herself.

"Give me ten minutes," she said, and scurried towards her bedroom.

Twenty minutes later, Rachel was dressed, with minimal make-up and hairstyling, and they were heading out of Thornthwaite in Jasper's convertible, the top thankfully up as the depressing drizzle was fast on its way to turning into a veritable downpour.

"So what prompted this picnic?" she asked as they headed up the hill, towards Windermere. "And where are we going?"

"Oh, I thought you could use some cheering up," Jasper answered. "And I could as well. As to where we're going…that's a secret."

Rachel eyed him uncertainly, unsure how to take his words. She needed cheering up? Yes, she was miserable, but how had Jasper known? And why did he need cheering up? And most importantly, was this meant to be some sort of date? She wasn't about to ask.

"A picnic in the rain," she said instead, determined to

keep things light. "Sounds like a fab way to be cheered up."

Jasper glanced at her. "Are you being serious?"

"Actually, yes." She smiled at him. "Definitely."

When you were determined to have a good time, Rachel reflected, it became instantly harder to do just that. There was no reason why she couldn't enjoy herself—Jasper was excellent company, amusing, interesting, and yes, attractive. As they climbed the twisting roads through the fells, the sun broke through the clouds; perhaps they wouldn't have to have a picnic in the rain, after all.

Jasper drove through the picturesque, narrow streets of Ambleside before emerging on the far side, in the wild and lonely valley of Scandale. Rachel gazed out the window at the dramatic sweep of fells, interspersed with clumps of woodland and bisected by ancient, drystone walls. It was both bleak and beautiful, fragile sunlight tinting the whole world gold.

"I hope you don't mind a bit of a walk," Jasper remarked as he parked the convertible in a lay-by off the narrow track. "I've been promised a view, and by George, I'm going to get it."

"I don't mind."

"Good." He handed her a folded-up picnic blanket and hoisted a rustic-looking wicker hamper, giving her one of his jaunty smiles. Rachel decided to stop worrying whether this was a date or not and just enjoy the afternoon—the fells, the watery sunlight, the good company.

They walked in silence for a few minutes along the road before heading up into the fells, the tufty ground strewn with rocks and stretching up and up to an impossible horizon. Although she'd lived her whole life in Cumbria, Rachel wasn't much of a hiker. She preferred looking at fells as opposed to climbing them, and perhaps Jasper sensed this, because he glanced behind with a quick, reassuring smile.

"Not much longer."

And so it wasn't—another five minutes and the promised view came in sight—High Sweden Bridge, an old stone bridge for packhorses from the 1700s that was, Rachel knew from reading *Cumbria Life*, considered the most romantic spot in the Lake District. Hmm.

"It's lovely," she said as she spread a blanket above the bridge, which *Cumbria Life* had assured her was the best place to propose in the whole county. Surely Jasper wasn't going to do *that*.

"Isn't it? I read about this bridge, and I wanted to see it for myself." There was the tiniest of pauses before he added in an offhand manner, "I'm glad to see it with you."

"It is a lovely spot," Rachel said again. She sat down on the blanket while Jasper began unloading the picnic—strawberries and cream, gourmet cheeses and deli meats, and a crusty baguette. Finally, clearly the pièce de résistance, he brandished a bottle.

"Champagne…?" Rachel said weakly, and he smiled and shook his head.

"Ah, no. As I recall, you aren't partial to champagne. Prosecco." He popped the cork while Rachel tried not to let her heart sink.

This was all so *perfect*. It was exactly the kind of fantasy scenario she'd once envisioned, when she'd been busy embroidering her life with daydreams. The beautiful spot, the picnic, even the man. Why shouldn't she be interested in Jasper Edgington-Jones? Why shouldn't she fall in love with him, even? She could recapture all those fairy-tale hopes she'd been so determined to turn into reality.

Except she knew now that she couldn't, and she didn't even want to try. She'd moved past that, had started to see how fragile and flimsy they really were. And more importantly, she was starting to realise what—and whom—she really wanted.

"Here we are," Jasper said as he handed her a plastic flute of Prosecco and then hefted his own. "To new starts and beautiful places."

"Hear, hear," Rachel said and clinked her glass with his. They both drank, and she tried to avoid his intent-looking gaze. She shouldn't have come. She should have realised what a picnic in the fells meant, what Jasper had planned.

"So." He stretched out next to her, resting on one forearm. "Have you been here before?"

"No, although I've read about it. It's a beautiful spot. Hard to believe that bridge is still standing."

"It's stronger than it looks, I suppose." He gave her a

half-sincere, half-amused look, classic Jasper. "Would it be utterly naff to say you are, as well?"

"Still standing?" Rachel joked. "Or stronger than I look?"

"Both." Now he looked really serious, the amusement gone like the mask it so obviously was.

"Jasper…" Rachel had no idea what she was going to say.

"I admire you, Rachel. You've had some hard knocks in life, but you're still smiling."

"Am I?" She hadn't been smiling that morning. She'd been as grumpy as anything.

"As far as I can tell you are." He cocked his head. "That takes some strength, you know."

"I suppose so." She didn't feel like a very strong person. She felt as if she'd crumbled at the first test, collapsed at the first hurdle. She looked away from Jasper's intent gaze. She was so not ready for this kind of conversation with him. "What about you?" she tried. "You've had a setback of sorts, haven't you, with your work? And yet you're here, looking as bright-eyed as ever."

"Ah, but it's all a mask."

Rachel couldn't tell from his wry tone if he was joking or not. "Is it?" she asked seriously.

"Of course it is." Still so light, too light. She couldn't tell whether Jasper wanted her to press or not.

With a smile he reached for the baguette and broke off a piece. "How about some food?"

"Now that sounds like a plan."

Jasper kept the conversation witty and light from then on, much to Rachel's relief. Still she couldn't quite relax enough to enjoy herself, which annoyed her. Jasper had planned everything so well, thought of every touch. There was no reason for her not to be completely and utterly charmed, and yet she wasn't.

Was this how Dan had felt?

The question slid slyly into her mind, shocking her with its power. Had Dan done everything right, been thoughtful in every word and gesture, and yet he had still sensed something was missing. Looking back, Rachel knew she had too, but she'd stubbornly ignored the absence. Convinced herself it didn't matter.

And who even knew if it did? Maybe Rachel didn't know how to feel that kind of all-consuming love for anyone, as she'd once said to her mother—except she knew that to be a lie, at least a little bit, because she felt something for Sam. Or was that just misplaced infatuation?

With her thoughts going in ever-increasing circles, Rachel couldn't keep her misery from showing and Jasper clearly sensed it.

"Why don't we walk across the bridge?" he suggested once they'd eaten, with Rachel only picking at the delicious offerings.

"Sorry I'm not very good company," she said, feeling wretched for ruining his planned picnic.

"You're very good company," Jasper assured her. "Come

on."

The sun had gone behind a bank of dense grey cloud as they walked across the narrow, arched bridge, and when Rachel stumbled, Jasper quickly caught her, his hands strong on her arms. It was the perfect moment, scripted by Hollywood, for him to pull her into his arms, but it fell utterly flat as Rachel gently pulled away from him.

"Rachel…"

"We should probably get back," she said, not meeting his eye. "I have marking to do…"

Jasper gave a little sigh, the small sound tearing at her heart. She was a terrible person. She couldn't feel the right things for anyone.

"All right," he said, and they packed up the picnic things in silence, Rachel feeling more wretched by the minute.

They drove back to Thornthwaite in similar silence, Jasper seeming pensive, Rachel miserable. As he pulled up in front of The Bell, she felt she had to say something.

"Jasper, I'm sorry…"

"For what?" His tone was light but Rachel wasn't fooled. Still she wasn't sure she wanted to spell out what exactly she was apologising for, for both their sakes.

"I feel as if I've rather ruined a perfectly lovely afternoon," she said after a moment. "I'm afraid I've been in a bit of a funk…"

"Entirely understandable. And you didn't ruin anything. I enjoyed spending time with you." His gaze lingered on her, his expression all too serious. "Is that a bad thing?"

"No…" She sounded woefully uncertain. "I'm just not sure I'm ready to…well, think of anyone like that, yet." She bit her lip. "If that's what you're implying, which it might be that you're not, and then I will be really embarrassed." She tried for a laugh but it wavered.

"That is what I'm implying," Jasper replied, unruffled, "but I can wait." He scanned her face, gauging her response, while Rachel remained abject. "Is that okay?"

"I don't know," she admitted. "I'm just… I'm not sure of anything, Jasper."

"Like I said, I can wait."

Rachel nodded slowly, too overwhelmed and uncertain to contest the point. She got out of the car, feeling petty and mean somehow for not being more thrilled about his kind-of declaration.

"I had a nice time today, Rachel," he said as she started to close the passenger door.

"So did I," Rachel answered, and Jasper smiled wryly.

"Good, then we can do it again sometime." It wasn't a question. "I'll see you tomorrow for dinner?"

"Dinner—"

"Roast at the vicarage. I'm going all out and doing a loin of beef. Very good cut of meat, so I'd best not ruin it."

"Right." She closed the door, turning towards The Bell, only to stop in her tracks at the sight of Sam standing in the doorway of the pub, the look on his face the stoniest she'd seen yet. His gaze flicked from her to the car to Jasper, who gave a little wave before gunning the engine and hurtling over the bridge. Without a word Sam turned and went inside.

Rachel hadn't thought it was possible to feel more guilty and wretched than she already did, but now she knew it was. Sam had looked…he'd almost looked *betrayed*, as if she'd done something wrong. And ridiculously, she felt as if she had.

Dragging her feet along with her leaden heart, Rachel headed upstairs to her flat. The day looked to end as badly as it had started.

Chapter Twenty-One

T HE NEXT TWO weeks passed in a blur of activity. Rachel managed to ignore her heavy heart only by working as hard as she could, preparing lessons, teaching twenty-five seven-year-olds, and managing Nathan in the classroom. The more time she spent with him in the classroom, the more she became convinced that he needed an assessment, and she spent several evenings mulling over how best she could convince Sam to agree to one, and coming up with no easy answers.

Besides work, her family life kept her busy; now that it was October, Anna's wedding was starting to feel imminent. With every trip up north she brought another few boxes of stuff to put in the vicarage, in preparation for her move there after the wedding.

She sent links to potential bridesmaid dresses online; unlike Rachel, who had had everything from a fancy boutique in Manchester, Anna told her sisters they could pick their own dresses, as long as they were all the same shade of crimson. It made the whole process a lot easier, and Rachel was secretly glad to miss the girly days at a boutique, sipping cocktails and squealing over different dresses.

"What *does* your wedding dress look like, Anna?" she asked one weekend when Anna was in Thornthwaite. Jasper, thankfully, had gone to London for a week, which gave Rachel a bit of breathing room from his waiting. She knew he didn't mean to pressure her, and he really wasn't, which was part of the problem. She felt guilty for letting him down, and annoyed with herself for not giving him a chance, but she knew she couldn't…and a lot of that had to do not with Dan, but with Sam. Not that it mattered, since she hadn't had more than a glimpse of the man since their argument over Nathan's assessment.

"It's very simple," Anna answered. They were sitting in the kitchen, sipping tea, a Friday afternoon after school, just as they might have done when their mother had been resident. Rachel could almost picture her by the kettle, swiping counters with a smile, or cutting generous slices of lemon drizzle cake or custard tart. Among a lot of other, more important things, she missed her mother's baking.

"Do you have a photo?"

"No, I'm keeping it a surprise." Anna smiled shyly. "It's not a big deal of a dress, though. Very non-meringuey. White satin, and the only lace is on the veil. And that's all I'm saying."

"It sounds lovely." A pang of unease assailed her. "You're not keeping it a surprise because—because of me?" Rachel blurted. "Because it might bring up bad memories or something?"

"No, of ccc...course not," Anna said quickly, but not before Rachel caught her stricken look. She *was*.

"Oh, Anna." Rachel shook her head. "The last thing I'd want is to cast some sort of shadow over your big day. You should show everyone your dress, if you want to. Well, not Simon, of course, but everyone else."

"I...like it bb...being a surprise."

"No, you don't," Rachel retorted. "You're stammering. That's always a sign that you're lying."

Anna flushed. "Or just that I'm nn...nervous."

"You don't need to be nervous with *me*." Rachel hated the thought that her own derailed dreams had affected everybody, not just her. "Anna, please believe me when I say the fact that you're getting married and I'm not is okay. It's *fine*. I won't be hurt if you talk about the wedding, if you show me a picture of your wedding dress, if you tell me how excited you are. I promise. I want to hear about those things. I really do."

"I know, Rachel," Anna murmured, her eyes downcast. "It's just...hard. I don't want to put my foot in it, or make you feel badly..."

"You won't. In fact, what makes me feel badly is when you don't talk about it!" Realisation had been trickling through her as they'd spoken; Anna hadn't talked very much about the wedding at all, and it was now in just over two months. Rachel hadn't let herself think too much about it, but now she realised how unusual it was. Her sister was getting *married*, she was a bridesmaid, for heaven's sake, and she knew hardly any of the details.

"Please tell me, Anna," she implored. "What music are you having? And what's the food going to be like? The flowers?"

Anna looked up, a shy smile lighting her face. "Well…" she began, and then launched into an excited description of all the above, and more.

An hour later Rachel tottered from the kitchen, her mind full of the details of Anna and Simon's wedding, which looked to be a lovely occasion. Rachel had enjoyed hearing about it, but it had taken more effort than she would have liked to sit and listen and act excited and interested—which she was, of course she was. And yet. There was always a dreaded *and yet*.

"I hope Anna didn't bore you to death with wedding talk?" Simon said, popping his head outside his study as Rachel made for the front door.

"Oh no, of course not," Rachel answered quickly. "It's lovely to hear about everything. It sounds as if it's going to be a beautiful ceremony and reception."

"I hope so." Simon hesitated, as if he wanted to say something more, and Rachel waited, regarding him warily. Surely he wasn't going to launch into some impromptu pastoral check-up? *But how are you really coping, Rachel?*

Please, no.

"Rachel…do you mind if I ask you something, well, rather personal?"

Yes. "No, of course not." Rachel gave as sunny a smile as she could. "What's up?"

"It's just…you might not realise it, because he always acts so carefree, but Jasper has been going through quite a difficult time lately."

This was about *Jasper*? Rachel felt a wave of relief followed by a deepening unease. Why on earth would Simon want to talk to her about Jasper? "Oh, yes? He mentioned something about being between jobs…"

"Yes, well that's putting it mildly." Simon looked undecided whether to say more, and Rachel rushed in to fill the silence.

"Don't tell me anything he wouldn't want me to know."

"That's part of the trouble. I think he would want you to know…if you know what I mean."

Oh, help. Jasper had told Simon something about her—about how he felt? "Er…" was all Rachel could manage.

"The truth is, he was fired from his last position because someone on his team embezzled money from the company. It wasn't a large amount, but it was enough for people to notice and Jasper took the blame because they couldn't figure out who it was. He's in London this week to attend a hearing."

"A hearing? You mean, like in court?"

"At the moment it's just within the company, since they can't actually accuse anyone without more evidence. But it tore Jasper up—not losing his job so much as the trust he'd placed in the people under him. The scandal of it made him lose his girlfriend, as well. She broke up with him a few months ago, when it all came out."

"That's terrible, Simon." And it was—she never would have known what sad secrets Jasper was hiding from his cheery demeanour. She'd known he was between jobs, of course, but she hadn't realised the loss had been tainted by betrayal and grief. "But…why are you telling me? Do you really think Jasper would want me to know all that?" He certainly hadn't volunteered the information.

"Jasper cares for you, Rachel. I don't know what your feelings are but I suppose I felt a certain duty to let you know where he's coming from, because he always acts as if nothing bothers him in the least. But that carefree Bertie Wooster act he's got going on is just that—an act. And I suppose I don't want either of you to get hurt." A blush touched his cheeks. "Sorry if I've stepped over a line."

"No, it's fine. I'm glad to know." And she would have to talk to Jasper at some point, to advise him not to wait. Now that she knew more of what he was going through, she had no intention of getting his hopes up when she knew in her heart she'd never care for him that way. "Thank you, Simon."

As she headed back to her flat above The Bell, the sight

of the pub gave her heart a little wrench. Had she completely scuppered her friendship with Sam? They hadn't shared so much as a hello in the two weeks since their argument, and although she was trying to soldier on, it made Rachel feel more miserable than ever. She wanted back the fragile camaraderie she'd had with Sam, and she missed her evenings with Nathan, as well. Over the last few weeks she'd started to rebuild her life again, but right now it felt as if the hopes she'd had as its foundation were just as flimsy as before.

The next morning she woke up with a leaden feeling in her stomach, both from the knowledge that she'd need to set Jasper straight at some point and the endless, empty Saturday in front of her. Miriam had made plans with a friend from school, and Anna and Simon were busy with wedding details. Esther and Will were occupied as well, going to Carlisle for some work get-together of Esther's, from her days with Natural England, and so Rachel would be all on her own.

She toyed with the idea of driving to Newcastle to see one of her uni friends, but when she texted Sasha, whom she'd lived with for two years as a student, her friend texted a sad face emoji and said she was in Suffolk visiting her boyfriend's parents. Rachel hadn't even known she had a boyfriend. The last year of her own wedding plans and their subsequent derailment had made her out of touch with just about everybody.

"Come on, Bailey," she said as she pulled on a pair of yoga pants and an old hoodie after switching on the kettle for her first cup of coffee. The flat was quiet, the day grey and dank. Everything felt lonely. "Time for a wee."

Outside the village was still quiet, the pub dark, the air still. A few mangy-looking sheep were in the pasture by St John's Beck, looking rather miserable. Rachel huddled by the bridge as Bailey sniffed everything in sight. Perhaps she'd take her puppy for a nice, long walk; now that Bailey had had her jabs she could go out and about, and although Rachel was far from outdoorsy she liked the idea of tiring both human and animal out, and then collapsing on the sofa to self-righteously binge on Netflix, or maybe pick up one of the paperbacks on her tottering TBR pile by her bed.

"Rachel."

Rachel turned, as did her heart when she saw Sam standing in the doorway of the darkened pub. It had started to rain, a misting drizzle that looked fairly innocuous but soaked her in seconds.

"Hi, Sam," Rachel croaked. She felt unaccountably nervous at just seeing him.

He jogged across the street, his expression serious. "Are you busy today?"

"Um, no?" Rachel stared at him in uncertainty.

"I wondered if you wanted to go out with Nathan and me," Sam said, not quite looking at her. "Nothing particularly exciting—just bowling in Workington. But Nathan's missed you and he asked if you could come with us today?"

"Did he?" Rachel felt rather ridiculously pleased by this, as well as disappointed that it wasn't Sam who had missed her or was asking for her. Ah, life. She'd take what she could get. "Are you sure you want me to come?" she asked, because it had to be said. "It feels as if you've been avoiding me these last few weeks."

"Yeah, well." Sam gave her a sheepishly apologetic look. "I'm sorry about that. I admit I was a bit shirty about the assessment thing."

"Okay," Rachel said after a moment. "I'm sorry, too. I was a bit shirty, as well."

"You were just doing your job, Rachel. I understand that."

She nodded slowly, unsure where this was going, or if Sam had changed his mind about having Nathan assessed.

"So do you fancy coming along with us?" Sam asked. "I understand if not."

Did she? The answer was overwhelming, irrefutable. "I fancy it," Rachel said, and Sam's full-on smile was enough to send any lingering doubts or worries scattering like seagulls after breadcrumbs. Returning his smile, she whistled for Bailey and started back across the street.

Chapter Twenty-Two

I T FELT ODD to be crammed into the front seat of Sam's old work van, heading up the A595 to Workington, with Nathan squeezed between them. Odd and uncomfortable, because Nathan was bouncing up and down the entire time, unable to keep still for so much as a second.

Sam looked unaccountably grim, but perhaps Rachel had simply forgotten how grim he normally looked. He certainly wasn't smiling.

They didn't talk much on the way to Workington, mainly because it was rather difficult with Nathan pinging up and down between them, but Rachel hoped things might relax once they were at the bowling alley. In any case, she didn't mind having a bit of silence between them; it felt like a way to bridge the awkwardness and aggression of their last meeting and whatever was going to happen today. A necessary no man's land, relationship-wise.

She soon discovered that Nathan at a bowling alley was much the same as Nathan at her flat, the playground, or school—not impossible, but definitely challenging.

First his bowling shoes were too small. Then the next pair were too big. Then the next pair were too uncomfortable, and when they finally found a pair he could live with, they moved on to the same ordeal with the bowling balls. Rachel was starting to feel like she was dealing with Goldilocks, but one who hurled shoes everywhere, spoke at the top of his voice, and generally made a scene.

She was both touched and gratified, however, that Sam seemed to know how to handle his nephew. He remained calm, always speaking in a slow, steady voice, firm but gentle, one hand on Nathan's shoulder, anchoring him in place. Watching him, Rachel couldn't help but think what a good dad he would be. What a good dad he *was*, because that was essentially what he was being for Nathan.

And Nathan listened to him at least some of the time. The rest of the time he was what Rachel had come to think of as classic Nathan—bouncing around all over the place, over the top whether it was in excitement or aggravation, exhausting and delighting her in turns.

"I haven't been bowling in years," she told Sam as she selected her own bright pink ball. A girl needed her accessories, after all. "Maybe even decades."

"Don't worry, the side ramps are up," Sam assured her, and she made a face. Although two minutes later, when she took her first turn bowling, she was glad for the ramps because otherwise every single attempt she made would almost certainly be a gutter ball.

Sam, predictably, bowled a strike his first two and then three turns. Rachel watched him, her arms folded, admiring his easy, confident stride that managed not to veer into irritating swagger.

"Is there anything you're not good at?" she asked, and Sam looked surprised.

"Plenty. Most things."

"I don't believe that."

He shook his head in disbelief. "Really?"

"Really. You renovated that apartment, you bought the pub, you've bowled three strikes. What can't you do?" As she said the words, she realised how truly impressed she was. How much she admired him. And yet Sam looked as if he thought she was taking the mick.

"I couldn't do school," he said at last. "Scraped by with five GCSEs. Three Cs and two Ds."

"Considering how much upheaval you had at the time, that's hardly surprising." Sam shot her an eloquently disbelieving look, and Rachel had to laugh. She and her geeky group of friends had all been about the ten A stars. "All right, fine. Three Cs and two Ds is rather a poor showing. But school isn't everything."

"No, but it is a lot, especially when you're fifteen." He sighed and shook his head before managing a wry smile that felt like a fist squeezing her heart. "Anyway, there's plenty else I can't do. Come on, Nath." He reached for Nathan's ball. "I'll help you this time."

Nathan, who had been methodically kicking the sides of the bowling alley, brightened at this prospect and Rachel settled back in her seat to watch man and boy together.

They played two full games before Nathan began to be bored—never a good thing—and Sam suggested they head for the lounge area near the video games. While he got them coffees Nathan parked himself in front of one of those enormous driving games, complete with seat and steering wheel, and watched the screen beckoning him to deposit a pound in the machine with tremendous avidity.

"He'll watch that thing for hours," Sam remarked as he sat on one end of a leather sofa and Rachel settled on the other, murmuring her thanks as Sam handed her a frothy latte loaded with sugar, just as she liked it.

"Will he?"

"I don't have to put any money in it, even."

"That's lucky." Rachel glanced at Nathan, who was staring at the colourful, moving screen with ferocious concentration. It was the same way he'd watched game shows in her flat, and Rachel couldn't keep an alarm bell from ringing inside her head. It wasn't quite normal, the way he watched it, but right now she wouldn't begrudge Sam a few minutes' peace.

She glanced back at Sam, who was sipping his coffee pensively, blue eyes slightly narrowed in a way that had become familiar.

"You're good with him, you know," she said quietly,

both because she meant it and she thought he needed to hear it.

Sam's eyes widened in surprise. "I'm trying. Not sure I'm succeeding all that much."

"You are."

He gave a slight shake of his head. "I don't really know what I'm doing. It's not as if I had the best example."

"No." When Rachel thought of Sam's childhood, her heart ached with sadness.

"Actually…" He glanced at her, a small, uncertain smile curving his mouth. "You know who I think of, in terms of who I want to be like?"

Bemused and curious, Rachel raised her eyebrows. "No, who?"

"Your dad." His gaze grew distant with memory. "I was only at the vicarage for a couple of weeks, but I remember your dad. The way he was with all of you and your mum. And even at that age I thought that was someone I'd want to be like, one day." He looked away, seeming embarrassed that he'd said so much. "Not that I'd ever even come close."

"You do, Sam." A lump was forming in Rachel's throat, one of pure emotion. "You do." She was incredibly moved and touched that her father had been such a role model to him, and that his time at the vicarage had had such an impact—which made another realisation slam into her. "Sam, do you…do you remember Jamie?"

Understanding dawned in his eyes and softened his features. "Yes, of course I do."

"What do you remember about him?" She almost didn't want to ask, because she knew it would be painful. Thinking about Jamie always was. But she also felt as if she'd been given a gift, or found a secret treasure—new memories of Jamie. Hers were so precious and so few, especially with the passage of years. She took them out sometimes like old photographs, examining the details, trying to find the truth.

"He played football with me," Sam said after a moment. "In the garden. He was only five or so, about half my size. One time I came in with dirty trainers and left muddy footprints all over the place and Jamie took the blame for me, because he saw how terrified I looked. I don't think your mum would have been all that bothered, but…"

"That sounds like Jamie." She smiled even though she could feel the pressure of tears behind her lids. "What else?"

"I annoyed him constantly, I think, but he was quite patient. Mostly, anyway. I always kept trying to wrestle him and he'd just take it, even when I played dirty, which was really rather bad of me, considering I was bigger than he was."

"I'm amazed I can't remember any of it. A couple of weeks, you said?" She shook her head slowly, searching through her memory banks for something, one little detail, but it was all distant and cloudy, as so much of her life before Jamie's death was. It was as if her brain had closed it off, made a definitive before and after.

"Well, I think you basically just ignored me," Sam said frankly. "I was a boy; you were a girl..." For some ridiculous reason that statement made Rachel blush.

"You must have been in my year at school," she said, willing her flush to recede.

"No, your mum drove me and Tiffany to our primary school in Whitehaven, because that's where we'd been going before."

"Whitehaven! That's over half an hour away."

"Yes, your mum was—is—amazing."

"And after you left? What happened then?"

"Back to my mum in Whitehaven, and then placed with a care worker in... I can't even remember, to be honest. There was a whole bunch of them." He glanced at Nathan, who was still watching the video screen with intense concentration. "I don't want that for Nathan. Whatever your faith in the system, Rachel, I know he'd be bounced around *because* he's challenging."

"Perhaps he wouldn't be bounced around at all, if he stayed with you."

"*If* he stayed with me," Sam repeated with grim emphasis. "Yes." He shifted restlessly on the sofa. "But let's not bring all that up again."

So they weren't going to talk about Nathan's potential— or not—assessment. "Okay," Rachel said after a moment. "Let's talk about something else."

The silence that stretched between them for several seconds felt strangely important.

"Have you sold that house yet?" Sam asked finally, startling Rachel a little because she'd been expecting something else, although what she couldn't have even said.

"No, but the estate agent thinks an offer will be coming shortly, which would be fab." She sighed. "You know, though, we never should have bought that house in the first place."

"Why not?"

"It was too expensive. But I loved it so much." She glanced at him, wanting him to understand. That sub-zero fridge comment still stung a little. "More for what it represented than anything else."

"And what did it represent?"

Rachel hesitated as she sifted through her thoughts. "The kind of life I've always wanted," she said slowly. "The kind of life I had growing up—family, children, laughter, love. I know our lives most likely seemed charmed to you, looking in from the outside, but after Jamie died it always felt like the perfect picture had a big smudge in the middle." She paused, searching for the words, the need for Sam to understand urgent and important. "I felt like I had a big smudge in the middle of myself."

"Why?" Sam's voice was both rough and gentle, and the pressure behind Rachel's lids that had thankfully eased now returned in force.

"Because I blamed myself for his death, at least partly.

Anna did too, I found out recently. I was running ahead because I wanted to get to school to see my friend, and she was behind me. Jamie was chasing her, but I went first. I should have seen the car."

"I'd always heard that it came out of nowhere."

"Did it, really? Mum and Dad were always so careful about having us look both ways, check all the way up to the top of the high street. I was in a rush."

"You were what? Ten?"

"Eleven and a half." She sighed, trying to blink back the tears. "I don't actually blame myself anymore. I haven't for a long time. It took therapy and prayer and time and healing, but I did just about get there."

"Good."

"But the house...even my engagement..." She could hardly believe she was saying this, and yet with each word she knew it was true. Terribly, tragically true. "It all had to do with Jamie's death, in a strange way. I wanted that life back, that we had before he died. I wanted to make it for myself, because it felt like...like something I've always been missing. Our family life has been wonderful," she added quickly. "My parents are amazing. But you don't get over something like that, you know?"

"Yes. I know." Of course he did. He might not have lost a loved one the way she had, but he'd certainly lost. They'd both been broken in different ways.

"I know Dan thinks I was a bit shallow," she continued

shakily, "and I don't really blame him, because I most likely seemed shallow—the big house, the Aga, the Range Rover." She shook her head. "And I admit my head was turned—I went a bit OTT, which is what I pretty much do with everything. But I just wanted the safety, the security. The warmth and the welcome. Does that make any sense?" She glanced at him, craving his compassion as well as his understanding, and although his expression was inscrutable Rachel could feel in her bones that she had both.

"Yes, it makes a lot of sense." He shrugged a shoulder. "I'm the same, in a way. I came back to Thornthwaite because it was the one place that had ever felt like home to me."

"Was it?" She tried to swipe discreetly at her damp eyes. "And why did you buy the pub?"

"It seemed like a going concern, and with my background I thought it would be a good fit. I know The Bell is seen as rough, but I try to keep it under control, and I won't serve anyone who has had too many." He cracked a small smile. "Although I need to keep an eye on the champagne, obviously."

Rachel let out a tremulous laugh. "What a way for us to meet."

"Yes, but I'm glad it happened." Her heart tumbled in her chest and she found she couldn't look away from that piercingly blue gaze. Was he saying what she thought he was...?

"I am, as well," she whispered, and Sam looked away.

"You've been good for Nathan."

Oh. The implication was clear—this was about Nathan, not Sam. It was hard not to feel crushingly disappointed, and yet even with that set-down Rachel felt a flicker of hope. Surely she wasn't imagining the connection she felt to him, the almost magnetic pull that had her leaning across the sofa?

"How did you manage to buy the pub?" she asked as she sat back. Maybe she was imagining it all.

"I worked hard and saved for ten years." He grimaced. "It wasn't easy."

He really was a self-made man—strong, independent, loyal, fundamentally decent. And sitting there, cradling a now-cold cup of coffee, Rachel knew she couldn't ignore the persistent and deep-rooted truth—she was falling in love with him.

"I think Nathan's had enough," Sam remarked as he nodded towards his nephew, who was now pounding the screen with the flat of his hands. "How about we grab some lunch before heading back?"

"Okay." Except she didn't want this day to end. Had they reached something new, or would Sam sink back into trying to ignore her?

"Rachel." He paused, staying her with one hand on her arm, his palm warm against her skin. "Thank you for saying all that...about Jamie. I know it's not easy."

Now she really was going to cry. "I wanted to." She drew

a quick, shaky breath. "We're…we're friends, aren't we, Sam?" Except that wasn't what she wanted to ask, because she wanted them to be more than friends.

Something flashed across Sam's face and then was gone. "Yes, of course we are," he said. "We're friends." And then he dropped his hand from her arm and went to fetch Nathan.

The rest of the day passed uneventfully enough—Nathan gorged himself on chips and left his sausage on the plate, and between both her and Sam they kept things on an even keel. Occasionally Rachel felt Sam's gaze resting on her, but when she looked at him he'd look away, and because he was so stony-faced she had no idea what he was thinking—and she wanted to know, very badly.

As they headed back to Thornthwaite, the silence between them was comfortable, or at least Rachel hoped it was; the conversation they'd had earlier had created a certain familiarity and even intimacy between them. Surely she wasn't imagining that.

Sam pulled the van into the little courtyard where she'd bowked on his boots over two months ago now. Nathan scrambled out of the van and raced ahead, flinging open the door to the pub.

"Nathan," Sam called, but then he shrugged, turning to Rachel with a little smile. "The flat's open."

Rachel got out of the van slowly, still not wanting anything to end. Now that they were alone she felt a growing sense of expectation building inside her, and she hoped Sam felt it too. He climbed out just as slowly, and they remained there, on either side of the van, neither of them speaking.

"Thank you for inviting me," Rachel finally said stiltedly. "I had a really nice time."

"So did I." They gazed at each other over the hood of the van, neither of them so much as blinking, everything silent and still. Rachel felt as if everything was happening at a distance, and yet so very close. Surely she wasn't imagining *this*. He wanted to kiss her; he was thinking about it, surely, *surely*. Here, in the dank courtyard that smelled of rubbish and old beer, where they'd first met, he was going to kiss her. He *had* to. She didn't know what she'd do if he didn't, but she knew she'd be crushed.

Rachel's breath caught as Sam walked to her side of the van and reached around her to close the door she'd left open, his arm brushing her shoulder. Her heart did a little jump and she turned to him, so close now she could see the little gold flecks in his irises. *Yes.* This was going to happen.

Her heart thudded in heavy, deliberate beats as Sam gazed down at her; they were so close their bodies were very nearly brushing. His hand was still on the door, his expression intent and yet also uncertain.

But she didn't want him to be uncertain. Rachel gazed up at him, hoping her feelings, or at least some of them, were visible in her eyes and expression. *Kiss me, you fool.* She wasn't brave enough to say it.

"Rachel…" Her name died away on his lips and then she didn't need to be brave at all, because Sam bent his head down and Rachel closed his eyes as his lips brushed hers. It was the softest, barest of kisses, and yet it felt more important than anything Rachel had ever done in her life. This wasn't a random snog or even the culmination of an intense and emotional day. This was a declaration and not just a desire. It was so much more than a kiss.

And yet it *was* a kiss, a wonderful kiss, the kind that made her stomach fizz and fireworks spark behind her eyes as she reached up to place her hand on Sam's cheek, his stubble rough against her fingers. He deepened the kiss so her whole body fizzed and her toes curled. She'd never felt like this before. *Never.*

And then Sam stopped. He broke the kiss and stepped back from her, looking both dazed and regretful. "I'm sorry. I shouldn't have done that."

"Yes, you should have," Rachel blurted. "You very much should have."

But Sam was shaking his head. "I don't want to mess you about, Rachel."

"Is that what you were doing?" She couldn't keep a note of hurt from creeping into her voice. She'd been offering her soul; had he just been going for a snog?

"You deserve someone better than me," Sam said resolutely. "A lot better."

Oh. Her heart twisted, melted, and ached all at once.

"Perhaps I'm the one who should make that decision, Sam—" she began gently, but he was already turning away from her, still shaking his head.

"That won't happen again," he stated in an awful, final tone, and as Rachel watched him disappear into the pub, she had a terrible feeling he meant it utterly.

Chapter Twenty-Three

"WHAT IS WRONG with you?"

Esther stared at Rachel in exasperation as she blinked the vicarage kitchen back into focus. It was Sunday night and she'd spent the last twenty-four hours swamped with misery, reliving the best memory of her life. She hadn't spoken to or even seen Sam in all that time.

"Nothing," Rachel said, completely unconvincingly. Esther rolled her eyes.

"Come on, Rach. You're looking like the walking dead here. Anna made the most delicious casserole and you haven't had so much as a bite."

"I don't mind," Anna said with a smile, although her gaze turned worried as she glanced at Rachel. "But you don't seem yourself, Rachel."

"She isn't," Miriam chimed in, and Rachel gave her youngest sister a warning glower, or tried to. Her relationship with Sam, or lack of it, was not up for discussion.

"What do you mean, she isn't?" Esther demanded. "Is this about Dan?"

"Dan?" Miriam scoffed. "Get a clue, Esther. Dan's history. You saw that ages ago."

"Tell me it's not Jasper," Esther said, and Simon winced.

"It's like that, is it—" he began.

"I'll talk to Jasper," Rachel said hurriedly. "Can we please not dissect my love life right now, or actually, ever?"

"So you have a love life," Esther said, and now Rachel was the one rolling her eyes.

"For heaven's sake, just leave it, please."

"Give her a break, Esther," Will said mildly, but his wife was clearly not to be deterred.

"If it's not Dan, and it's not Jasper…"

"It's not anyone—"

"It's *Sam*," Esther crowed, and Rachel shut her mouth. She wasn't going to say a word, not one word. Unfortunately, she didn't have to.

"Sam West?" Will said, startled, and Esther nodded, her narrowed gaze trained on Rachel.

"You've fallen for a bad boy, Rach. Honestly."

"He's not a bad boy," Rachel snapped. "Don't be so judgemental, Esther."

Esther held her hands palms up. "I was just joking—"

"Well, it's not funny. Sam's worked hard to get to where he is, and he hasn't had an easy life at *all*." Rachel gulped as she realised with a rising sense of panic just how close she was to bursting into noisy tears in front of her entire family.

She lifted her chin and tried for a dignified glare, but

then she saw all the looks everyone was giving her—ranging from surprised to downright stupefied.

"My goodness," Esther said faintly. "You really do care for him."

And that's when she burst into tears. Will and Simon beat a hasty, alarmed retreat while Esther, Anna, and Miriam all gathered around as her sobs slowly turned to snivels.

"Sorry," she finally hiccupped. "I don't know where that came from."

"I do," Anna said as she rubbed her back. "You've had so much to deal with, Rachel. First the wedding…"

"Please, let's not talk about that." Rachel fished for a crumpled tissue from her pocket and gave a hearty blow of her nose. "I'm over *that*."

"But still, it's all bound to come out, isn't it? And then Mum and Dad leaving…"

"Yes, but we've all been dealing with that, and in any case, we're grown women." She thought of Sam being taken from his parents at such a young age, and Nathan too, and she almost started sobbing all over again.

"It's still a lot to deal with," Anna said stubbornly, and Miriam and Esther both murmured their agreement. It took Rachel a few stunned seconds for realisation to dawn.

"You're trying to excuse it," she said slowly. "My…my feelings for Sam. Because of the wedding and Dan and Mum and Dad…you think I only care about him because of all that?"

Three uncertain and fairly guilty faces stared back at her. "Why couldn't I like him—love him, even—for who he is?" Rachel demanded, all traces of tears gone.

"Love him? Rachel, you barely know him," Esther scoffed.

"I know him better than you think," Rachel shot back. "I admit, maybe not enough to love him, but to care for him, yes. Definitely yes." She gazed at them all in turn, trying to understand why they all looked so uncomfortable. "Why do you have trouble believing that? Because of who he is?"

"Not exactly," Esther said, sounding uncharacteristically reluctant to spell it out. "But you have to admit, he's had quite a different life to ours—"

"He lived in the vicarage for several weeks," Rachel cut across her. "Did you know that?"

"Did he?" Esther looked surprised. "Mum and Dad had so many people through over the years…"

"Anyway, what did you mean, not exactly?" Rachel's three sisters all exchanged looks that made her want to scream. *"What?"*

"Rachel," Anna said, her voice far too gentle, "it's just…Sam's not exactly your type, is he?"

"Perhaps I didn't know what my type was." She glanced accusingly at Miriam. "What do you think, Miriam? You seemed to think it was reasonable to care about him when I talked to you the other day."

"I'm not sure caring about someone is ever reasonable,"

Miriam said on a sigh. "It's certainly not sensible."

"Dan Taylor was eminently sensible," Esther remarked. "Don't you think you might be rebounding here, just a little? Going in the opposite direction after you've had a bad breakup?"

"You said yourself it wasn't a bad breakup," Rachel reminded her. "This isn't what's happening here."

"It's just," Anna tried again, "you've always had such ideas about what you want your life to be like, Rachel. The big house, all the kids…" She trailed off uncertainly. "Do you know what I mean?"

Rachel wanted to be offended, and in truth she was more than a little hurt, even though she understood where they were coming from. "Yes, I had those dreams, once upon a time," she said. "And I admit they may have seemed a bit shallow on the surface. I let myself get carried away by the trappings." She drew a shaky breath. "But I'm different now, and Sam is different. I don't want what I used to, at least not exactly." She still wanted the home and the family, the love and the laughter…but she was starting to understand just how different that could look and feel.

"Isn't this all a little fast?" Esther interjected. "You barely know Sam West."

"Yes, well, we're all getting ahead of ourselves, aren't we?" Rachel answered with a sniff. "Because I'm not at all sure he cares about me."

This was met with a thunderclap of silence before Esther

asked in her usual, blunt way, "So what has happened between you?"

Rachel shook her head. She was not going to desecrate the memory of the best and most real and honest kiss she'd ever had by telling Esther about it like it had been nothing but some semi-sordid snog. "I'm done talking about this," she announced instead.

Esther looked offended. "Don't you want our advice?"

"No," Rachel answered, deciding to be as blunt as her sister. "I don't. I want Mum's advice." The realisation reverberated inside her, solid and true. Her mum would know what to say, what to do. Her mum always did.

She didn't get a chance to talk to her mum until later that night, due to the time difference between Thornthwaite and Jinan. While Miriam stayed at the vicarage to watch a movie with Simon and Anna, Rachel sat curled up on the sofa in her flat, hugging a pillow to her chest, as her mother's face froze for a second in a rictus smile before the connection was established and there she was, on the screen, her face as familiar and lovable as always.

"Hey, Mum."

"Rachel! It's so good to see you. How are you?"

"Fine." Now that she had her mum on the screen, Rachel didn't know how to explain what was going on. And really, what did it matter? Sam had said he wasn't interested in a relationship, because he thought she deserved better. What recourse did she really have? "How are you, Mum?"

"Busy. We've just gone out to some surrounding villages for the first time and it's really incredible. The people have so little, and yet they're so warm and open and friendly. Honestly, Rachel, if I'd known what it would be like, coming out here, I never would have dragged my feet."

"You didn't drag your feet," Rachel protested. "You were willing to go—"

"There's willing and there's *willing*," Ruth answered with a smile. "It took your father far too long to convince me that this was the right course of action, but I'm glad we're here. So glad. Anyway." Her mother gave her a direct look. "What's going on with you? How is teaching? And how is that puppy?"

"Bailey's fine." Rachel scooped up the puppy from the floor to give Ruth a close-up of Bailey's lovely, squishy face. "And teaching is going well, a little trickier this year, but nothing I can't handle." Hopefully.

Ruth gazed at her from thousands of miles away, eyes slightly narrowed. "So what's troubling you?" she asked, and Rachel almost laughed. She couldn't fool her mum, even when they were on different continents.

"There's a man," she blurted, and surprise rippled across Ruth's features before she nodded.

"Ah." There was a world of understanding in that one syllable. "And what man would that be?"

"You know him, actually." Rachel hadn't told her mum much about her living situation except that she and Miriam had found a flat in the village, and now her words tumbled over themselves as she sought to explain. "His name is Sam. Sam West. He owns The Bell—"

"Sam." Ruth smiled in memory. "I remember him, of course. He stayed with us when he was little—oh, about seven or so."

"That's right." Of course her mum remembered Sam. Ruth had always had a knack for not just remembering names of people but their life situations, as well.

"Sam is the man you're talking about?" Ruth couldn't keep a hint of surprise from her voice. "How did you meet him?"

"He owns The Bell, and I'm living above it. And I teach his nephew in Year Three."

"All right." Ruth waited, but Rachel didn't even know where to begin.

"I'm not sure what I'm even asking you," she blurted. "There's not much to tell. We're…friends, and I've helped him and he's helped me. And he's a good man—I know that. He's been through some difficult things, and he's done some bad things, but he's really made a new man of himself."

"That all sounds very positive," Ruth said gently. "But I suppose the real question is—do you have feelings for him, Rachel? And does he have feelings for you?"

"Ye-es." Rachel's voice wavered. "I do. And I think he does for me, but he doesn't want to do anything about it because he thinks I deserve better."

"And what do you think?"

The question rocked Rachel, because she hadn't been expecting it. What *did* she think? "I suppose," she admitted painfully, "I would have agreed with him, once upon a time. I had such plans for my life, Mum—"

"I know you did, darling."

"I just wanted what you and Dad had—the house, the family, the dog and the Aga...all of it. It felt perfect. It *was* perfect, until..." She stopped, but Ruth filled in the words, her voice quiet and sad.

"Until Jamie died."

"Yes." Rachel sniffed. She was going to cry again. "I think my whole life I've been trying to get back to the way things were before then."

"But you know as well as I do that you can never go back," Ruth said quietly. "And however it looked to you as a child, Rachel, it wasn't perfect. Nothing is. And happiness comes in many forms, not just a big, old house, a family, a dog, or any of those trappings, as lovely as they are. The important thing to think about, to decide, is what kind of life God is calling you to."

Rachel squirmed a little, because she hadn't really been thinking about it like that at all. She'd been thinking about what she wanted, what kind of life she envisioned for herself. But what if happiness was to be found in something else entirely? And not just happiness, but *importance*? Meaning? Something that had been missing now for a while.

"How am I supposed to figure that one out?" she asked a bit grumpily. Of course her mum would spiritualise things. And yes, maybe it *was* spiritual, but still. Rachel wanted answers, clear-cut and specific.

"The usual ways. Talk to people you trust, examine your heart, pray." Ruth paused. "I'm not there, darling, so I can't tell you what to do, but I can tell you that all through my life I've been straining towards learning this lesson—which is that we are called to do what is hard and right, and love is usually both of those things. That first blush of romance fades and you're left with a lot of struggle and striving— which is where the miracle happens, and where love really grows and flourishes." She smiled, her face suffused with gentleness. "That doesn't mean if something is hard it's also right, but it does mean that we shouldn't shy away from something *because* it's hard, and only choose the things that are easy or fun. Only you can examine your own heart in this."

Rachel sat back, exhausted just by the thought. Why couldn't things be right *and* easy? "Do you love Sam?" Ruth asked, and Rachel swung back to stare at the screen.

"I don't think I can say that yet. This is still… In some ways we are only just getting to know one another…"

"But…?"

"I think I could love him," Rachel said slowly. "But I'm scared to." The confession felt both shameful and liberating. "Because I don't want to give up all those dreams. Because he's not the sort of man I thought I'd fall in love with, even though in the important ways he is—honest and brave and loyal. And because I know getting involved with him will be messy and difficult—his nephew is very challenging, and he has custody of him, and he has his own past..." She trailed off uncertainly. What was she really saying? That she wasn't willing to muck in with life in all of its complicated mess? That the dream of the life she'd had was more important than the wonderful, current reality? Or just the plain, unvarnished truth—that she was afraid to get hurt?

"I think," Ruth said with a smile in her voice, "you've found your answer."

IT TOOK RACHEL three days to work up the courage to examine her heart as her mother had advised, and then another three days to work up even more courage to follow it. All the while Sam was avoiding her—hurrying past when she saw him outside the pub, ducking into a storeroom when she came into The Bell. Rachel told herself she didn't mind, because she wasn't ready yet.

But then, on a cloudy Saturday morning in mid-October, she knew she was. She'd taken care of other things first—a painfully awkward conversation with Jasper, who had taken her hesitant rejection in good form, although Rachel knew she'd hurt him. Dan had called her to say the estate agent had a firm offer on the house, which felt fitting, to let that dream finally die. Nothing stood between her and Sam except, of course, Sam himself.

Her sisters had given her space to work everything out in her own mind, although as Rachel dressed that morning she wouldn't have minded having a bit of moral support. How did you go about convincing a man to take a chance on you? She had no idea, because she'd always been the one to be asked, pursued, even chased. She'd enjoyed it—the thrill, feeling wanted. Now she was on the other side and it felt incredibly daunting.

"What are your plans today?" Miriam asked on a yawn. She was sitting at their little table, drinking a cup of vile green tea and feeding Bailey bits of toast even though Rachel had asked her not to.

"I'm going to talk to Sam," Rachel said in a manner of someone making a formal announcement. Miriam's eyebrows rose.

"About what?"

"The fact that he needs to start dating me." She let out a tremulous laugh before setting her jaw. She was really doing this.

"Wow." Miriam looked impressed. "Good luck with that."

"Thanks." Rachel squared her shoulders. "Hopefully I won't need it."

Nothing, of course, turned out the way she'd hoped.

Sam didn't answer when she knocked on the door of his flat, and the pub was still closed and shuttered. Where *was* he? Nerves fluttered in her belly and up her throat as she contemplated her next step, or lack of it. She'd been picturing a quiet, reasonable, mature conversation somewhere private, but of course it wasn't going to go like that. Nothing in her life ever did.

By mid-afternoon Rachel's thoughts and feelings were in a ferment; she'd been waiting around most of the day, keeping an eye out for Sam, and slowly but surely losing her nerve.

"There he is," Miriam announced helpfully as she pointed out the bedroom window to the high street, where Sam was strolling down by himself. "Go get him."

"I can't," Rachel whimpered, and Miriam gave her an Esther-like look.

"You've been waiting all day to have it out with him. Now's your chance. He's alone."

"He's in the *street*—"

"No, he's just gone into the pub. Perfect." Miriam gave her a little push. "Come on, Rachel. Whatever way this goes, you need to follow it through. You'll be disappointed otherwise, and you'll always wonder if you and Sam could have made a go of it."

Rachel didn't move and Miriam gave her another gentle but firm push. "Go on, then."

And so she did.

Chapter Twenty-Four

THE PUB WAS dim and quiet as Rachel came in from the door in the back, blinking in the gloom. A few old codgers were sat by the bar as usual, hunched over their pints, so she'd have an audience for whatever she was going to say. Perfect.

"Sam?" Rachel's voice wavered, little above a whisper, but Sam heard her anyway. He turned from his position behind the bar, eyes narrowed, an empty pint glass in one hand.

"Rachel?" He didn't sound particularly pleased to see her.

"Where's Nathan?" she practically squeaked, just for something to say.

"He's playing out with a friend. Toby someone."

"Toby Smithson? Oh, that's good." Toby was a rambunctious boy with a generous heart and he'd been Nathan's table partner for the last few weeks. The boys had seemed to get along, and Rachel was glad Nathan had made a friend.

"As long as he behaves himself." Sam's stare bordered on

unfriendly. "What do you want?"

Rachel stared back at him, having no idea how to take that first, flying leap. This was *such* a bad idea. Panic filled her, making her take a stumbling step backward, ready to bolt. She didn't even know what she was going to say to him. *Please date me? I love you? You had me at hello?*

"Is something wrong?" Sam asked, which just showed how crazed and terrified she probably looked.

"No. Yes." Rachel cleared her throat, and then took a step forward. "I wanted—needed—to talk to you."

Sam rested his forearms on the bar. "Areet." He waited, unsmiling. Of course.

"Could we...could we go somewhere private?" At this one of the farmers lifted his head to give her an interested look.

"Something private, eh, Sam? You're one with the lasses, hey?"

"It's not like that." Sam glowered briefly at the man before turning his implacable gaze back on Rachel. "I can't leave the pub. You can say whatever it is you need to here."

Coward. Rachel knew he could leave the pub; there was naught but two old farmers in it and he'd left it before. He just didn't want to give her a chance to say something emotional, to talk about that kiss.

Courage rushed through her along with adrenalin, and she drew herself up. If Sam thought he could outmanoeuvre her, he had another thing coming. Several, in fact.

"All right, fine," she said, giving him a level look. "I want to talk about us."

Sam flinched in surprise. "Rachel—"

"And about the way you kissed me a week ago now."

One of the farmers chuckled, a dry, rasping sound, while the other one lifted up his empty pint glass.

"Pull me another, Sam. I'm staying for this."

"Rachel," Sam hissed, grabbing the empty glass and pulling a pint of Guinness glaring at Rachel all the while. "Now is not the time—"

"Now *is* the time," she retorted. Weirdly she was almost enjoying this now. "I've already spent a week settling in my own mind what I feel for you, and now I need to know what you feel for me."

Colour flared in Sam's face. "I already told you—"

"You told me I deserved better than you," Rachel said steadily. Inside her, everything trembled. "And I disagree."

Sam shook his head, his lips pressed together. "That doesn't matter."

"So I don't get a say?"

"No."

She stared at him, hardly able to believe the conversation might be over before it had begun. That was it? Sam folded his arms, his jaw set, as he waited her out. Rachel felt like screaming, sobbing, and stamping her foot all at once.

"Ach, Sam," one of the farmers said as he took a sip of his Guinness. "You're being a bit hard on the lass."

"Yes, you are," Rachel said fiercely. "Do you think I haven't thought this through, Sam? Do you think I haven't realised what this means?"

"You don't really care about me, Rachel." His voice was quiet and sad and so very certain.

"You can't tell me what I feel."

"She's right there, lad," another farmer chimed in. Rachel had never been so grateful for the stony-faced old codgers and their tersely given wisdom.

Sam was starting to look as if he seriously regretted having this conversation in the pub, but Rachel wasn't letting him off the hook now.

"I care about you," she declared. One of the farmers whistled under his breath. "At the beginning I told myself I wouldn't. I didn't want to, because I thought I knew what I wanted my life to look like—"

"I know what you want your life to look like," Sam cut her off, the words exploding out of him. "I saw it that first day, when I drove you to the big pile on the fells. You want things I could never, ever give you, Rachel."

"And I told you last week that it had never been about the things. It was about what they represented, Sam. Happiness and…" she *would* say it "…love."

Something flickered across his face and then was gone. "I can't give you those things, either."

"Are you sure about that? Because I think you can."

He stared at her for a long moment, his jaw bunching,

torment in his eyes. Rachel longed to reach out and hug him but she wasn't brave enough, and there was still a bar between them, as well as a lot of other things besides.

"Look at me, Rachel," he finally said in a low voice. "Look at my life. This pub barely breaks even and I live in a grotty flat—"

"Your flat is not grotty. It's cleaner than mine."

"And you know why it's so clean?" Sam growled. "Because I picked up the habit of keeping things tidy in *prison*. Did you forget that detail?"

"I haven't forgotten anything, Sam," Rachel said softly. "Not one thing."

"And what about Nathan? You know what he's like. You want to sign up for that? What happened to your five kids, all piled in the Range Rover?"

"I'm letting go of my old dreams because I have new ones now," Rachel answered, her voice growing stronger with every word. "New ones that are about you, and Nathan, and the life we could have together if we were both willing to give it a chance. I'm not saying it would be easy, but my mother had some wise words for me the other day. She said loving someone was hard and right, and that when you get past the fun, easy stuff, that's when love grows. So I'm asking you for a chance to find out if that's true." Her heart was beating so hard it hurt. "That's all I'm asking for, Sam," she whispered. "A chance to find out if we have a chance."

Sam stared at her for a long moment. Why did the man

have to be so darned inscrutable? Why couldn't she tell what he was thinking, at least a little bit?

"All I've wanted," he finally said, his voice low, "is a life like yours. A family like yours." He shook his head. "But I learned a long time ago that it wasn't for me."

"Why not?" Rachel asked, her throat and heart both aching.

"Because I've made too many mistakes, and I can't handle another one. I say yes to you, Rachel, and then six weeks or six months or even six years down the road and you've had enough. I couldn't...I couldn't take that." He lowered his head, his gaze on the old, scarred wood of the bar. "I can't risk it."

It felt as if Rachel's heart was both contracting and expanding as Sam's painfully honest admission reverberated through her. "Everything is a risk, Sam," she said, her voice aching along with her throat and heart. "Everything. You could walk out of here right now and be hit by a car. You could fall in love with the safest person in the world and realise it wasn't right." *Like I did.* "Or you could decide something—someone—is worth taking a risk for, to figure out if forever is possible. This isn't easy for me, either." She waited, her gaze fastened on his lowered head, willing him to look up and *see* her. "I spent this last week thinking and praying about it, and I know now I'm willing to take that risk with you. I want to take it, even if I'm terrified. But I guess the real question is..." her voice and her courage nearly failed her now "…are you willing to take that risk with me?"

The ensuing silence felt endless, an agony of waiting and utter unknowing. She'd gambled everything. She'd put her heart right out there; she hadn't stayed safe. She'd thrown her already-trampled dreams in the dust and was reaching for new ones…but what if Sam wasn't with her on this? What if he decided it—she—simply wasn't worth it?

Then he looked up. "Rachel," he said, and she couldn't tell anything from his tone, but she liked the way he said her name. She loved it.

"Yes." She stood there, waiting, her heart in her eyes, in her mouth, on her sleeve. And she knew in that moment that this was worth it—Sam was, because her mum had been right. Love wasn't easy, or safe, but it was so worth it. She hadn't had that with Dan; she hadn't felt this way, as if everything rested on this moment. As if she'd found the thing she was made for, the person she was meant to be.

Still Sam didn't say anything, but he looked at her, and there was so much emotion in his eyes that that was nearly enough.

Then one of the farmers pulled the brim of his flat cap down low on his face and muttered, "I think this is when you kiss her, lad."

"I'm not doing that in front of you lot," Sam answered, and then he came around the bar and reached for Rachel's hand. In a daze, she followed him out to the dank little courtyard where it had all begun. Still holding her hand, he turned to her, his expression fierce and almost frightening.

"Did you mean all that, back there in the pub?"

Rachel gulped. Nodded. "Yes. I did."

"All of it—about me, about caring, about taking a chance?"

Her heart felt as if it were beating its way up her throat. "Yes, Sam—"

"Even though things will be complicated? Even though Nathan can be a right pain in the—"

"Yes."

"Even though there will be social workers and assessments and my prison record will come out—"

"Assessments?" A smile bloomed across her face. "Do you mean—"

"Yes, I do." He took her by both shoulders, gazing at her with such startling intensity Rachel felt as if she were under a microscope. She felt scrutinised but also beloved. "Tell me you meant it, Rachel."

"I meant it." She understood in that moment, with a sudden, breathless clarity, that she meant it in a way she never had with Dan. Dan had been right all along— something had been missing between them, something important, and for the first time she knew absolutely to the tips of her toes and the depths of her soul that he'd been right to call it off. And she was right to be here, smiling at Sam, waiting for his answer.

And she got it—in his kiss. His mouth came down on

hers and Rachel's eyes fluttered closed as the whole world seemed to right itself.

Sam's arms came around her and he held her tightly, as if he would never let her go, and Rachel hoped he wouldn't. Then a voice, sounding grumpy, was heard from the pub.

"Hey, can we get some service in here?"

Epilogue

CHURCH BELLS PEALED out, the notes seeming to shimmer on the crystalline air as they echoed through the village and settled on the snowy pasture. It was three days before Christmas and Anna and Simon were about to get married.

Rachel stood in the porch of the church, trying not to shiver in the freezing air as she adjusted Anna's veil. Next to her Roger smiled with a suspicious glint in his eye, and then got out his handkerchief to discreetly wipe away the stray tear. He and Ruth had returned to Thornthwaite a week ago, and it had been a joyous reunion, full of new beginnings—Miriam, nearly eight months pregnant now, and Esther, only two months along. And then of course they'd re-introduced themselves to Sam and met Nathan. The Holley family was expanding in all sorts of ways, and they would all be spending Christmas together in three days' time.

The last two months had been the best of Rachel's life, but also some of the most challenging. Her mum had certainly been right. Navigating a new relationship was fraught, especially with so many obstacles to overcome. A few weeks ago, the results of Nathan's assessment had finally come in and he'd been officially diagnosed with partial Foetal Alcohol Syndrome, something that had devastated Sam even as both he and Rachel had acknowledged this was a step forward, and they could now begin to work on strategies and therapies to help Nathan. Sam was also applying for permanent custody of Nathan, with his sister's approval; the hearing would be sometime in the new year.

Rachel and Miriam had both moved out of the flat above The Bell—Miriam to go her own, unexpected way, and Rachel into a small terraced cottage on the high street she'd bought after Fellview had sold. It had a garden for Bailey and a little more space for her. It made sense, in this new period of life, to put down roots, and to give her and Sam a bit of breathing space as they tried to go about romance the normal way and date like two people who had only known each other for a few months, which was what they were, even if it didn't always feel that way. It felt like so much more.

Already her family were good-naturedly hinting at wedding bells for her and Sam—when would there be another vicarage wedding? For now, Rachel was happy with this one. She had new dreams, fragile, barely birthed ones, and she wanted to see how they grew.

"Are we going to get going with this?" Esther asked as she came into the porch, dressed in a crimson sheath dress. "Otherwise I might need to have a snack in the middle of the service. I'm constantly starving." Esther was eight weeks' pregnant and not quite glowing yet, but joy seeped from every pore. Rachel knew how longed-for this baby was.

"And I might go into labour," Miriam said with a smile and a theatrical groan. Her own dress was the same shade of scarlet, but with a much-needed Empire waist and flowing skirt. "I look like a red whale in this dress."

Anna smiled at them all, looking lovely in her simple gown, her lace veil flowing over her shoulders. "You all look beautiful. Absolutely beautiful."

"As do you," Rachel said. "You're radiant, Anna." She'd never seen her sister look so happy, and she was glad.

"I feel radiant," Anna admitted. "I feel like the best is about to begin." Which was how Rachel felt—perhaps how they all felt. She glanced at Miriam, wondering what lay ahead for her youngest sister.

From the church the organ music started to swell.

"Shall we, my dears?" Roger asked, looking around at his four daughters, and Anna nodded.

"Yes, let's get this party started." She gave a nervous giggle.

The three sisters lined up in order of age—first Miriam, and then Rachel, and then Esther, and then Anna and Roger behind. Ruth had already been seated by Will. As Rachel took her turn to walk down the aisle, she searched the pews for Sam and Nathan. Her gaze caught on Dan, who smiled at her, and she smiled back. A while back they'd reached an understanding, and they were friends again. Truly friends.

Then she saw Sam, and her smile became a full-watt beam of joy as he grinned back at her, love shining in his eyes. No, it hadn't been easy these last two months, but it had been wonderful. Still smiling, Rachel started down the aisle.

The End

Read the last Holley Sisters story,
A Vicarage Homecoming, about Miriam, out soon!

The Holley Sisters of Thornthwaite Series

Book 1: *A Vicarage Christmas*
Anna's story

Book 2: *A Vicarage Reunion*
Esther's story

Book 3: *A Vicarage Wedding*
Rachel's story

Available now at your favorite online retailer!

About the Author

After spending three years as a diehard New Yorker, **Kate Hewitt** now lives in the Lake District in England with her husband, their five children, and a Golden Retriever. She enjoys such novel things as long country walks and chatting with people in the street, and her children love the freedom of village life—although she often has to ring four or five people to figure out where they've gone off to.

She writes women's fiction as well as contemporary romance under the name Kate Hewitt, and whatever the genre she enjoys delivering a compelling and intensely emotional story.

Thank you for reading

A Vicarage Wedding

If you enjoyed this book, you can find more from all our great authors at TulePublishing.com, or from your favorite online retailer.

TULE
PUBLISHING

Printed in Great Britain
by Amazon